Lies

A PLACE

THE EXISTENCE SERIES BOOK 2

THE EXISTENCE SERIES

REMEMBER
BEYOND THE END
LIES A PLACE
FOR THE ETERNAL

For more information on the series,
sign up for Tara Allred's newsletter at
www.taracallred.net.

OTHER BOOKS BY
TARA C. ALLRED

SANDERS' STARFISH
UNAUTHORED LETTERS
THE OTHER SIDE OF QUIET
HELPING HELPER

A PLACE

THE EXISTENCE SERIES BOOK 2

TARA C. ALLRED

Special thanks to:
Brittany Boman, Jennie Collingwood, Jann Cook,
Dr. Dan Franck, Aubrey Gubler, Marni Law,
Staci Mitzman, Ashley Reinhold,
and Dr. Vonda.

Patella Publishing
First eBook Edition: 2022
First Paperback Edition: 2022
ISBN: 9780986421594

Cover design by Melissa Williams Design
Typesetting by Amit Dey

Published in the United States of America

Patella Publishing

IN MEMORY OF
CHARLES WHITING

who lived an extraordinary life, overcame incredible odds, had a zest for life, and shared that zest with others, making us better because of our associations with him.

*"All our life…is but a mass of habits,
—practical, emotional, and intellectual, —
systematically organized for our weal or woe,
and bearing us irresistibly toward our destiny,
whatever the latter may be."*

—William James

PART ONE

ONE

LEILANI

I watched the nurse's thick, calloused hands intently. Her grainy, sweet voice sent an alarm to my head. "You'll need to give yourself a shot twice a day." With those hands, she produced a long needle. "When the calendar tells you to begin administration, you'll need to do this..." She inserted the needle into the vial, then filled the syringe to the 10mL level.

With her flowery scrub top raised, she pantomimed inserting the needle into her hairy stomach. "You understand?" Her head lifted. Her asparagus-colored dreadlocks nodded at me. Before I responded, she straightened and approached me with her needle raised high.

I pulled back. Sitting next to me, Yam placed his hand on my knee. I touched it, covering mine over his, and our fingers interlocked.

The nurse cleared her throat, a scold was there. Yam and I both withdrew. "It's okay," she said. I met her eyes and she nodded at our hands. "You can comfort her. I will allow that touch."

Yam slid his hand back into mine. For a moment, I closed my eyes, picturing his hand strumming the guitar strings, him singing, us laughing. Since our first kiss, back home on the island, I had hoped we might kiss again, but such contact was not allowed while we were in Ashyr's care.

"Leilani." I opened my eyes to find the nurse staring at me. "Can you give yourself these shots?"

My fingers tightened around Yam's. "I can."

Without asking, the nurse raised my tank top high, revealing my belly button and the lower edge of my bra. Yam turned away, as if giving me privacy. But as his hand felt like it might leave too, I gripped it firmly, leading him back to look at the large needle with me.

"You will go like this." With a mechanical motion, the nurse drew her arm back and then moved it forward toward my belly.

Unintentionally, I gasped. My body pressed against Yam.

The nurse laughed. "I didn't do anything."

I protected my belly with my free hand. "Well...I thought you were coming at me, like you..." There was too much panic in my voice. "Like you were going to do it now."

"I'm not." She laughed again. "But I need you to, so I know you can."

I closed my eyes, wanting the needle to disappear. I pictured myself back on the eighth floor of my secure living quarters. Since I'd been in Ashyr's care, each evening, around the same time, I watched the colorfully attired people on the gray streets below pairing up through some ritual between them. As night came on, they disappeared. Lights spread out like a fan through the city. Their ritual served as my daily entertainment, watching their bright specks dance below me. People living, while I waited.

Waited for this.

"Leilani." The nurse called me back. "If you can't give it to yourself, Jate will."

I realigned myself in my seat and tensely dropped my protective arm to my side. "Let me see it," I said strongly. While my other hand stayed locked on Yam's, I reached for the syringe. "I can do it."

My handler, Jate, smelled. On first meeting her, the foulness made me want to lose my first meal in L.A., a tasteless lunch of soda crackers and bland cheese. Yam had warned me that the food here was not good. What he hadn't warned me about were the smells.

I stared at the needle now. On that first day, when I had asked Yam if he had smelled Jate, or his handler, Kandi-Greene, who also made me hold my breath when we met, Yam had only grinned. "You'll get used to it." Later he explained, "It's the perfumes. Hairspray. Deodorant. Those are the smells."

"It's horrible," I said.

"It's how everyone smells here. You're going to see a lot of new things. Smell a lot of unique smells. Everything is different here. You lived in a bubble."

In my imaginary discussion with Dad...in a fantasy world where I had forgiven him for lying to me...where I magically *understood* why he had kept the truth from me, letting me believe the island we resided on was on Earth and not his invention floating in its own orbit in the sky, he would explain by saying, "We know how to keep clean with little impact to our sphere. The island has a huge impact on us and we on it." Something like that.

"Show me." The nurse nodded at the syringe in my hand.

Yam had explained I would get used to the smells but as I stared at the needle and thought of Dad, and the island, and what he would say about the smell, between the nurse's odor as she hung over me and the needle in my hand, nausea stirred up the bland roast beef sandwich from lunch. "I thought you said we weren't doing it now," I said, trying to push down the fear.

The nurse's eyes shifted to the hand-holding; a scowl formed around her lips. Then her eyes returned to the needle. A look of sadistic glee spread over her face. "Do it," she said.

Between the syringe in one hand and Yam's hand in the other, I felt she was now punishing me for our touch. "You said...." the fear kept resurfacing in my voice, "I needed to wait...until the time on the calendar..." I cleared my throat. "Wait...until I start this."

The nurse nodded. "That's saline solution." The gleeful look was still there, tight against the extra makeup on her face. "It won't hurt you. But you need to show me you can do this. Can you?"

I tried to laugh it off, like *of course I can*. But the sound, hollow and disgusted, turned against me.

"Do it." The nurse's large arm touched me, right around my forearm.

I pulled back from her, letting go of Yam's touch too. He shifted to look at me directly.

"Can you do it?" he asked.

"Sure. Sure." I couldn't quite meet his eyes.

His hand pressed against my knee. "I can come give them to you. Every morning, every night."

"So can Jate," the nurse replied.

"I can do it," I said, speaking to the floor.

"Then," the nurse cleared her throat, "go ahead."

I touched the spot directly below my belly. *Three. Two. One.* I jabbed it in and tried not to wince at the pain.

"Very good." She took the syringe from me. "Begin once the calendar tells you to."

* * *

Yam's pacing reminded me of my dog, Huck. He looked at the window like Huck looked at a fence: a challenge that needed to be conquered, an exit to somewhere else. I kept my voice level and cool. "A bit anxious?"

He turned. "Just…"

I finished for him, "…ready to be out of here?"

After a short nod, he headed for the corner, for his guitar that had saved us. Our daily ritual, him playing for me, me singing along sometimes—even though he sang better than me. A few days ago, he said he was writing me a song that he wasn't ready to share yet. So I changed the mood with a teasing tone. "Is today our day?" I asked over the strumming. "You finally ready?" I gave him a hopeful smile.

But he didn't smile back. "Ready for what? To keep sitting here, doing nothing while Ashyr forgets about us?"

These weren't Yam's words. The impatience, the frustration—these had been my words countless times. Other than our handlers, we saw no one else. Other than my first visit to the clinic, we had never left the building's floor that housed our two little apartments.

I tried to soothe the moment like he had done for me countless times. "Play me your new song. Please."

In the oversized chair, with the black coffee table between us, he shared no smile, just shook his head. "Not yet."

Usually I could spark a smile from him, but not today. A few more strums from his guitar then he set it down with a heavy sigh. He leaned back against the chair and stared at his hand that bounced up and down on his lap.

I missed holding that hand. Soon after our first days, right after my lesson on administering my own shots, we sat on the couch holding hands until K.G., short for Kandi-Greene, saw. Then a long lecture ensued. *No touching!* Jate was called in. Immediately, I was put on birth control.

"In case you fall into archaic ways," she had said while her ankles bounced up and down. Jate was like a dark purple bean. She was tall and her limbs seemed to bend and curl constantly. Elbows extended while wrists bent at her waist. Or a knee folded to create an L-shape with her legs. Or her moving ankles, up and down, like a human jumping bean. Meanwhile, her face remained covered by her dark purple hair. She hardly said anything and when she did, it seemed more out of exasperation, like I was a babysitting job that was taking its toll.

"We have strict instructions." K.G. cracked his knuckles while he spoke. Yam's handler was a block: a four-point square from shoulders to torso. He wore a bright pink polo that fit tightly against his chest, although it looked like he had a thin pillow shoved underneath. Copper-colored bangs formed perfectly looped curls against his forehead. More hair curled around the chains that attached from the tops of his ears to the gauges in his earlobes.

"And," K.G. added, "we need to make sure nothing goes against those instructions."

"They're worried," Yam whispered, "that we're going to have—"

"Don't say the word." K.G. covered his ears. His face cringed as if Yam had offered an obscenity. Then he pointed back and forth between Yam and me. "Do you understand? There is no touching!"

Yam shrugged as if K.G.'s words meant nothing to him. So I nodded back. From then on, Jate made sure that with every morning meal, a tiny pill was waiting for me. When she first delivered it, it was the first time I saw her smile through her long, straight hair. "Once your cycle starts, there will be more meds...plus the shots. But for now, we have to ensure your cycle indeed begins."

I didn't like the way her lips curled up at me, or the tiny little pill, or what was still to come—the process, the huge demand on my body to create lots of eggs for Ashyr.

Now, as I watched Yam's hand bounce against his knee, I hunted for our day's conversation topic. "What do you miss most right now...about home?"

He shook his head like he didn't want my help over his grumpy mood. "You first," he finally said.

I nodded. It was my job today to bring some positive vibes, but as I started to answer a longing grew in intensity. "The water. I miss the water," I said. "And my time of being with it every morning. The smells in the air." Even though Yam had been right, because once I started using the soaps, lotions, shampoos, conditioners, candles, air fresheners, and everything else that existed in my secured living quarters, I not only got used to the smells, I stank too. And that was what I missed, the breeze of fresh air.

"They can't fix it."

His words cut right through my memory—me standing in the water, the waves lapping over my calves, the feeling of awe rushing through me. Instead, his tone brought the fear, the wrong note, the unfixable state of the island.

"I thought you said they could?" I asked lightly. "You said Ashyr gave our dads what they needed to repair the oxygen levels, right?"

"Something keeps happening, so they can't keep the levels balanced long-term."

"They built the islands." It still felt funny to say those words. "They've kept both our homes running for all these years." *In secret from me...* but I left out the self-commentary. Instead, I remained calm for Yam. "They know how to make it work, so they'll get everything working again."

"This is different."

"How do you know that?"

"I talked with Baba today."

My eyebrows shot up. "When?"

"Earlier this morning. I haven't been able to reach him for days." Yam spoke as if his focus had turned somewhere else. "He's been too busy investigating this."

"How did you talk to him?"

"Just..." he shook his head. "Let me relay the information."

Once before, he had said that. He asked if I wanted him *to relay information* to my dad—just like that, so matter-of-factly, like he had another phone with him that was different than the device he'd first given me, which died after our second day.

Apparently, that phone required a special charger that was in his drone, which our dads were currently using to fly back and forth between their islands. So now I had silence, no communication with my family. But he still had a working one. When I asked to see it, he dismissed me. "It's just something my baba made for me."

"Can I use it to talk to my dad?"

"Not yet. Besides, they're busy."

"Just let me talk to my dad."

"I'll let you know when you can."

And that was it. Once before, when I had asked why Jate and K.G. looked so odd, Yam had dismissed me, saying "Everyone looks different here. It's the accessories. Just accept it." It was this same tone, this attempt to silence me. He used it whenever he mentioned communicating with his dad. So here it was again, another moment where that unrest inside grew—at Yam, at my dad, at all the people who wanted to control my life.

Before I even knew I was stuck inside a giant bubble, I had felt trapped. But now, outside the bubble, I felt even more trapped. Like I'd been thrust inside tight, lead-laced shoes, trapped and bound. Ashyr handing me off to Jate, forcing me to wait until I gave him my eggs. Me waiting for Yam to let me talk to my dad. My parents not reaching out to talk to me and make sure I was okay.

"I should be there with him. Helping him," Yam said.

"Not here," I said quietly, the unrest growing stronger inside.

"Yeah," he said.

"Waiting."

"Waiting," he said.

He looked around my living quarters. I did too, at the gray tones on the cupboards, walls, ceilings, sofa. Other than the black coffee table and the white drapes, as well as a white vase and a black table and chairs, the room just held a palette of grays. Color came when Jate or K.G. entered the room. Same with when I looked out the window in the evening. As the dusk settled on the people, the gray streets and gray buildings were offset by the brilliant colors of reds, blues, oranges, greens, pinks, magentas, teals, turquoises, peaches, and yellows that moved through the streets.

"Something isn't right. I can tell," he said.

"So let's get out of here."

His eyes questioned what I had just said.

I turned my head. "Or…" I focused on the black-and-white checkered board on the gray end table. "Let's play chess." How sick of this game I was. As I moved the board onto the coffee table, I redirected the conversation again. "Have you noticed there aren't children here?"

"Leilani," he said slowly. He waited until I glanced at him. "We finish what we came to do." I looked back at the board, turning it to give him the white colors this time, only to hear, "Then we go home."

I jerked my head toward the outside window and kept focused on my new conversation. "Whenever I watch the people, I never see any children with them."

"They are at the nursery." He picked up a pawn. It was his turn to go first. "Or the care center, or whatever they call it." He sounded so frustrated.

After he placed his pawn, I moved mine. "I want to see the children."

"Yes. Let's see the reason we are here." His frustration shifted to sarcasm. "Let's see the ones we are helping."

"Maybe I'll ask Jate or K.G. to ask Ashyr. Maybe he'll let us see the children."

"Sure." He moved another pawn. "Maybe he will."

TWO

ASHYR

Like an expectant parent, Ashyr bounced into the seat of his private drone. Numerous times, he had shown up at these appointments regarding the status of developing eggs, but today was like no other. Today's status meant a check on what would save all his children.

As the drone lifted into the late morning traffic, Ashyr's hands glided along his recently dyed hair. Jet-black roots lifted upward into an orange and blonde inferno, the perfect hairstyle for the occasion that put Ashyr back on top. No more heavy secrets ahead.

While the drone glided along, he used his inhales and exhales to dream over the approaching news. As long as follicles were maturing, eggs would follow. With the medication, the percentages intrigued him. The harvest should be high. His fingers bounced against his knee as he ran through the numbers. From follicles to harvestable eggs—eighty percent. From harvestable eggs to fertilized, embryo status—another eighty percent.

On the low end, he could estimate twelve follicles leading to ten eggs, eight to fertilize. The outcome—three to four fetuses—a completely doable number.

But...as long as they didn't overstimulate her production, what if there could be twenty-four follicles...or more? From twenty-four to twenty eggs...sixteen fertilized...then...six to eight fetuses developing! A jackpot to work with—half for stem cell growth to cure the current generation of youth, the other half to restart his next batch of healthy children.

As soon as the drone landed, Ashyr shot out. He headed straight to the elevator, then down to the ground floor to meet the receptionist.

"Hello, President Harmon." She stared with adoring eyes, like she clearly had been waiting for him.

He grinned back. "Have my guests arrived?"

Her high cheekbones raised toward the rotating doors behind them. "Perfectly timed. I think one's coming through now."

A youth headed straight toward Ashyr. From his bun, large strands of auburn hair fell, unkempt. The rest of him was neatly shaved, but the black shirt was misbuttoned. The right side hung lower than the left, with the shirttails partially tucked in, partially tucked out. And the kid's breathing—disorganized and completely out of control.

For any other youth, Ashyr would reprimand the appearance. But this one was on loan. "Welcome," Ashyr overemphasized calmness in his voice. "Welcome, Yam."

"Is she here?" His eyes were wide. He leaned so closely, Ashyr had to step back.

"I believe we are still waiting on..." Ashyr turned to the receptionist, "Miss Leilani?"

"She's gone," Yam said from behind.

Ashyr turned back. Even if his *Baba Brody* wouldn't approve, this kid needed an EnRapture experience. Some soothing effects would be good for his highly exposed nerves. Again, Ashyr spoke softly, "She and her handler will be arriving soon." He turned back to the thin-lipped receptionist.

"No." Yam touched his arm.

The receptionist gasped. Ashyr spun back and waved the touch from his skin. "Where's your handler?"

"She's gone." Yam's head shook like a fish caught on a line. "She left us."

A tight laugh pressed against Ashyr's rib cage. He spoke over the kid's response. "She'll be here shortly, with her handler..." Again, he turned to the receptionist. "Jate, right? That's the name?" Before a confirming nod, Ashyr returned to Yam. "Leilani and Jate will be here soon. And now, answer my question. Where is your handler?"

Blankness covered Yam's face. "You need to talk to Jate."

Youth who avoided answering Ashyr's questions received a warning. But in this situation, Ashyr instead felt his upper lip curl. He spun around and lifted his head at the receptionist. "Let's connect with Jate."

With a narrow smile, the receptionist said, "Certainly, President Harmon."

Such respect. In fact, under the circumstances, such character should be rewarded, even if the pout of her lips could benefit from some additional accessorizing. Ashyr pulled out one of his own Golden Invites and handed it across the desk. "Reach out to me."

Her eyes grew wide; a giddy laugh slipped out of those pencil-lined lips. "For an experience?"

"Yes. With me." Ashyr tapped at his own seal.

"Thank you." She clung the invite to her chest before waving it over her ring to be recorded.

Determined not to turn around, Ashyr kept the smile on her. "You're welcome."

Then she followed her instructions, punching in the request until the hologram of Jate emerged. All Ashyr could see was dark purple hair with neon pink highlights, and a nod that followed, which concerned him.

"Eye contact," he demanded.

With a whip of the neck, her hair parted. Unmistakable moisture filled Jate's eyes.

"Where are you?" he asked.

"Back at the..." but the words trailed off.

A grunt exploded from Ashyr. "Why aren't you here? At the clinic?"

"I can come." Her eyes blinked through the moisture. "But I won't have Leilani."

Yam stood close. His breath prickled against Ashyr's neck. "Where is she?" Ashyr asked.

In unison with Jate, Yam answered, "She's gone."

"How?"

"I don't know," Jate said.

Yam leaned in close, bumping against Ashyr's arm. "Check her meds," he said.

Ashyr shifted back, only to meet Yam's eyes. "Why?"

"I'm not sure..." Slowly, Yam's head shook. "I don't think she took them."

Ashyr spun back to Jate. Hair again covered the hologram face. A nod followed. "I'll check," Jate said.

The face disappeared, replaced by the hold image of colors rotating in a circular fashion. Ashyr's jaw tightened.

At last, she returned with no eyes present, just dark purple hair. Then came the nod. "One pill gone. No shots taken."

"She's gone," Yam said again.

Ashyr shut off the call.

Foster did this. No one else would. *You traitor.*

"You knew about this." He spun around to face Yam. "Didn't you?"

"What?" The boy looked confused. "No."

"You just said it yourself. She didn't take the meds." *First, Foster, you took Mariana from me. Now you took Leilani.* "Why didn't she take the meds?"

"I don't know." Yam took a step back.

"Because she never intended to be here, did she?" A vein throbbed near Ashyr's temple. *You take and give nothing back.* "You. Your families. They lied to me."

"No. We didn't."

"Then where is she?"

"She…" Yam's focus fell to the ground. In a whisper, he said, "Maybe she's been kidnapped."

This was preposterous. *It doesn't require much, Foster, just respect. Respect for all that I have here.* "How? By whom?"

The kid just stared at the floor, shaking his head slowly. "I've been with her every day."

Ashyr spun back to the receptionist. "We need answers. Who worked with Leilani? Give me the nurses who trained her to administer her meds."

The receptionist's fingers moved fast against the tablet. "Nurse Scroll."

"I want an exchange with them ASAP. I want clear, undiluted facts. Nothing fancy in the exchange, just the pure memory of working with Leilani. I'll be in the first collection room. And…" Ashyr pointed behind him. "Send a secured drone to pick up this youth. Contact his handler, find out why he isn't here with the kid now. Make sure he is there, waiting for the drop-off. Tell him Code LD." Then he faced the kid. "Foster won't stop this."

"He didn't."

A plan burned in Ashyr's head. "We send out a massive alert. We blast it across every person's registry. Every EnRapture club. Use every airship in my fleet. And we throw out a reward. One that can't be refused. We find them." He drew his shoulders back. "You do not reach out to your *baba*. You especially do not reach out to Foster." He nearly yelled at the kid. "Understood? We find her in no time. We get her back here. We use whatever follicles she has. One or twenty-four. Doesn't matter. A contract is a contract. And Foster delivers on this."

"He didn't take her," Yam said.

"We'll see. Won't we?"

THREE

YAM

Deep breaths in, long breaths out. Ujjayi-focused breaths. Yam sought the sound like the ocean in his exhale. But such a sound only stirred memories of Leilani: him on her beach, her kiss, her island, their homes.

For the past six hours and forty-three minutes, Yam had worked to control his breathing. Since Leilani's disappearance, his treatment had been that of a high-risk runaway.

What if she had been kidnapped? Kidnapped would be easier to face. Just as long as she was found safe.

He picked up his guitar again. If he wasn't playing or attending to his breathing, anxiety came like an impending storm. But within only a few strums he was back on his island, playing for her during that first day they had met.

He'd been quick to fall. Too quick. More strums and he was seeing her there in these quarters. The weeks of them stuck together in this place. Day after day, every day, her and him getting through this awful time—together.

Where was she? His fingers took on a life of their own. Quickly, they plucked at the chords of his song in progress—her song. He hated those notes now.

Earlier in the day, he gripped his written lyrics, prepared to rip his work to shreds, but he hadn't.

If only she had taken the medicine. He focused on his breathing, the Breath of Fire. Active exhales to regain control, to reconcentrate, to be mindful of the moment.

If he could just notify Baba! How he missed Baba. He should be there, helping Baba.

Anxiety whirled closer to his lungs. Without clear thought, he made a poor attempt at Kapalabhati breathing. Ashyr—quick, explosive exhales, as if trying to push the anxiety out of his lungs—accusing Baba, or at least Foster. Tight. Short. Sharp breathing, dripping like gasoline drops over an impending blast—there was no way they took Leilani!

He didn't care what Ashyr said, Yam had every intention of notifying Baba as soon as he could get to his FID, the Fluid Interface Device, tucked in his jacket that he'd left at Leilani's place. All day, he'd been waiting, trapped in his apartment like a caged animal.

The moment the elevator door beeped from the hallway Yam released a sudden softer exhale. He closed his eyes and lowered his shoulders. The hand of anxiety withdrew. The electronic lock disengaged. A knock followed.

Yam yanked the door open to find K.G.

"Have they found her?"

"Nope." K.G.'s eyes looked bloodshot. "No word of her yet."

"Ashyr said this would be easy. He said he would send out a blast and she would be found."

With a covered dinner tray in hand, K.G. motioned to enter.

Yam shifted, letting his handler in while heading straight down the hall toward Leilani's door. It was locked.

When he turned back, K.G. stood in the hall. The dinner tray was gone.

"I've been locked in there all day." Yam pointed at his door then shifted to point at hers. "I need to get in. I left something important in there."

K.G. shrugged his broad shoulders. "I don't have access. Everything's changed today." He shook his head as if scolding Yam. "Her disappearing. And you...not in my care this morning. I'm going to be reassigned."

Again, Yam tried the door handle, only to receive the same results.

"For now," K.G. said, "in order to meet your needs, I have limited access to this area."

Yam spun around, waving a hand at the exterior doors. "Great! Then help me. My *need* is to be out there searching for her."

K.G. shifted to stand between Yam and the exit. "I have clear instructions. You are not allowed out."

Out, like Yam was a bug shooed into a jar, left alone to wait for scraps of leaves from the outside world. He tried again. "My essential need is to talk to Ashyr."

K.G. folded his wide forearms. "That is unarrangeable. Ashyr is waiting at his place, hoping there is some news soon." Then a grin rounded his lips. "Well...he's not just waiting...but...he's being taken care of."

"What does that mean?"

"Uh..." Kandi-Green shrugged. "The twattle is..." He whirled a finger around as if teasing Yam with a level of coyness, "it seems Ashyr is staying busy right now." The chubby finger stopped its little dance. "He has a long list of EnRapture partners lined up around his penthouse. Hundreds have come to offer support. Condolences. Their exchanges to help Ashyr at this time." He reached down his V-neckline shirt to produce a handkerchief. The handkerchief rolled around his finger. "The day has been bombarded with announcements about her disappearance. A bit of disruption to our normal routine." He offered a light sniffle, but his voice lacked emotion. "Everyone's talking about this special youth that's so important to Ashyr. And how she's gone missing." With the handkerchief, he dabbed at his red eyes. "Once I finish up here, I'm headed to the condolence party too."

Yam processed the baby face, the exhausted eyes, the lack of real sympathy. "Do you think she was kidnapped?"

Eyes grew huge, followed by a childlike shrug. "I know what Ashyr tells me."

"Which is what?"

"I don't know where you two came from. I don't know why Ashyr cares so much about her. But I do know he says someone from where you came from has meddled with the important work here."

Yam gripped at the top of his bun. A breath struggled in his lungs. "I need to see Ashyr!"

"No." The handkerchief disappeared again, back down through the V-neck. "Right now what Ashyr needs is comfort."

Suddenly, Yam took control of his breath, a deep inhale followed by an exhale of a clear plan. Get the FID. Get help. Find Leilani. Go home.

To do this, Yam needed out of this bug jar.

Roughly six feet ranged between the short, square body of K.G. and the locked door that led to the elevator. When Baba was Yam's age, violence surrounded the globe. *Violence and hatred. Harm to other humans.* Yam could hear Baba's words, his claim of *why* he built an island and left the world behind.

But within these circumstances, right in this moment, what would Baba do? Well…Baba had pulled a super-old, unloaded, pointless gun on Ashyr. Not to use, but to persuade a change. A demand for Ashyr to leave. And that was Yam's answer: in place of a weapon, Yam's aikido training—not to harm, but rather to persuade a change. No violence. But a…

All right, it was violence.

But it'd be a quick, well-calculated move. He wouldn't hurt his handler. Nothing major. Just the element of surprise. The wind knocked out of him while Yam grabbed the key fob and swapped their situations.

A calm, empowered breath in. A shift with the right foot. A plant with the left foot. A strong exhale out. A nod and a smile. Then Yam launched. His right leg flew around. His left leg hit its target, straight into K.G.'s hip, and the square body fell to the ground.

He wanted to pause and check, make sure he hadn't hurt his opponent. Instead, he dashed for the pocket, grabbed the key fob, and darted to the metal doors. After a brief fiddle and a beep, Yam exhaled.

He was already down the fire escape when the pounding began.

FOUR

YAM

As he burst out of the building, the evening air greeted him. After being trapped inside for weeks, the refreshing air eased Yam's racing heart. Briefly, he held his pent-up eagerness in place, listening until in the distance he heard the low hum of people. Then, like coiled springs on one of Baba's PIGS, Yam's muscles sprang into action, and he ran toward the noise.

His body only slowed when he spotted the thick crowd. Soon he was surrounded by intoxicating smells of perfumes, colognes, body sprays, soaps, hairsprays, and synthetic fruity scents. Flowers, banners, and people in masks and capes blocked Yam's path. Repeatedly, he said, "Excuse me," only to have feather boas dance over his arms.

Someone's large back pushed him into another body. A scowling, purple-painted face spun around. "Watch it." Before Yam could apologize, another moved between them. A poster sign rubbed against his arm. *We love you, Ashyr!*

His body revved to keep moving, but to do this he would need to break free from the chaos. He moved to the shadow of a tall building. Another sign passed. *She will be found.* His weight pressed against the building's cold cement wall. With closed eyes, he calmed his breathing. Bit by bit, he shut out the loud noises and visualized the hum of his helipod. The building's coolness transported him as if he were leaning against the drone's window.

From his mind's eyes, he was looking down at the tall buildings, using the FID to navigate his flight, gliding toward his destination. Had traffic been heavy on his descent into the city, the FID would have recalculated, redirecting his path with ease.

So he used this plan to move from the building toward an alley to his right then to a dim, quieter street on the other side. Soon he walked alongside a small group with strong voices.

"All will be well."

"Does anyone know who she is?"

Yam turned at the words. One's skin pattern was striped like a zebra. Another's coloring resembled a tiger.

"She's important to Ashyr," a voice in the group said.

"She must have a high ranking."

"She's a youth, isn't she?"

Yam couldn't stop looking, until one with a divided complexion, dark on the right and pale on the left, met his eyes and said, "Must be a valuable one when she graduates."

Yam sped forward, focusing on his breathing, and left the group behind. Then he made another slip through an alleyway back into the thick of the crowd. From a distance, another sign waved at him: *Let EnRapture calm your fears.*

To reach Ashyr's building, Yam crossed a small park and pressed past the flowers, the banners, the people in masks, capes—some carried megaphones. Music blared near his ears. More body odor and hair spray. Textures of silk, lace, satin, and leather brushed against him. A person with butterfly wings on their back, a stiletto heel on the right foot, and a mid-calf-length boot on the left stepped in front of Yam. "You touched me."

With pressed lips, Yam fought the eye roll. Rather than discuss with another purple-painted face about this madhouse they were in, Yam slid under a barricade. Yells erupted behind him.

"Hey!"

"Who do you think you are?"

"You can't do that."

"Stop him."

He jogged straight up to the entrance right as a security guard met him. "Where's your registry?" The guard's honeycomb fingernails motioned for Yam to deliver. "That little stunt just lowered your ranking by two percent."

"Ashyr wants to see me," Yam said quickly.

"You and everybody else here."

"No. Really."

The guard's magenta eyebrows raised. "He paged you? Unless he paged you, you're not allowed to be where you are." He had shoulders like a bulldog, and a waist trim and packed with strength. Against his teal uniform, his name badge read *Kit*. Yam stood slightly taller, maybe by an inch, but the guard almost doubled Yam's size in solid mass.

"I don't have a registry," Yam said.

Humor lit across Kit's face. He tilted his head toward the crowd. "Then head back to your pod. No youth at this event tonight."

"No." Yam kept his feet planted. Perhaps another martial arts twist. A spin under and around this Kit to yank open the doors…which would likely be locked. Besides, if he were to try the same move he used on K.G., it'd take a lot more force to knock this one down.

"I don't want to hurt you, kid." The guard stepped closer. "But you either leave or I tase you."

Yam felt the inner smile. Kit had just supplied the solution. He drew his shoulders up and positioned his weight. It all came down now to watching Kit's movement. "Do what you have to do, man. It's your job."

Eyes raised. A hand moved to the taser gun at his belt. "Fifty thousand volts! Seriously, kid. Just leave. If you don't have a registry, return to your group pod and hang out with them. Work on building your skills. Maybe in two years, you'll get lucky and have a shot at some time with Ashyr. Pretty damn unlikely—but dreams aren't bad." He nodded his head in the opposite direction from the building. "Just scram, kid."

Yam took a step back, positioning himself, keeping his distance open and ready. "No." He watched the hands. The movement would happen soon. But when Kit didn't shift, Yam egged him on. "You've got it wrong. I'll never touch that stuff. I'd rather die than be put in a situation like that with Ashyr!"

One step, then the guard reached back but with the other hand. The switch threw Yam. For half a second, he delayed. Then, with a quick recover, he launched. His arm swung for the neck. His knee pressed into Kit's, sending him to the ground. He used his other knee to press into the man's back, twisting the wrist so the firing would hit Kit instead. Except, rather than the expected taser shot, an object dropped to the ground.

"What the hell?" The guard, on his back, pointed at the black object that painfully bounced down the sidewalk.

Yam kept his knee in place, securing Kit so he couldn't move, while through jagged breaths, he tried to process the situation. No taser shot...and now he had a pinned-down man to deal with. The crowd yelled. A good five feet away, Yam looked to the taser—which it was not.

"You want me to radio him or not?" Kit spoke into the concrete.

Yam eased his pressure against the guard's back. "You were supposed to tase me," he said weakly.

"And I would have," he said with a grunt, "had you been like everyone else."

Suddenly, hands gripped Yam, pulling him off the guard. Then the arms disappeared as fast as they came. Still, three people boxed Yam in. "What do you want us to do with him?" one asked as Kit rose to his feet. Another one handed him the dropped radio device.

"Nothing." He brushed off his uniform. "I'll take him into the lobby and get this straightened out."

"Can you handle him?" a third voice asked.

The guard's dark magenta eyebrows raised. "Of course." But he pulled out handcuffs with a chain attached. A loud breath and then he reached for Yam's arm. Once Yam was handcuffed, Kit tugged at the chain, leading him through the building's door.

As soon as they got inside, he dropped the chain.

"I thought you were going to tase me," Yam repeated, apologetically.

"Yeah. I should have."

"Why didn't you?"

"Like I said, had you been like everybody else, I would have. But you're not. Are you?" He glanced at the handcuffs then back at Yam's face. "No one talks about EnRapture the way you just did."

"What?"

"That you'll never use EnRapture with Ashyr. Nobody talks that way. Nobody would even think such a ridiculous thing, much less speak it out loud. So yeah, what's your purpose? If you aren't here for that, why are you here?"

Yam let out a slow, controlled breath. "Thanks for..." he raised the handcuffs, "not tasing me."

"Thanks for not breaking my wrist. That was intense. If you weren't a lout, I'd ask if you wanted a job." While he rubbed at his wrist, he nodded at the tinted windows out toward the crowd. "I'm not sure how long this sympathy mob is planning to stick around."

As if in prayer, Yam gripped his hands together. "We need to find her. Before tonight's end. So please, just help me see Ashyr."

For a long moment, Kit eyed Yam. "You got information?" While Yam delayed answering, Kit punched at his tablet. "I make no promises, but…" He rubbed at his chin. "Tell me your 'why' and maybe I'll see about getting you in…maybe…in about ninety minutes."

The crowd's energy had shifted to peering in hummed silence toward the lobby doors. "No. It needs to be now," Yam said.

Kit looked again at his tablet. "Can't be now. And first, I need a strong *why*."

With hands still cuffed, Yam stepped farther into the building. "Just point me in the direction and I'll figure out the rest."

The guard looked up. He tilted his head as if processing something. "I think you're confused. Just 'cause I opted not to tase you doesn't mean I'm looking for you to help me lose my job."

"I have confidential information, which makes my need to see Ashyr urgent."

Kit chuckled. Then he shifted, eyeing Yam as if examining a possible delinquent. "You sure this isn't somehow connected to EnRapture? Running low on supplies, maybe?"

Yam shifted his stance slightly, rolled his shoulders back, and debated his options. Maybe, even while still cuffed, he could launch a surprise attack. But first, he'd need the guard to relax as well. "You really don't get it, do you? I hate that stuff. I don't even want to be here among all you Ashyrites. It's just a society of distractions. No one here thinks for themselves. It's just a huge craze of self-indulgers. Fake gratification with no real experience. There's no progression here."

"Whoa!" Kit raised his eyes. "So you're looking to see Ashyr for a one-way ticket to Australia, huh?"

Yam shrugged. "Most of my family's already there."

With a laugh, Kit reached back toward his taser. "Should have figured. So they've been shipped out. You're just looking to join them, huh?"

Yam shifted his weight back, prepping for the launch just as soon as the man's hand moved. He could do this. It all came down to focus, his legs, and an element of surprise. "We aren't from here," he kept talking. "And no...we never would be a part of *here*."

A grin suddenly broke over the guard's face. His hand relaxed by his side. "Where are you from, bud? It's definitely becoming clear you aren't from *here*."

"Just let me see Ashyr."

The guard tilted his head from side to side. "Tase the kid. Get the kid a spot in line. Send the kid to Australia. Or back to wherever it is he came from.

Huh?" He leaned toward Yam. His hands gripped his belt buckle. "Which option sounds best?"

Kit's eyes told Yam he'd lost any "right" moment to spring. Shifting plans, Yam glanced at the tablet that governed Ashyr's schedule. This place had to be full of locks, fingerprint pads, visual scanners—all stuff that required this Kit as Yam's ally.

With a hopeful breath, Yam opted to risk it all. "Ashyr wants something really bad. More than," he motioned at the crowd, "this sympathy-fed EnRapture lineup. And I'm in a position to give Ashyr what he wants. So help me."

The guard peered intently, as if waiting for Yam to feed him more.

So Yam did. "Tell me what you need." He leaned forward. "What do you really want? Because I'm in a position to help you out. In return for helping me see Ashyr, I can get you whatever you want, from him."

The only response was a low laugh.

That was not the response Yam had been aiming for. "You don't want anything? You don't need anything?"

Another low laugh, then Kit said, "This is when we pull out our registries and start negotiating some deals around our exchange. Only problem is, you said you don't have one. That and you speak your negotiations like a true amateur."

Yam kept his focus. "You've got to want something beyond EnRapture."

"Very few people around here want anything other than EnRapture."

With cuffed wrists, Yam pressed the heels of his hands into the sockets of his eyes. "I just want something like...common sense, instead of this EnRapture—"

"If you're not from here, then you don't get us. This is our culture. It's how we coexist."

"In peace," Yam said sarcastically.

"In peace," Kit said strongly.

"Let me talk to Ashyr." Yam's fingertips rubbed at his scalp. "Let me negotiate with him. Let's see what he can give you. A bonus of the pills. More stock for you."

Kit firmly shook his head. "What do you have that he wants?"

Yam pulled in a long inhale, begging a future Baba to forgive him. On the exhale, he said, "A chance to see some classified artificial intelligence that is quite important to Ashyr."

The guard pressed his lips together. He nodded and said, "I want an experience with Ashyr. Funny, huh? You'd think, me working for him, day in, day out, he'd have offered that to me by now. But no. So yeah, bud. You deliver. Give us this swap, and I'll get you in."

"I want in immediately."

"If you really can deliver, you're next up." He picked up the tablet and dragged items across the screen. "Then," he looked up and smiled at Yam, "this is all assuming you really do have some strange pull with Ashyr. So I get to see him right after you, and you fill in for me down here."

Yam nearly laughed. "I wouldn't know how to fill in for you."

The guard rubbed at his wrist and gave Yam a wink. "I bet you can figure something out."

FIVE

YAM

The automated voice announced his entrance, "Greetings, Yam." From the wide sofa, Ashyr shifted to a reclined position. With half-raised eyelids, he met Yam's face and heaved out a groan. "What do you need, kid?"

The words Yam truly wanted to say stayed in place due to his stern frown.

Ashyr filled the void with his own supply. "This whole day's starting to blend. Violent quests. Daring adventures. Climbing a mountain, an exotic dance workout, sexual conquests, creativity in so many forms. Art in color, shape, sounds, lust. Captures. Feats. Games. Actions. Interested in a sampling? I can make some arrangements for you."

"What are you doing?" The question came as if Yam was his mother.

"Research." A sinister look crossed his face. "For Foster. Want to know what I've learned?"

Yam kept still and gave a stoic nod.

"That I haven't yet reached a max level—if EnRapture has a max level of consumption, I'm not there yet. Foster would want to know that, from our old slum lab days. Old-fashioned him with his lab notebook, handwritten observations, his results, his modifications."

"What about Leilani?" Yam's shell cracked with her name.

A light laugh, while disgust filled Ashyr's smile. "No leads. Because it's hard to find a lost girl who isn't among us. Little did I know Foster could sink this low."

"We need to find her."

"Oh, we are." Ashyr yawned. "Be sure to tell Foster we've got the entire tribe out looking for her."

"No. You have your tribe lined up around your building using this loss as their gain."

"You're loud." Ashyr shook his head as if warding out Yam's voice. "They're sharing information, really helpful stuff, that confirms what we already know."

"Bull." With a wide hand, Yam pointed at the coffee table between them. It was lined with masks, gloves, empty pill bottles, earbuds, and colorful accessory items.

"My gifts," Ashyr spoke lovingly to the table. "Some from tonight. Others from my favorites. See that one." He pointed to the center. "A cat nose, a real taxidermy one. Given to me the night..." As if his strength slacked, Ashyr pressed against the arm of the couch. "Well, you remember that night..." Weakly, he raised an arm and pointed at them. "You and I, we first met at that detention center. My business partner, Serena, gave it to me that night."

"We need to protect her," Yam said.

"I know. But she's been too busy. Doesn't even reach out."

"She's in danger."

"No. She's got something big in the works. That's why I haven't heard from her."

Fuming at Ashyr's lack of focus, Yam spoke firmly. "She, Leilani, can't use EnRapture."

"Oh, *she*." Ashyr closed his eyes and circled his head in a small movement. "Serena. She's good. One of the best of the best. I miss her."

Yam reached for the cat nose and flung it directly at Ashyr. "We need to find Leilani."

Ashyr looked up as if displaced. He blinked his eyes a few times at Yam. "Yeah." He picked up the cat nose from the couch and rubbed his fingers over it again and again. "What do we need to do? We need to help Brody and Foster remember." His eyes met Yam's. "We had an agreement. A trade...and I live in fairness."

The repeating was getting old. Still, Yam said it again, "She is not with Foster."

"Well..." A renewed strength surfaced in Ashyr's voice. "I own this place. EnRapture works, and it would bring her back if she were here. Instead, what we have is Foster, the traitor, and a ticking clock." He gripped his head as if those last two words had been too much for him. He closed his eyes and waved a hand at Yam. "Tell Kit no more tonight..."

"She's here—somewhere in this city!"

"Quiet," he said meekly. His eyes flickered up and down. "We need Foster to bring her back," he said calmly, still grabbing his head.

"We can't." Like claws, Yam's fingers pressed into his scalp. "Because she's not there." He drew in three loud rhythmic breaths. In desperation, his hands fell to his side. He took one more breath in, before adding, "I promised Foster I'd protect her."

An explosive laugh burst from Ashyr. "Me too, kid. Promised Foster directly. But he couldn't leave it at that."

Yam just kept repeating his words. "We need to go find her."

Ashyr shrugged his shoulders. "How about we get you back up in the sky, and you bring her back."

"She's not there!"

"You are an insistent one, aren't you?" Ashyr shifted, placing himself in a more upright position against the armrest. "Here's the plan. Go back to your quarters. Tomorrow morning, you make your donation. Then you're free, kid. Other than our original contract to tell no one why you came here, you are free to go find her. Go for it. Pretend the impossible, that she's here among my people. Or go home, back to your family, and learn she's back with Daddy Viper. Your choice."

"How would I get home? Your airships are banned—one ruined our islands."

Ashyr shrugged, like it was not his problem. "All right then…." He rubbed at his ring. "One more EnRapture experience before heading to bed. Or should I call it a night? Either way, it's time for you to go. I'll notify my guard—"

"Wait." Yam dashed around the coffee table, placing himself uncomfortably near Ashyr.

Ashyr shifted into the crevice of the couch as if alarmed by the proximity. "I stated the conditions. We're now done here." He waved Yam away like a cat. "I keep my word. Give me your donation and your deal is complete with me."

Yam took one more step forward. His shoe touched the edge of the sofa. Other than the fear of facing a future Baba over what he was about to do, Yam spoke with confidence. "I have something you want to see."

A weak laugh came from Ashyr. "Leilani?"

"No." Yam stared forward and formed his words. "Some of my baba's work."

Silence hummed.

"A device to communicate with others," Yam added.

Ashyr still pressed into the sofa, but his eyes held Yam's.

"His AI work." Yam slowly counted, waiting patiently, then added, "So let's make a deal." While a smile overtook Ashyr's face, Yam continued. "Get me into Leilani's room, which is where the device is, and...give your guard an EnRapture experience with *you*...and then..." Suddenly, he gulped for air, the fear of facing Baba overtaking him.

But Asyhr moved it forward. "Your father's work." His body softened into the sofa. "Not

Leilani…but this is closer to being fair." He now sat almost upright and gave Yam a new look of respect. "For the night, I'm done with EnRapture. My guard can have a Golden Invite for another time. As for the rest of your deal, go ahead. I'm listening. Tell me more."

SIX

YAM

Tearing through Leilani's personal space, Yam couldn't locate his jacket. It'd been here—but now it'd vanished.

The night before, he ended up sleeping at Ashyr's. Not that he'd wanted to. But after Yam had shared the generic functions of the FID, Ashyr dozed off with a large smile on his face. Twice, Yam made noise to wake him, only for Ashyr to mumble, "Sleep first, then we'll go get what we need."

Yam refused to explore Ashyr's place. Finding a bed meant lying in one, and Yam would prefer the floor over that. So he took a spot near the entrance and fell asleep. When he awoke, Ashyr stood above him, sipping at something in his mug. "You're a strange kid. I have plenty of rooms here."

Slowly, Yam sat up, wishing he had space to run through his morning routine of stretches to help soften his sour mood.

Instead, he faced Ashyr's alert and cheerful face. "Let's go! It's time to get out of here. Let's go see your pop's work."

On the ride over in Ashyr's private drone, Yam's muscles only tensed further. Perhaps sharing the FID with Ashyr would only make everything worse.

But now, standing in Leilani's bedroom with her clothes thrown to the floor, nothing could be worse. The FID was gone!

With his foot, he shifted through the brightly colored t-shirts, denims, shorts. He dropped to the floor and rummaged through the teals, pinks, and blues. Nothing matched his jacket.

Anywhere.

He picked up a nearby flip-flop and threw it across the room. As if his mum was there, he could hear her words, "Are you *in* control? Or *out* of control?" She would ask him to note the clues. What emotions might overrule a person's control over their own behavior? Then she would surely ask him again, if, at this moment, he was *in* control.

No.

He was on the brink of losing all control over his actions and behavior. And seeing Ashyr's amused grin in the corner was not helping the situation.

"Of course." Ashyr folded his arms and leaned against the doorpost. "This all makes so much sense. They played you too. Our buddies took the girl *and* the device. Doesn't surprise me. Shouldn't surprise you either."

"They didn't take her!"

Ashyr's palms shot up as if he meant no harm. "We still have no sign of her. No one coming forward to give us anything. Looks very suspicious to me."

Yam went into her bathroom. From the drawers, he pulled out the soaps, lotions, shampoo, and conditioner that the place had come stocked with.

Ashyr spoke from behind. "You know, it's like I keep saying, we just need you to go home. Then bring her back. We do this in one week, and we have hope. We have time. We can still carry out the procedure."

"That means we have to find her." Yam hit a box of feminine tampons under the sink. The box tipped, causing its contents to tumble across the cupboard floor. He slammed the door closed.

"Then let's not waste time. You go get her. Otherwise, it's death to everyone she could be helping right now. Death to the next generation."

He wanted Ashyr to shut up. His chest moved up and down as he passed Ashyr, back into the bedroom, where he stripped the bed of the comforter. Trinkets, from when he'd raided her drawers earlier, lay scattered across the floor. Pens, earrings, a bracelet, a miniature framed photo of her and her parents— he stared at all she'd left behind.

"We can't turn back the clock," Ashyr said. "If Foster wants to cooperate, return that which he has agreed to…well then, like I've already said, without the meds, we'll have a smaller harvest, but, we could still make this work."

"Not if she's tried EnRapture, right?" Yam met the cold blue eyes. "Am I right? Won't that sterilize her? You can't have what she has if she uses EnRapture."

Ashyr scowled. "Why…" He glanced at the sides of the room then met Yam's face. "Why would she do that? Brody would never allow it, would he? You trying EnRapture. No. He wouldn't. And neither would Foster. It's honestly a pity, such a tight leash they have you kids on." He raised a chin at Yam as if challenging him. "The training stuff would be fine. Some of what our youth use—it'd be good for you, both of you."

"What about full strength?"

Ashyr gave Yam a mocking grin. "There's a process here. Order among our society. You would be fine. She would be fine. I'm not worried about her and EnRapture."

Yam shook his head. He couldn't think. Not about Leilani. Or about EnRapture. Or the danger she was in. Instead, he needed clarity of thoughts. He needed Ashyr to stop talking. And the FID—he needed the device to guide him, to work alongside him with his thoughts, to replace all this other noise of Ashyr being Ashyr. Of Baba being unreachable. Of Leilani being gone.

Yes, Mum. I have lost control. He wished he could tell her that, instead, he spoke to Ashyr, "What facts do you have to support that they took her?"

"The fact is she can't survive without a registry." A victorious grin followed, as if Yam's question had just validated Ashyr's accusation. "That's my proof. But what do you have?"

Like a hot drink, Yam wanted to spew out all the reasons. She left because Ashyr abandoned them.

She never took the medicine. She had used all of them. But he pressed his lips together and let all the heat burn from inside.

When he opened his mouth again, he forced out calm words. "Sometimes you just know. Our parents have not been here. Truth is truth. And that is the truth—they didn't take her. It just doesn't align."

Ashyr's laugh was barely audible. "Guess you don't know them like I do, kid. Give it time and you'll see them for who they really are. She can't survive out there. She has nothing to offer. So no kid, your theory is wrong."

SEVEN

LEILANI

As directed, I kept the twelve paces between us. But sometimes, the distance shrank. When we entered the dark alleyway, I had to make sure I could still see his silver hair reflected in the moonlight.

The day had been long, full of waiting, but a different type compared to waiting for Ashyr. Today felt like instead of others owning my life, I did.

My new friend, Draven, had said I could find him outside the youth center on the basketball court. I waited. And eventually, he was there.

When he saw me, we spoke briefly, with him instructing me where I could meet him that evening.

So more waiting until dusk came. In the distance, I could hear murmurs. As if I was still looking from my window above, I imagined people, in their colorful dress, now pairing up, until the noise dwindled.

Finally, Draven came.

Only for a new wait to begin.

When I met him at that dark corner, he quietly said, "We need to find a safe place, exotic girl. Don't walk near me. Just follow me."

So I did, through narrow streets that at times lost the moonlight. His boots crunched ahead, and I strained to make out his hair as the light came and went. He said we needed to get away from the city, and he was leading me to a quiet, deserted portion. But for now, moving somewhere, just being outside, with the companionship of the cool air, felt good.

At times, the rhythm of his boots grew more rapid. Gaps between buildings let more moonlight break through. He veered to the left, around a corner, and into another tight alley. Soon buildings hugged us in blackness, until I could no longer make out his hair.

I slammed against him.

"Watch yourself." His breath came out jagged. "We'll have our touch soon."

His boots sounded again. I waited until I caught the movement of his silver hair. As I followed it, I remembered how its brilliant lack of color fascinated me when we first met at the youth care center.

After being stuck in our quarters for weeks, I was thrilled to have an outing. But Yam declined the field trip. I couldn't believe he didn't want to go. But I wanted out of our prison. "Are you going to be okay? Alone?" he had asked.

The truth was I felt so much relief. Him not coming. Me needing space. Just a little change. All that time together, he had become my first unrelated best friend—still, a little break, an environmental change, sounded nice. I told him I'd be fine, and I was.

All the arrangements had been coordinated through K.G. with the word back that Ashyr was thrilled to give me this chance to see where the *off-spring* would go after fertilization.

Now, less than a week later, I created a new field trip, one with my new friend Draven. As we walked through the dark shadows of L.A., it felt great to be free.

* * *

I almost smacked into Draven. Again. This time on a corner with an aged sidewalk beneath. My mind had been lost in the memory of Yam, of sneaking out, of leaving him. Now, Draven paused. As the moon shone down, I circled the area. To our side, a five-story structure had a chunk of concrete missing. So did another building.

A lot of life had once been here. But now the buildings were damaged and past repair. Destruction from the past. What Dad had deemed *the end of the world*. While we remained motionless, I debated which questions to ask my guide. Did I want a history lesson right then? Or to keep us moving?

Draven hunched over. His hand pressed against his back.

"What's wrong?" I asked.

He just shook his head. "A little pain. It'll go away as soon as I have an EnRapture experience, which will be soon. We're almost there." Then he was off walking again, but not as fast this time.

I walked near him, almost side by side. "Don't get too close," he said. "We're still not out of the city."

But seconds after I let him take the lead again, he paused and leaned against a tower of cement left from a decaying structure. In the moonlight, sweat glistened on his brilliantly silver-white brow. His breathing came out in chops, like a knife cutting a carrot over and over again.

I checked my breath. At one point, we'd speed-walked and I breathed a bit fast. But not like him. His breaths were laborious, as if he was in pain.

"Are you ill?" I sounded so dense while playing my role well, the exotic girl from far away who had a secret she couldn't share. Thankfully, Draven didn't answer me. He just stared down at the ground and tried to silence his breathing. I looked away. This was his moment...and I couldn't watch it.

Instead, I slipped into my memory of first arriving in L. A., of Ashyr blitzing a hello, making Yam and me sign our names to a contract, our promise that we would not share why we were there, in his care, working toward a solution for his people.

Yam and I both understood our purpose could be misunderstood and stir these people into a state of alarm. It was the *Up in the Sky Silence Pact*, as Yam and I called it, and we respected it.

Other memories came, ones I didn't want. Like Yam's words that we needed to do what we came to do then go home. Like my mom's voice. *Are you being selfish, Leilani?* Isn't everybody selfish? Weren't my parents being selfish when they built an island and left other people behind? Wasn't Ashyr selfish, tricking me to come here to meet his own needs for his people? Who wasn't selfish?

Besides, this was my one opportunity to have an EnRapture experience, to feel what it was like to be a part of these people. Then I would go back. I wasn't leaving forever. I'd go back. Back to being *unselfish* with Yam. Back to waiting for Ashyr. I'd undergo the surgery, even though I wouldn't take the shots or the rest of the medicine.

But I would do it. The procedure. What I told them I would do.

Except now, as the moon served as a spotlight on Draven as he fought his inner battle, all I wanted was for him to start walking again.

When he didn't, I wanted him to wipe his brow. Or stop the jagged breathing.

Instead, he held out his hand. "Here, exotic girl."

"What?"

"I need your hand," he said between breaths.

"Why?" He had made it perfectly clear we were not to touch.

"Let me pretend for a moment. Like we are sharing an experience, like my mind would be elsewhere, right now, away from this pain."

I stayed in place.

"Come on." He nodded his head slowly toward the dark, empty street in front of us while his body pressed against the decayed building remains. "It's safe here. No one can see us. I just have a spasm in my back, some annoyance, an injury that's slowly healing.

And once I have an exchange, the pain will leave again. But…since you've never done this…right?"

I pressed my lips together and nodded.

"Well, until we can get to the underground bar, you don't have a registry. So let me at least show you. Do you know what happens?"

I shook my head.

"Well, this pain will leave soon. Give me your hand." He pointed at it, and I broke out of my statue stance. His fingers and palm slid over mine, then his fingers locked down. He gave me a calm smile and his breathing softened. Inside, I felt a flitter. A happiness. Then his palm disappeared. But his other hand that held my hand from below stayed in place. Using a finger, he traced over my palm. "When we connect, the glove will be the conduit." His index finger pressed into four places on my hand. With each touch, I felt a surge of electricity penetrate through me.

"Your neurons will send me the message, the experience you want to share with me. You decide the emotional journey you wish to take me on. And I choose the same for you."

His finger just hung there, pressing into my palm. My fingers folded down, nearly touching the top of his hand.

Then, slowly, he stopped holding my hand from below, but his finger still pressed into my palm. His thumb hovered so closely. I held my breath, waiting for it to touch my skin.

At last, it did. His thumb and index finger pressed into a portion of my hand, like pressure points on both sides. Then he lowered my hand to my side.

In place of his touch, his eyes held mine.

His voice was a whisper. "I've nearly graduated, and I've had a lot of exchanges to prepare me for what's next. But you've had none."

"Until now," I replied softly.

"I've been in training since I was twelve, exotic girl from another place." He expressed no humor on his face. "I'm good. I mean I'm really good. One of the best. Ashyr himself once said that about me. So you—for your first experience—it's going to be really good. Quite possibly the best of the best. Remember it won't always be that good for you. I hope you understand that."

I nodded. My breath felt quick and light and I wanted his hand to touch mine again. I swallowed as he continued. "If you plan to live here, you need to learn fast. Do everything you can to advance quickly. Use the registry we're about to get to build up your ranking. Then once you have a start, seek out the best help you can find. I'm an excellent first—an ideal beginning—but the registry we get you...you'll be going straight into adulthood. There will be no training experiences. Do you understand me? The rest of us have a training portion—so you need to learn fast."

In the darkness, with only the moonlight overhead, I kept watch on his soft eyes and nodded my agreement. I would go back eventually, but for now, my choice was to be here living like they lived.

EIGHT

YAM

Twenty minutes earlier, an EnRapture party launched, leaving Yam to walk the streets in peace. While others celebrated some holiday in Ashyr's society, Yam used the time to clear his head.

Between his guitar case, duffle bag, and backpack, he felt like a cross between a turtle and a mule. K.G. had packed his belongings—had them out ready for him when Yam returned from the clinic after his donation. With a pleasant "bye-bye" and a huge smile, K.G. loaded Yam up and practically shoved him out of the building.

Once again, among all his belongings, Yam searched for the jacket and the FID, even though he already knew they weren't there.

So it all was simple in theory, his mental *to do* checklist: find the FID; reach out to Baba; let Foster know; get home. So simple to understand what needed to be done. The difficulty was in how to accomplish each task.

It didn't help that the task *Find Leilani* kept clawing for its place on the list. Of course, he needed to find her. She was as important as the FID—and finding *it* likely meant finding her.

As he walked, he passed an accessory shop designed to look like a giant wrapped package. The windows were dark and mysterious. The signage in front said Step into Aweshocking. *Accessories to discover your unique you.*

Earlier today, as he had waited at the clinic, before they sent him back for his deposit, he had overheard the chatter. It was more information than he ever wished to hear again: changed body parts, the modifications of appearances, the ways to allure others—all through accessories. Now as Yam passed one shop after another, he noted how they thrived on the mystery, alluring customers through the next great shock—a hunt for a new trend or thrill that would take one's registry right into the next tier for higher-ranking partners.

He sped up only to feel the burdensome weight on his back. Perhaps the wisest thing he could do was just turn around and ask Ashyr to provide his one-way ticket out of here. But his feet continued as if their duty was to hit the streets, searching, like he would be able to find her with nothing but his belongings to help him through this crazy world.

Why had she left? The question burned at his mind, his eyes, his heart. *Why? Why? Why?* He pushed out the question. *Just keep walking. Just take the next step.*

Snippets of his song-in-progress hit him. He had pictured sharing it with her, the lyrics that revealed how he had felt about her. Yam and Leilani—that's how it was supposed to be. He would teach her the words and they would sing it, passing the time—*together*. And then—*together*—they would return home.

He set down the guitar case then unloaded the weight of the duffle bag and backpack. The street showed no signs of people, just rows of businesses. Off in the distance, he could hear the music, the Rage Party, the noise, the competitions, the crowds, the world Yam wished to be far from.

A brochure had been discarded among the flowerbed of rocks and black-eyed Susans. The building next to him was an EnRapture care center. He stepped closer to the pamphlet, refusing to pick it up yet drawn to the words that captioned a flashy man in a purple costume and a lion's mane headdress.

The best care during your accessory rehabilitation period. Daily EnRapture partners with 400 or higher ranking available around the clock to give you the very best exchanges, making your stay here easy and enjoyable.

Yam shook his head and kicked at a rock that had spilled out of the flowerbed. He had no clue what he was doing, where he was going, or how he would survive. He picked up his gear again, loaded up his back, and resumed walking. The act of moving seemed the only way to clear his head... to find direction, his courage, the strength to find the device. To find her.

But the truth was, even if he tried to look, he was useless. Without Ashyr's support, Yam was a young, broken kid in Ashyr's system. He didn't belong anywhere. Therefore no one wanted to talk with him. Without the ability to perform an exchange, no one had any time to help him.

As Yam stared at the *Missing* poster outside a high-end EnRapture club, Leilani's eyes met his and he couldn't help but get lost in the irony. From running supplies, he knew certain places to go. But not for this. For this, he was broke. Nowhere to go with no plan emerging. Yet here, Leilani's photo stared back at him. No skills, no street smartness for Ashyr's system, and yet she'd been able to remain hidden for the past two days. No one had turned her in. Which, due to Ashyr's reward, seemed odd even amid Yam's disgust.

How was she surviving?

Living in the shadows of the streets? Perhaps she had left the tribe's boundaries. Found a way outside of Ashyr's region. But how would she get anywhere? She had no transportation.

Unless she stole someone else's transportation.

Or...maybe she was surviving. Maybe she had found a way to work past Ashyr's system. Maybe she was playing against Ashyr's system and thriving in some way.

He turned the idea around and around as if it were the old Rubik's cube his dad had once tossed into a junk crate. As a kid, Yam loved that thing, staring at it, studying it, trying to solve all the mismatched colors. Eventually, he had succumbed to the temptation and peeled off the stickers to relocate them and fix it himself.

Fix it himself.

If he were to fix this, the only way he could do so was with Ashyr's support. Or find someone to work with inside the system. Because he couldn't survive on his own...and neither could Leilani. Which meant Yam had one other option, one other person he knew. He needed to find Aria.

NINE

LEILANI

The first time I met Draven, the events played out like we were meant to be. On that day of my special field trip, K.G. led the way to a single-passenger drone that waited on the roof for me. With a new view, I watched the city as the drone weaved through the buildings. The people, like colorful ants, scurried along the streets and soon I would be joining them.

When the drone landed, Ashyr was waiting for me on the care center's roof. His eyes carried that same look from before, on the island, when I had told him I would join him in L.A. How pleased he looked as I stepped from the drone.

His bangles clanged around his wrist as he waved me toward the elevator. "You're going to be amazed. It's always amazing! These children have the ultimate care. Every need met. Every want satisfied. Think, Leilani, think what you wanted as a child. What did you ache for? If you were here now, it would be granted."

With no pause for me to answer, he moved swiftly into the elevator. But I did answer, silently. I ached to leave the island, to get away, and experience something new.

Inside the elevator, a man with large, folded arms eyed Ashyr closely. "I have an expiring ticket here," he said. "You promised me, no matter what time, when I saw you next, it'd be the right time to cash in. I'm here. And I see you. So the moment is now."

Ashyr pressed his lips together. A quick chuckle or grunt sounded behind his lips. "Well…" He looked from the man to me. "Well… well…" Then, as the elevator descended, he faced me completely. "Seems we have a situation here. An emergency, if you will. See, I have a promise I must follow through with, and…" He spun back toward the man. "Well…" He waved his arm toward me. The bangles crashed together as he searched for something, some words, and suddenly I felt it: forgotten again, an inconvenience, a babysitting moment where Ashyr felt required to find someone else to care for me.

As the elevator doors opened, I hid my agitation to say, "I can wait."

"No. No." He waved his arm again in my direction but didn't look at me. Instead, he stepped out and looked past the lobby toward the entrance gate. "I'll find you someone."

"Don't rain-check me again," the man said, his step a bit close to Ashyr. "You don't want word out that you don't deliver."

Ashyr raised a hand to silence him. "Ah, yes, Viki," he called to a person who appeared within our view. She headed toward us with very long, gorgeous curls, a brightly painted face, and a strong, powerful nose. The tank top was low and thin, designed for a body builder, and her arms and chest were hairy and muscular. At the waist, she wore a flowery belt buckle, followed by a pencil skirt that stopped mid-calf to reveal her hairless, shapely legs. Her high heels tapped loudly as she looked at Ashyr. I stared longer than I should have. I fixed it with a smile, but Viki only focused on Ashyr.

"I need a rescue," he said. "A trade for a trade."

The voice cooed back like a bird. "I'm always up for a trade."

"Take her, this Miss Leilani." His bangles clashed toward me. "Give her a tour. Show her the place. Don't ask her questions. She won't answer them. Right, Leilani?" At last, he looked at me.

My only response: a simple nod.

"She needs to see what we do here. Show her the workings and our successes."

"Lovely. I'll give her the 431 tour."

"Perfect." Then Ashyr was gone, leaving me in the lobby instead of showing me what he built. Gone like Dad. With no goodbye before he left.

*　*　*

The silver hair stopped ahead. "We made it." Draven nodded at a sign, dark and broken. Among the shattered light bulbs, one remained. Its hazy glow faded in and out with static infrequency to reveal the words *Southern Exposure*—the underground EnRapture bar.

"It'll be okay here?" My voice cracked as an uncertainty suddenly emerged.

"Pretty sure—at least from what I've heard, they don't ask questions. Through my training, I should be able to work out an exchange to get a registry. As long as I can find a willing partner, we should be good."

He stepped down into the dark steps, toward the entrance, and farther into the shadows. He reached for the door. Hastily, his hand drew back as if he'd been burned.

"What?" I stepped down to be near him. The single bulb glowed on. "Whoa!" I caught it. The black and white flyer. The large header: MISSING. The reward: EnRapture experiences to increase ranking by 200%. My face in the center of the poster.

My left heel hit against the stairwell. I couldn't look at Draven. I didn't know if he was looking at me. Surely he was thinking about the reward, of turning me in. It was over. My short little escape, my hopes of freedom, of living—it was over.

I drew my foot slowly up a step.

"Are you going to …" My bold tone failed right as the light flickered on for me to meet my eyes on the poster.

In the fuzzy light, I also caught the amused smile on his lips. "Well, you seem to be worth a lot."

My foot glided up another step.

"With no EnRapture experience, huh?" The tone of his voice had shifted. A finger went to his chin, tapping it as if processing his options. "It doesn't quite make sense..." He turned fully around to face me. "Who exactly is offering this reward?"

I needed to find a lie. Fast.

Ashyr had to be angry right now. Very angry. And Yam—I couldn't even think about Yam.

The poster made me feel like a criminal.

I just needed a registry—like Draven had promised. From there, I could make it on my own. And with a registry, if I wanted to, I could change my identity. From all Yam had shared, changing one's looks was so common here. It was like eating bread. Everyone did it. So I would too. A new look and a fresh registry that I would use to build up through experiences. I could do this. If that's what I wanted to do. Or I could go back—on my own. When I was ready.

As the light flickered again, I met perfect circular eyes, open and wide. "Is it the Council? Maybe even Ashyr? Who's looking for you?"

I drew in a breath. "How about we have that experience you promised me first? Then you take me back. It'll be a win-win for both of us."

He rubbed at his chin. His eyes never left mine. "A win." His lips twisted up as the bulb went out. "An increased ranking of 200%. I'll be the youngest person to ever have had that kind of ranking."

I nodded against the sadness I felt from his words. He would use my situation for his gain.

Just as I would use him for mine.

It was all that was fair.

TEN

LEILANI

Sounds made me jump. The darkness felt like a friend and a foe. After all my waiting, this wait felt the longest of all. I crouched down in a doorframe of an abandoned building, close to the EnRapture bar but not too close, while Draven secured a registry and kit for me.

I tried not to think, yet all I could do was think. I had to stick to my plan. Stay in control.

Once Draven reappeared, he gave me a nod.

"Stay near, but not too near," he muttered as he passed. Then he was off again like a snake, winding me through the dark alleyways. No updates. No discussion. Just a speed that hadn't been there before. His exchange at the EnRapture bar must have helped...that and the offered reward.

I expected him to stop at any moment, but he just kept walking—swift steps, almost leaps, from building shadow to building shadow.

"Too close," he said when I reached him at the edge of the last building.

From there he stepped out into an open space of fields, a single road, and railroad tracks. Cautiously, he looked around. Then he gave a small nudge with a finger. I was to follow him. Close. But not too close.

The more lost I got in my thoughts, the more determined I became that Draven would not take me back. Not for a reward. I would return on my terms.

When he reached the tracks, his fingers barely nudged the next command, a gesture for me to move forward, past him. "Just follow the rails' path," he muttered.

I did. And I hated it: him walking in the shadows, watching me, tracking me like I was his prey. What if Draven wasn't going to fulfill his portion of our bargain? What if he was leading me straight to Ashyr?

Sometimes when I turned back, he was there. Sometimes he wasn't. Sometimes for long distances, it was just me and the rails, and a twig snapping in the silence behind me. All this felt silly, dramatic, like I had stepped into an elaborate fiction tale. I wanted to turn back and question him. Why such ridiculousness? No other person was around. Why the long travels? Where was he leading me? I should demand answers—and keep control of this situation. But each time I considered challenging him, I heard Yam's voice instead. *They do things different here. It's best to stay clear of the people or have someone you can depend on to help you get around.*

For right now, I had to trust Draven. I could at least trust that he didn't want to call attention to himself. And if a reward was out for me, I couldn't draw attention to myself either. Not until I got what

I needed. So I kept walking until I heard a whistle to my left.

He stood near a wide field. He didn't turn around again; he just kept moving along. I took his cue and followed, keeping a distance, trying to watch my steps in the darkness while I tromped through the brittle hay-like grass in my beach sneakers, trusting they would protect me against anything that required protection.

My breathing had picked up. I was getting tired. Hungry and tired.

To not get too lost in my needs, I tried to focus on something else, like the field-trip-care-center day, when Viki shared "the toddler and preschool abode." Her cooing voice carried on, speaking about the well-equipped security, so "the little critters didn't wander off."

While Viki was lost in her presentation, a young boy popped up in the window. He had red hair, center-parted, and large ears that reminded me of the primate science poster on my bedroom wall back home, of the bonnet macaque right in the center.

The little monkey waved at me. Then he giggled. I giggled back.

He pointed at his nose. So I pointed at mine. He laughed. I smiled back.

"Come along." Viki's shrill voice broke into our game. She already was at a hallway crossroad.

I gave a small goodbye wave, only to see a whole chorus of children emerging around him. They too now waved, smiled, and laughed.

Again, the little boy pointed at his nose. I pointed at mine. All the others followed.

"Come along," Viki repeated.

Breaking away, I followed Viki until we ended up in a large room with basketball hoops. Older kids, dressed in royal blue and bright yellow gym clothes, played ball until I sneezed. Then a kid turned around. Followed by another. And another, and another. Only the sound of the unattended basketball filled the room.

Viki shattered the silence. "This is a fine sampling of our children. Peers grow from infancy to adulthood here. All siblings. All family. All caring and watching out for each other."

I stared at these kids, pre- or early teens who stared back. I tried to smile, but they didn't return the expression. In their midst, I was a stranger; their looks informed me I was as different as I felt.

"Come," Viki said again. And she was gone.

I followed her down the quiet hall. We passed more windows, with more faces popping up. I stared at them while they stared back. I caught some of Viki's words: *adult care, teamwork, support network, no one ever is lonely*. The faces that watched me pass were different than mine. The look in their eyes, the number of peers that surrounded them, all the things they knew about this place that I didn't understand...a big gap existed between me and them.

Suddenly, Viki stopped. Near the end of the hall, a large man watched us. She nodded at him.

He nodded back. When she spoke again, her voice dropped to a much lower tone. "I forgot something." She sounded masculine. "A small, minor emergency. Something I can address briefly. Could you—" She spun around, then pointed to the cafeteria sign. "Here." Her heels pounded against the floor as she headed toward the sign. "Have you eaten?" she asked like this was a brilliant question. Her ruby lips gave me a wide smile.

"No," I said, while clearly understanding two things. I was a nuisance here. And everyone knew I was out of place.

She stepped inside. I followed, only for again a shift to happen in the room. This time the group staring back was closer to my age. The place was a palette of colors with their inked faces, their dyed hair, and their bright clothing. The expressed styles were like nothing I'd seen before. Maybe punk. Spacey. Fantastical. Just completely different. And I couldn't find how to place myself in this room with my faded jean shorts and my pale pink t-shirt.

Viki left me and I stood alone, near the center of the room, while all eyes watched me.

She hustled a kid from a table. He had the most brilliant silver-colored hair. She soon had him near my side. "Draven will help you. He'll take you through the line. Help you pick out your food. Whatever you need. Once you're finished eating, I'll be back."

And before I could respond, Viki was gone, leaving me face-to-face with this Draven.

"Where are you from?" he asked.

I shrugged. "Why do you think I'm not from here?"

He moved his head in a half-circle, spanning his eyes over the crowd of youth who watched us. "It's pretty obvious you aren't from our batches," he said. "We haven't seen you around."

I hunted for words to answer. I had my pact with Ashyr. So I wasn't exactly sure what I could say.

"There's been some talk," he filled in my gap with his words. "Some rumblings that the council has brought in some new youth, different from any of the batches. Are you one of them?"

I just stared at him. It didn't matter what Ashyr made me promise. Word was already out.

"I hear where you come from is pretty exotic." He spoke as if I'd confirmed his words.

"I could be from here." My tone sounded so hollow, so false.

He drew back, giving me a clear view of the cafeteria. I heard the whispered tones and made eye contact with faces that watched me.

"Why am I different?" I asked more quietly.

A huge grin spread over his ebony-inked lips. "Ah, so the rumor is true. Other youth, not from the batches, are being held by the council. Interesting." The grin widened. Then, with his hand, he waved away the attention of others and stepped around to block my view. In a soft, nearly kind whisper, he added, "If I ask nicely, would you tell me why you're here?"

I liked his smile. And I liked how his eyes danced playfully toward me.

I held top-secret information. News that could spur uncontained fear for everyone in that room. And it was fear that didn't need to be spread, which was why Ashyr had kept me separate from all of them. I understood this. I got the reasoning. But at that moment, I was tired of adults and their secrets. My parents acted like everything was confidential— and that hadn't really worked. Ashyr had treated me closer to a discarded handbag than a guest who was there to help his people. So right then, I wasn't sure whether I wanted to keep helping Ashyr in the way he wanted me to.

But I also hadn't come to spread fear.

As this kid tossed his silver hair back and his dark lips lifted into a smile, I settled on a compromise. Due to the cute pleading in his eyes, I decided to go for a bit of reserved honesty. "I live in the clouds. On an island. It's like a flying saucer spaceship with an ocean and stuff."

"And stuff." His lips curled as if amused, like he was working to suppress a laugh. "So you don't want to tell me. That's cool. Based on your imagination, sounds like you offer some great exchanges."

"I'm serious," I said, trying to show that in my tone. But his adorable smile, which seemed to keep fighting toward a laugh, caused me to break into a smile too. "Plus…" I just shook my head. "I don't share…*experiences*…not what you guys call experiences."

He tilted his head. He looked from my eyes to my toes and then back. When he locked in on my eyes, my heart raced a bit. "You've tried EnRapture or no?"

"No. I haven't."

"The training stuff?" His eyebrows raised. "You've tried that then."

"Nothing."

His eyes grew bigger. Slowly, he nodded. "How interesting."

"Is that why everyone is staring at me?" I looked past him to see that, fortunately, they no longer were. Instead, they were busy eating or leaving their tables to visit with others, as if my novelty was gone. But when I looked back, it seemed the crowd's fascination had all shifted into this one boy's eyes.

"That's not common here." He stepped back like he was still admiring me. "But I guess if you live in the clouds..." He gave me a wink.

I just shrugged. The more his eyes stayed on me, the more my smile grew.

"If you ever want someone to show you, give you a chance to try EnRapture, I can definitely help with that. I'm from Batch Two, nearing graduation, if that means anything to you." His eyes stayed on me.

"No." My playful tone grew. "What you just said means nothing to me. But you can explain."

"Oh, I will." He raised his head, confident, cute, and flirty. My first outing, my first real encounter, and it seemed to be going extremely well. "So," he continued, "do you want an exchange—an EnRapture experience with me?"

"I do." My words sped out too fast. Way too rapidly, along with my heartbeat. "I really do."

"Okay." He stepped forward. His smile appeared pleased at me, at himself, at both of us. "Great. When? Now?"

Of course, right then, Viki appeared in the doorway, all the way across the cafeteria. Even though Draven and I had never left our initial spot, her head scouted around, hunting for me. While she seemed blind, I shifted so Draven's body blocked me from her view. Such timing, when all was going so well. "I can't now. But soon. How do I find you?"

He turned to catch what I'd been looking at. "I take it you're going to need to slip away? That your exoticness keeps you with…well, as the rumors have said, with some high-class company?"

"Company that keeps their eyes on me a little too closely."

"So," Draven slid into a nearby table, his eyes drawing me down with him. We both hunched low. "Can you get away?"

"I'll figure something out."

"Do. Then come back here. I'm always outside the building near the basketball courts around four. Understood?"

"Understood."

Then Viki appeared at our table.

ELEVEN

LEILANI

At the end of the field was an old barn in need of a paint job. "This is the warehouse," Draven said. "We should be safe here."

"Have you been here before?" I asked.

He lifted his head. "I've heard about the place. Inside are some simple spots. Nothing fancy, but as I said, I provide the fancy. After, we can sleep here tonight. Then head back in the morning."

Based on these unsettling looks Draven gave me since the *Missing* poster, I would need to slip out before he awoke. But for now, my legs needed a rest. And sleep sounded good.

"Are you sure you want to do this?" he asked.

"Of course," I said firmly.

But then why was I running my fingers through my hair, again and again? This was Mom's nervous gesture, something which had always annoyed me. Yet here I was doing the exact same movement. I didn't even stop as Draven extended a glove as if out of nowhere.

"Take this, and let's go inside," he said.

It shouldn't have been hard to just take the glove. Just lift a hand, extend my fingers, grip it and take it. But I didn't.

"Look." He drew back the glove. "I'm risking a lot here. Seems you're a fugitive or something, exotic land and all. You must have some high stakes on your head. Whatever it is, it's pretty important you get back to where you need to be."

"I'm not in a rush."

He eyed me. "Others may be."

I shrugged.

"As far as my registry goes, you carry no value for me to have an EnRapture experience with." He raised his eyebrows as if challenging me. "I don't need to go through with this. Do you understand that?"

"Okay, then why did you agree to do this anyway? Before the reward, before you knew otherwise, why did you come?" I crossed my arms, sounding far tougher than I felt, but glad to voice a question that had been nagging at me.

The corners of his lips raised. He met my eyes directly and held them. A softer smile surfaced. "Leilani." A second time, he raised the glove for me to take. "I agreed to this. To give you your first EnRapture experience." He wasn't looking away and a flutter happened near my stomach, then it spread all the way through me. I glanced at the glove. I stepped closer and took it.

"Put it on." He nodded at it.

I slipped it over my hand. The glove felt light and airy. Small nodes, like half-sphere metal balls, cradled against my palm; feeling them against my skin stirred anticipation. Something amazing was about to happen. My breath turned light and brief. I extended my hand, waiting for him to take it, only for him to laugh at me.

"What?" My hand withdrew, feeling stung. I wiggled my fingers inside the glove, holding to the sensation there instead of listening to the noise of his laughter.

"You gotta take the pill first. We don't just hold hands. There's no point to that; nothing would happen. What did you think?"

His tone only stirred my fingers to wiggle more. Nervousness ran from my heart to my feet. My breath felt stuck and a bit confused. As I looked at him again, he still held a grin on his face. But it wasn't warm. I felt silly. Clueless.

I had come this far. There was no turning back. I was stronger than the little girl he was treating me like...a girl who had lived a sheltered, protected, oblivious life on the island.

I was more than that.

I was tough. I was strong. I was capable of making it out there like others my age. And I would show Draven—and Ashyr. My parents. Yam. Everybody. Including me. I could do this—on my own. I could make my own choices, and live my own life, and have the understanding I needed.

So I didn't know the order of what was involved in all this. That was the point. He was supposed to teach me. That's what he agreed to. So I would forgive him. His laughter. His insult. In fact, I sent a laugh back, even if it sounded a bit stiff. "Oh." With my gloved hand, I tossed my hair back. The movement felt terrible, an odd combination of Mom's nervous hair toss colliding with the confident briskness my hand felt while covered in this sleek, light glove. "I need the pill first," I said.

But he didn't say anything. Instead, he gave me a puzzled look. I felt the burn in my cheeks.

"Wow!" he said, only to laugh again. "It's like you're an alien. Like you really don't belong on Earth. You really don't have a clue about this."

"An alien." I tried to laugh again, but it came out short, like more of a huff than a laugh. "I just have a different life, that's all."

"You know..." He suddenly stepped so close our shoulders nearly brushed against each other. Then his arm rested against the barn structure. I remained frozen in place. Otherwise, had I leaned back, I would have touched his arm.

"Being someone's first," he said. "That's why I'm here. Do you know why? Because it leaves a mark. It's a starting point. Where they build everything from. Foundational. Memorable. One of our teachers shared a quote from Ashyr. He basically said, 'After you reach a hundred, these experiences all blend. It's hard to recall where one starts and the other stops, what separates one from the other. And then you just keep blending them in a melting pot as you craft your own signature experiences, created for others to crave. Once you find your special recipe, others will seek you out, then you will fight to stand out among all the rest. But that first experience… if you are lucky enough to be someone's first, they immortalize you. They call you out from all the rest. You have a permanent place in their minds. A cavity of their memory goes undiluted, reserved just for you.' Ashyr said he loved that placement. That spot. It's why he invests so much in us trainees. Why he likes to offer special rewards to his youth. And now, this is my moment. So when you asked why I agreed to this, that's your answer." Without touching me, his voice came extremely close to my ear. "You will remember me for as long as you possibly can. I will stand apart in your memory, over all the rest. That's why I am here." And then I heard him swallow. I swallowed too.

He stepped away. I drew in a large breath, fighting the breathlessness in my lungs.

He moved in a circle around me, then paused at the barn's entrance. He nodded at me. "Do you want your first EnRapture experience, exotic girl?" He walked backward through the door. "Are you ready for the pill?"

I swallowed for another attempt at air and nodded. Then I followed him into the barn.

TWELVE

LEILANI

A delightful perfume, different than any other smell I've encountered, an enticing fragrance. In through my nostrils, all the way through me. Like blood. Like my veins become one with the pleasing scent. What is it? Sweet. Spicy. Intoxicating. A scent just Draven. A mixture that lures me deeper, neurons firing, pulling it in around me.

I like it. Love...I'm in love with the fragrance.

A lull, a deep, out-of-body voice—I can't make out the words, just the hum of a sound. Low, rhythmic chants. With moans. Moans that offset the chants.

Draven gave me earbuds before this. Earbuds that blocked out all noise. But the sounds came from inside my head. From Draven. Waves and waves of sounds pulsing through me.

Suddenly, I want to scream. Pure pleasure. I press my lips together. Delight, like strong, melodic wind chimes, ripples through me. A touch of lips against mine. A quiver inside. Bubbles, coming, going, drawing me back into the sea, rushing forward inside me.

I desire something.

I desire it so much, yet I don't know what it is.

Yet the call for it whirls through me, an awakening, a new me emerging.

My mouth salivates, like a pang of hunger is there, but for more than food.

Then Draven delivers. I feel the pressure. Strong pressure. Within my mind, something presses down on my lips. Seductive. Perhaps a woman. Perhaps a man. Perhaps both. Or neither. I can't make out the source, only the feeling, my lips parting, feeling the sensation, the warmth, the pressure. A longing grows deeper again.

A reflection of my face. A merge of myself. Another kiss. Me kissing me.

Suddenly, I am in the woods. Trees. Daylight. Astoundingly bright. So astounding I can't take it in. I block my eyes. Redness peers through my eyelids. A redstart warbler hops into my line of vision, floating, fluttering, chirping at me.

I stretch out my arms, only to feel other arms holding me back. I try to open my eyes. To step away.

A wait. Fear. A void. Emptiness.

I have left me.

Me.

Helpless.

Depriving me of me.

My breath catches in my throat.

Rebirth. A fire of an awakening.

A form of Draven wrapping me in his arms. He is there. There to assist me. I hear words. Something about his heart dripping into mine. A drip of his heart. Then flames around us. Flames that rush into my veins. The burning—too much for me.

My breath catches. I'm queasy. Unsure. Fear races out of my breath.

Then the flames lessen.

His tight embrace softens.

The wanting is back.

His voice, a lull again, near my ear, inside my ear, dancing through my mind. "I make appointments with all. It's who I am. Who we are. No single person left away."

A suck of air. In. Out. Then in. Then out.

Calmness. Soft sunlight. Pastures. Clouds.

Drained strength. Exhaustion.

Then silence.

Darkness.

My body doesn't feel like me; a strange rhythm flows through it.

* * *

The nodes on the glove unlocked. I lay flat on my back. Draven's hand slipped from me.

I hunted for my breath again. My voice. My vision. My own sounds. My own clear thoughts.

It required a sluggish, painful, cloudy effort to communicate with my hand to pull the goggles from my eyes. To move at all.

Too much effort. Instead, I remained still. Totally still.

Listening, I waited to hear Draven, wishing for him to slide his gloved hand back into mine. To take me through it again.

Another experience. With him. Another sensation like that. Another fix.

One clear thought: I wanted EnRapture again, soon.

PART TWO

THIRTEEN

MARIANA

Inside the Australian hangar, three men stood. Two were like bookends, dressed in blue jeans and leather sports coats. They kept looking from the man in the center to Mariana and Sunny, who approached them. "What is this?" the man in the middle, with the hunched shoulders and thin legs, called out to Sunny.

Seconds earlier, as they exited the drone, Sunny had reached for Mariana's hand and whispered, "Just smile."

Mariana did just that. But as silence followed, Sunny's grip tightened, and Mariana felt her smile turn rigid.

For hours before, surrounded by darkness and the drone's dull noise, Sunny had encouraged Mariana to sleep. Like a bear hug, the encapsulated ride helped Mariana as she floated in her sea of unknowns. What was to become of the island? How was she to prepare for her people if an evacuation was required?

But now, while the dark eyes from the man in the middle stared at her, waiting for her to respond, silence pounded in Mariana's heart. An entire night to reach Australia, only for Sunny to wait until the last minute to prepare her for this.

So much of the ride, she had wanted to cry, scream, pout, throw a tantrum—anything to stop the events spinning her family's life into chaos. Like a soothing mother's tone against a child's nearing meltdown, Sunny would say, "Just breathe." Then right before they landed, she had said, "Let me do all the talking. It'll be better that way."

"Let's not start this rough, Tarthur," Sunny at last spoke using that same motherly soothing but firm tone to the man. "Listen, and we will get through this."

He folded his large arms. His shoulders bowed out, resembling the posture of a gorilla. He leaned closer toward Sunny. "Then speak!"

"A big change is happening in our family." Tightly gripping Mariana's hand, Sunny stood perfectly straight. Meanwhile, one of the tall men folded his arms, mimicking the posture of the hunched man. The other bookend stood behind and stretched his arms, exposing the significant muscles and holster under his thick sport coat.

In an attempt to keep her smile still, Mariana pressed her teeth firmly around her tongue.

"This is soon to be my son's mother-in-law," Sunny said. Mariana's breath caught. Sunny's grip tightened around Mariana's hand. Quickly, Mariana recaptured the smile and silently begged Sunny not to break a bone. The man stepped toward her, and her entire body stiffened.

"And?" He peered at her face. Her chest froze.

For the first portion of the drone ride to Australia, Sunny had reassured Mariana, "You're going to be okay. Your people are going to be okay. If they can't save the islands, you are their path out."

Mariana couldn't process that—an evacuation of one hundred and ninety people using a one- and two-person drone. Thinking of this only caused her breathing to escalate.

"Breathe," Sunny would say, over and over again. Later it became, "Sleep. You need to sleep now. Tomorrow will carry enough worries for the day."

And now she faced those worries in the gruff gorilla-like face of a man Sunny had called Tarthur.

It had been at sunrise in the drone when Sunny had rustled through a bag. It didn't sound like she had slept on the ride. Mariana hadn't. But Mariana had kept silent in the hopes that Sunny might. As the sunlight found its way into the craft, Sunny tossed a pair of khakis, a light t-shirt, and a thick button-up work shirt into Mariana's lap from her seat in front. "Um...before we arrive..." she said. "You will want to quickly change your clothes." Then in the front seat, as Sunny's dress raised above her head, she nonchalantly added, "Um, also...it'd probably be good for you to know... there's been a recent modification around here."

The clue had been there. The shift in Sunny's voice. The slow, choppy phrases. While Mariana changed, Sunny talked. *Over six months ago. Fires. A lot of them. Extremely bad.* Then Sunny added, "I probably should have mentioned things before, but you've got more than your fair share of worries right now. So..." A strange harshness followed. "All you need to remember is your goal in being here is to give your people options. That's it."

Now the gorilla man glared at her and every muscle in Mariana wanted to flee. "What's your name?" he asked.

Her feet ached to step away. She opened her mouth, only to feel the pressure in Sunny's hand.

"Speak," he said.

Mariana closed her mouth, and the forced smile was gone.

"What's wrong with her?" Tarthur said. Annoyance filled his face. "We need a name so we can get her a visa." When she still didn't respond, he turned to Sunny as if exasperated at her muteness. "Why is she here?"

"Her name is Mariana Grady." Suddenly, Sunny shifted Mariana out of the way, so she instead faced Tarthur. "And she's here to plan a wedding."

The two tall men started circling them. The hunched man, Tarthur, kept his eyes on Mariana. "This wedding." His eyebrows shot up at her. "You're going to have it here?"

"*If*," Sunny said firmly, "we have it here, then she will need to bring in the guests. And...there will be lots of guests who might attend."

"How many?" He still watched Mariana but when she offered no answer, he looked to Sunny. "There will be an entrance tax. On each head. Is Brody willing to pay that?"

"*If* we have it here," Sunny said, "There's still lots to decide."

"*If*," he mocked her emphasis. "Then we will negotiate an entrance and *exit* tax."

Sunny's fingernails pressed deeper into Mariana's skin. "I will share that with Brody."

"Then what?" His question came as a growl toward Mariana. "Your daughter lives here? She works for me?"

"Later," Sunny said firmly. "We'll talk about all this later. Let us first explore our options for this. Then we decide."

The dark eyes met Mariana's again. "We don't have guests. Unless you pay a tax. When people come, they come to fill a need. And when they don't fill that need, we remove them."

"She's not here for that, Tarthur," Sunny said.

"We mine for materials to create *anything*."

"Did you hear me?" Sunny placed herself closer to him. "She's not here for that. And under the circumstances of *why* she is here, some hospitality is in order."

He swung his shoulders toward Sunny. "We have purpose here! So what about Brody; did he send her?"

"To help me plan a wedding for my son." A firmness was in Sunny's voice that Mariana had never heard before. For quite some time, Sunny and Tarthur looked at each other.

"You know," Tarthur said, "there's much I'd do to see him. So…" his voice was sickly calm. "Is this the hospitality you want me to offer? Should I be expecting him for this wedding?"

Sunny lifted her head. The handgrip loosened slightly. "Most likely not."

"Of course." He gave a soft nod to the men now standing behind Sunny and Mariana. "There'll be a tax for her being here. Do we get the drone until you decide?"

"Per Brody's arrangements," Sunny said.

He nodded. "Per Brody's arrangements." A softness filled his voice. "I hope you shared my last message with him. I'm still his fanboy. He and I, we combine my mining plans—"

"We left in a hurry," Sunny interrupted him.

He paused and lifted his bushy eyebrows at her. "But you have gifts?"

She released Mariana's hand to look at the drone. "No." Her breathing sounded choppy.

Without Sunny's support, Mariana wrapped herself in a hug.

"Just need to give it time, don't we?" Tarthur shook his head at her.

"No," Sunny again said firmly. "Listen, Tarthur. Several guests might arrive here—"

"*If,*" he cut her off.

"*If,*" she repeated, staring at him with her hands on her hips.

He copied her and for a moment neither moved. "Wedding will be when?" he finally asked.

Sunny gave the slightest shake of the head. "We don't know yet." She turned to Mariana and touched her in a gentle, tender way. "When do you think we can decide?"

"I give you a month," the gorilla man announced. "A one-month visa. Then you come back here, and we work out the negotiations around this *If* wedding. And these guests. And the gift Brody will provide." His eyebrows shot up at Sunny. "Understood?" Before she answered, he spun back to Mariana and raised his head. "Do you understand, Ms. Grady?"

Mariana nodded.

"Say it," he said.

Sunny let go of Mariana's hand and nodded.

"One month," Mariana said.

FOURTEEN

MARIANA

Once out onto the unpaved street, the questions began. "What just happened back there?"

While one of the tall men had issued Mariana her visa, Tarthur, with the other tall man, escorted Sunny over to the drone. After they finished up, one of the men handed Sunny a bag. Now, with an empty street in front of them, Sunny sank onto the dirt and with quivering hands opened it.

Marianna joined her. "Sunny, what's going on?"

From the bag, Sunny retrieved a pair of heavy work boots. "Here. They're already broken in. Give me what you're wearing."

Mariana pressed her toes down into the canvas tennis shoes, already replacements from her sandals, changed in the drone before they landed. Sunny's hands pressed the boots closer with a renewed firmness. "Hurry. We need to get going."

Mariana took the boots, but she didn't do anything with them, whereas Sunny had hers laced up and was already moving. "Come on. We have a bus to catch. I'll answer your questions as we walk. Fast."

*   *   *

The problem was that even though Sunny's legs were shorter than Mariana's, she walked with such speed that it seemed she intentionally didn't want Mariana to catch up.

On Sunny's heels, Mariana passed buildings that looked close to a century old. Rotten wood fences. Boarded-up windows. Weeds growing over a path that perhaps had been a sidewalk long ago.

Eventually, the road turned a brownish red, with burnt brush and dead trees ahead. As she plowed into this patch of desert, Sunny never paused.

From far off in the distance, a chilling laugh sounded. It rang like mockery, like Mariana was a fool. Like she knew nothing of her situation.

Sunny owned her explanations. Like why she didn't tell Mariana about all this before. Even before the crisis with their islands, she could have told her about this place—and *why* she had moved here. As if an imaginary Sunny were in her head, Mariana heard the reply. "*You were so worried about Leilani leaving with Ashyr. You didn't want to also hear my worries.*"

Still, on the drone ride, they had the entire night's travel to Australia. Sunny could have told her then.

The more Sunny sprinted ahead, the more annoyed Mariana became. Twice she called out to Sunny, but it seemed to only encourage Sunny to widen the distance between them.

Ahead, Sunny waved her hand. Soon Mariana did the same through a cloud of bugs. The imaginary Sunny's voice appeared again: *How would knowing have changed anything, Mariana? Had you known, what would you have done differently? Tell me what other options you had. You need to be here.*

Tall, dry weeds replaced the burnt brush. Barbed wire fences and some scattered cows broke up the scene in front of them. Otherwise, it was wide open.

Mariana tried to speed up, only to slow down. At last, she stopped and called out again. "Sunny! What are we doing?"

Momentarily, Sunny turned back. Her hand beckoned Mariana to keep walking. But as soon as Mariana got close again, Sunny moved quickly. A strange growl erupted from Sunny. "Just trust me."

Out beyond, dark chilling laughter erupted again.

"What is that?" Mariana yelled ahead.

Sunny looked back briefly. Mariana grabbed the moment to catch up. "Kookaburra," Sunny said between short breaths.

Mariana's breaths were heavier. "That's coming from a bird? It sounds like it belongs to Halloween."

"It's called a laugh." While she didn't pause her stride, Sunny gave her a quick smile. "It's how the kookaburra families establish territorial boundaries. Imagine that. Through a laugh they tell the other kookaburras where they live. *Boundaries.*" She forced the word out.

"What's happening?" Mariana asked quietly, working diligently to keep the pace.

"It's spring here. Just barely coming into it. The days are warming up. But the nights are cold. I haven't lived in a place of seasons since I was a little girl. And here, it's the opposite." Sunny's phrases matched her stride. "I love it. Even if I feel upside down every time I realize what month it is."

"Sunny?"

"The brush is starting to make noise again. Do you hear it? Full of life, a transformation. The last time I was out collecting firewood, I truly thought I saw a rock wallaby. They're extinct, supposedly, but I swear I saw one with a baby. It made me smile all day."

"Why are you here?"

"Winter, out here, it's contemplation and rebirth. But spring, it's growth. A time of change. We're all changing, and you feel it here. Different seasons than what I once knew. But no less magical either."

Mariana tried again. "Where are we headed?"

"Let's deal with the questions later. I can't think straight to answer them right now."

Such a response stopped Mariana. Meanwhile Sunny kept moving.

Mariana waited.

But Sunny made no pause. She ventured forward toward rocks and sand. Eventually, Mariana followed, drawing in the strong smell of eucalyptus as red dust kicked up around her. They passed dead trees, green shrubs, tan and brown ones too.

Eventually Sunny did stop. From her pack, she produced a canteen and handed it to Mariana. "You first. There is only one, so leave me some."

After a long drink, Mariana whispered, "Is the plan for us to walk all day?"

"We'll get there before it's too late."

"For what?"

Sunny reached for the canteen and took a moderate drink before tossing it back into the pack, which she hoisted over her shoulder as she started off again. "Come on. One foot in front of the other."

Again, Mariana didn't move. "I'm confused, Sunny."

This time Sunny turned around. "Maybe you're supposed to be confused right now, and you just have to be okay with that." But after only a few strides, her friend paused. She turned around again. "I'm sorry. You want to know what just happened. He, Tarthur, put me in a race. I needed to cool down, find a more level place, some control, so you didn't have to hear my wrath." She started walking backward briefly and waved Mariana forward. "Keep up with me, and we can talk."

The invitation did its job and while Sunny turned back, Mariana jogged to be by her side. Right away, Sunny volunteered words in a hushed, out-of-breath voice. "It was a power struggle back there. And he won. He got the better of me. And I don't like that, so...thanks for that time...for letting me cool down."

"I'm still confused, Sunny."

"We're racing to catch a bus, for the miners. If we can catch it, we have a way to our town. If we don't..." the words faded.

"Because you brought me here?"

"Uh..." Sunny looked out ahead. Her steps hastened a bit. "Part of it. He knows you are here for other reasons. He didn't like that I took control of some of the negotiations. The bag handoff was his way of telling me the bus skipped the stop for us. But if we move fast, we have a second shot at the next town. So as long as we keep moving, we'll get there."

"And if we don't?"

Sunny kept her eyes forward and her voice even. "The power struggle will get worse. For me. For Tarthur. We just get to the bus and get through today, okay?"

Against the burn of her hamstrings, Mariana kept up. "You know there are many more questions."

Sunny shrugged. Her eyes stared ahead at the emptiness before them. "Here's how it goes. We have a pool of three categories. In category one—I'll share those answers. In category two—I cannot answer those questions. That's information that's not my place to share. And category three is what I don't know. And there's plenty of that. For now, just make peace that you don't get all the answers. Okay?"

"Well...some are better than none."

"Why am I here, right? Should we start there?"

"Yes. That seems like a good place."

"It's complicated. Everything about here is complicated. You either fight it or accept it. I recommend accepting it."

"So share. Give the complicated *why*—so I can accept it."

"Over six months ago," Sunny's pace paused slightly, "the outcasts in the center, as Ashyr has called them—well, these criminals decided to change their circumstance. So picture an egg yolk when it breaks. Well, that's what happened here. They not only broke out of their contained membrane, they then strategized how to turn all this upside down. They aimed to bring back The Honoured Society, from the 'Ndrangheta era. They call themselves *drang* for short. But we tend to just call them the mafia.

"They're organized in all their efforts. Became organized arsonists...and drove the people from their homes by fire. Organized conspiracists...and offered the homeless promises of safety in specific areas, which is where we are eventually headed to. Basically, they are organized with their fraud, gambling, extortion—all of it. And...at that awful time, while the entire sky seemed ablaze with fire...and when the drangs used terror and chaos to lead the people to precisely where they needed them to be, and when the drangs promised relief to the destitute people for a price, the good people here took it."

"*Negotiations,*" Mariana repeated the words Tarthur had used earlier.

Sunny nodded. "Negotiations. The people work for the mafia now. And…some jobs are worse than oth…" Her voice cracked. For a moment, she just shook her head. "There is a lot of work in the mines. Mine work that allows us to have shelter, food brought in, and enough resources for the mafia to tax us highly on it all over again."

"The mines? He talked about creating anything."

Sunny kept looking ahead but nodded her head as if it was a fair question. "Sometimes there are things bigger than ourselves that lead us to end up in situations we don't want to be in, but we are here. Because it's where we are supposed to be. It's that simple. If you understand."

"I don't."

"Then you will."

Mariana paused her steps. "I don't think you're answering my questions."

"You'll understand in time."

"Your answers…" Mariana shook her head while tension rose in her voice. "Sunny, they aren't really answers."

At last, Sunny smiled. "They aren't riddles. We just can't understand some things until we've experienced them for ourselves. Then we understand."

"How is that not a riddle?"

"It's just all I can say right now."

"Because of Category 2?"

"Because I'm tired. I didn't sleep well on the drone. I have a lot on my mind. And Tarthur wants to scare me."

"Tarthur, the gorilla man."

Sunny's smile turned into a one-note laugh. "Yes."

"He is scary."

Sunny turned away. Although her feet kept walking, her shoulders started to shake. "He got to me this time. We just need to get to the station before the bus heads out. Then it will be all right. That's all I can say right now. If they get to me today, I'll lose my focus. We all will. And we can't lose that. Not on the bigger goals, the most important goals in front of us. So please, keep walking. That's all we can do right now." Then, as if she had renewed energy, she sprinted forward, only to leave Mariana behind again.

FIFTEEN

MARIANA

The town they had walked to was not a town at all, but rather a trading post, a changing of the guards. As soon as they neared the first structure, Sunny's pace quickened to a small jog. She walked right up to a man who had a shotgun slung behind his back. "Did we make it?"

"Nope. Bus left about ten minutes ago."

Sunny's shoulders collapsed. Her head shook. She turned away. Her shoulders rose high again. Her fists balled up near her eyes.

Unsure of what to do, Mariana sank to the ground. She stretched out her weary legs and watched Sunny, who now paced in a figure-eight pattern in the sand. Her hand kept covering her eyes; her shoulders rose at times and fell at other points. *Power struggle* clung to Mariana's thoughts. Is this what her arrival had done?

"Hey you," a man called from the door frame of a second structure.

Like a lightning bolt, Sunny whipped around. Her face broke into a smile. "Please say you are here for us."

"Well…" His leather hat lifted. The grin carried up into his eyes. "I overheard enough to know it was a good thing I was out this way. Figured maybe sticking around today wasn't a bad plan."

"Thank you, Leif."

His boots pounded down the structure's steps. Then broad shoulders wrapped around Sunny and her body seemed to collapse into his arms. When she finally pulled back, moisture covered her face.

"Let's get you home," he said.

"Thank you," she said quietly. Then she motioned Mariana over. As Sunny wiped at her face, she drew an arm around Mariana. "This is my dear friend, Mariana Grady. She and I, with our husbands, the four of us, we have done some amazing things together. And this…" she waved a hand toward the man, only to pull the hand back to her lips as if her words had choked on some residual emotion. "This is a man who is never short of miracles, Mayor Leif Ackerman."

He extended a hand, far more aged and calloused than his kind, youthful face. His shake was solid. "Just call me Leif. We don't often get visitors here."

Right then, the guard with the shotgun moved near them, causing Sunny's shoulders to stiffen. "She's here to explore whether this would be a good place for a wedding, for our children's wedding." Her words moved between the guard and Mayor Leif.

While the guard just nodded, Leif raised his eyes at Mariana, then shifted a look back at Sunny. The smile left his eyes. "Well, congratulations then."

With her eyes still on the guard, Sunny's smile never faltered. "Well, I hope you have room to give us a lift back, Leif."

"I'm his escort," the guard said.

Leif tugged at his hat brim and his eyes disappeared under it. "I came to pick up some supplies and to deliver this month's taxes. And yes," he shifted toward the other man, "we've got room for both of them."

"Then let's head out." Without a smile, the guard walked toward a Land Rover between the buildings.

Before Mariana could move, Leif's hand was on her shoulder. "I look forward, at some point, to hearing about this upcoming wedding...and how we can help you as needed." The pressure in his hand grounded her, like the red soil beneath her feet was stable, secure enough to give her what she needed. As the hand lifted, she offered a smile and a nod. When she exhaled, she felt the first ounce of lightness since her arrival.

"Hold on," Sunny spoke to the guard. "Mariana, facilities are in the second little building to your right. Take care of what you need; we have a five-hour drive ahead with no stops." Then Sunny turned to Leif. "So how did you know we were here?"

"Your things arrived hours ago. They're all loaded up in the Rover, waiting and ready to go."

"My shoes too?"

"Yep. Tarthur's already taken what he needs."

"Thank you."

* * *

In the back seat, with the bumps, the potholes, and the sound of a loud engine, Mariana could barely make out the limited conversation between Leif in the passenger seat and Sunny, who sat beside her. From the all-night drone ride to the early-morning interrogation-gorilla-man, followed by the silent four-hour walk with Sunny, Mariana now bumped around in the Land Rover over roadless terrain, feeling tired, dirty, and hungry.

"How's Misty?" Sunny's voice sounded eager.

"As good as can be expected," Leif said.

"And my girls?"

"They are fine, Sunny. Just fine."

While the driver sighed loudly, Sunny pressed her head against the headrest. She, too, let out a loud, long exhale, so intense Mariana felt its weight, too, from her own seat. As the vehicle lapsed into silence, Mariana glanced at Sunny with eyes closed, head bowed, lips trembling as if sharing inaudible whispers.

Mariana closed her eyes too. But the bumps sent her head tossing back and forth between the headrest and window. Her neck muscles tightened, and her body stiffened in preparation for the next jostle. In time, she gave in and lifted her eyes to watch the barren wilderness. Red, tan, brown, weeds, dry grass, sun baking the ground. Even through the Rover's window, Mariana felt the air's harshness. The elements were unkind out here.

She closed her eyes again, forcing her mind into clean, humid, soft air. She let the memory wrap around her like a light, comforting blanket as she strolled down to her beach, steps moving in her mind, the trees, the flowers, the thriving nature lifting the weight in her heart. While her eyes moistened, she tried to be grateful. For sixteen incredible years, their vibrant ecosystem had been real, an actual life of paradise.

Eventually, the jostling of the vehicle shifted to a strong rocking. While the engine hummed a coarse lullaby, her head began to droop. The last time Mariana had traveled in a gas-fed vehicle on a road was a lifetime ago. Not that what they were traveling on felt like much of a road. In her calming state, she revisited her travels on the island, visiting Caroline on foot, and for Zane, she would either walk, bike, or use a solar-powered golf cart.

But soon the island memories flittered into dreams of bouncing on a country road in a gas-fed vehicle as a teenager. Her two older siblings had moved on, it was just her and her parents. They thought she was sleeping. How Mariana wished she was dreaming instead of listening to their tones. They weren't speaking directly, but Mariana understood they were justifying one's extramarital affair to counter the other's. When everyone lived at home, it had been a happy place. But after her sister left, followed by her brother, everything changed. Her mother decided it was time to stop mothering, time to fulfill other needs. Which led to her father fulfilling other needs too. During their battle of needs, Mariana was forgotten, while others came and went. On that car ride, her mother announced she would be leaving.

At her high school graduation, it was Mariana who told her siblings that their normal family was over.

The end of paradise.

The next time she opened her eyes, a small town appeared through the dust-covered window. Small homes were mapped out in a square before them with dirt-lined streets. She wiped at her eyelids, remembering her strange dream of the past. Another lifetime ago.

Through tired eyes, a drained mind, and a pained heart, Mariana at last clued in that Sunny was talking to her. "For this group, the population is six hundred."

All Mariana could do was nod. A pain tightened against her lip. She was biting it. Tears burned behind her eyes. She kept herself composed, closing her eyes briefly, calculating the math. The population—600. And then there was Mariana's population: 190 needed a home—maybe. *Maybe...maybe...maybe*, the only word that brought hope now.

As the Rover bound over the uneven road, she saw the unkempt wooden homes, with nothing but barren dirt as their yards. No children out playing. No dogs. No flowers. But birds. Somewhere overhead, once the vehicle parked and Mariana stepped out, she spotted a robin, with its red cap and breast, a black belly and tail with white tips. The sighting stirred a soft smile and she listened.

Songbirds cheering her on! She spotted the choir, lots of them perched in sparsely leafed trees. And above all that, in the dusk-filled sky, above everything else, a bird glided overhead.

Foster would be happy to learn of this. Of birds. Of movement and life. If there were birds, he would say there could be a future here. If the island truly was unsustainable, if the *maybe* turned into a goodbye, then they would find peace and hope because of the birds.

Sunny touched her arm then handed Mariana her bags and directed her toward a simple peeling yellow house. More paint peeled along white pillars that supported the wooden porch. Steps creaked as Sunny led Mariana toward the door, and those creaks triggered movement inside.

"Mommy!" A daughter came running, followed by another. Soon both had their arms around Sunny.

Next to a grown woman, an older daughter hung back. Both watched Sunny through the kitchen bar window.

"Hey, hey." For a very long time, Sunny kept her arms wrapped around the girls, locked in place between the screen and wooden entrance. Finally, Sunny released the hug to head straight into the house toward her oldest daughter. Another long hug, followed by the same. Arms wrapped around the other woman, her complexion dark, her hair thick and curly with a red headband pulling it back. When they released, the two just stared at each other. Nonverbal words were exchanged. The other woman, at least half a foot taller than Sunny, nodded and gave Sunny a soft grin. Sunny wiped at her eyes. They both smiled and hugged again. This one lasted even longer than the first.

"Girls!" Sunny announced after she stepped away. "Please meet my dearest, dearest, friend from long ago, Mariana Grady."

Still near the screen door, the youngest approached Mariana. Left fingers pressed against her lips like she was struggling with something trapped inside her mouth.

"Go ahead and ask her." Sunny nodded at the girl.

"Can I hug you?" The voice came out as a silent, shy whisper.

Mariana's cheeks burned against the sudden smile. "Sure." She leaned down to feel small arms wrap around her neck. Then a brief kiss brushed her cheek.

As the arms left, Mariana remembered Caroline at that age, twenty years ago while they were in L.A., and Leilani, over ten years ago. Those little arms, and how they hugged her like that, there on the island. And since then, so many hugs. Sixteen grandchildren. Birthdays. Holidays. Special dinners. Visits. All those moments—planned and spontaneous—wrapped in that little hug. Mariana tried to compose herself.

"This is Amayrani," Sunny said, her hand brushing through the little girl's hair as she leaned against Sunny.

"But I go by Rani." The girl looked at her mom as if she had failed to properly introduce her.

"She does." Sunny squeezed Rani close. "We don't have many visitors around here. I'm sure you can't understand why." She gave Mariana a wink. "So when we do, Rani always wants to hug them, connect with them in the way she knows best. Because you give good hugs, don't you?" Sunny wrapped her little daughter into a sudden hug, and then picked her up as if she were two years younger.

"And this here is Aya."

"I'm almost seven," Aya announced.

"That's right," Sunny said. "Less than a week away."

"Party, party, party," the other woman said, nodding her head at Sunny.

"You bet." Sunny released Rani before heading back over to the bar to place her arm around her oldest daughter. "This is Ivy-Mai."

Mariana nodded. "I almost got to meet you."

"Yes. You did," Sunny said. "Mariana was going to be my midwife for your delivery."

"And then life changed."

Sunny nodded. "And then life changed."

As Mariana met Sunny's eyes, the message was to leave it at that, which was fine. Of all the nights, this was not the night to revisit when both islands had determined to stop visitations between each other, to reduce the risk of introducing any foreign particles into each other's biospheres. Such irony—Mariana didn't have the emotional capacity to revisit it.

But Mariana had always marveled at Sunny. She, who had existed alone other than a very small handful of family. Birthing her three daughters alone, without the support of other women. Yet here she stood. Surrounded by other females in this small little home.

"And this is my sister, Misty. You met at our wedding years ago, when Misty was a much younger flower girl."

"Hello," they both said in unison, followed by simple nods. A heaviness clung to Misty's rich brown eyes. Mariana turned away, remembering scraps of Sunny's story, that this was a half-sister, that Sunny had been raised by her grandparents until her father remarried. But that was all.

She scanned the home, smaller than Sunny's shoe palace back on her and Brody's island. Simple windows, simple doors, ancient oven, old lights, smells of years ago, yet a smiling mom hugging her children. And there it was, that deep, almost overpowering longing for home.

SIXTEEN

LEILANI

The old, abandoned house carried an absolute stillness, such silence, reminding me of the warehouse that looked like a barn. That place where I had my first EnRapture experience with Draven.

On the house's wallpaper, there were circles, at least on the parts that still clung to the wall. Circular dots, like exploding flowers. And where the walls were bare, dark-fuzzy spots dotted some of the corners.

Shredded curtains covered the windows, sometimes letting the haze of light come through. And when there wasn't light, there was too much blackness. No electricity. No running water. Just a roof. And a bucket to gather raindrops. And rain. Lots of rain.

I lay on the mattress that Draven had put on the floor for me. I wore the hoodie he gave me. Its purple, rich blues, teal and white mixture gave me warmth. The bare mattress pressed against my cheek while the single sheet entangled around my feet. My jeans were ripped. Jate got me those jeans. I couldn't remember how they'd ripped. I guess she brought them to me ripped.

I twisted just enough so my hair blocked out the sun. While at Ashyr's place, at some point, I colored it to pass the time. Actually, Jate had done it, unhappily. I wanted bright colors, a drastic change, like pink, blue, purple, like the others. She gave me the faintest reddish tint; that was it.

The sun worked through the dirty windowpane. Even through my hair, its rays burned at my eyes. I tried to remember what Draven had told me. I should remember. Instead, I closed my eyes. More sun rays that turned my eyelids red. I replayed my experience with Draven. Only to replay it again. Around and around. Replay after replay.

I needed to remember it. Never forget it. Every sound he shared. Every feeling. Every emotion.

Except parts of it were already fading. Even with all the repeating of it, I couldn't hold onto the intensity felt, or the acute accuracy. Details kept slipping into other forms. No wonder the youth went to school to learn what they knew. This required training, skills and techniques developed to capture all this. To know what was important and what needed to be retained.

My skills lacked. A huge disadvantage awaited me. With only one experience to use, Draven said I needed to mold it. Again and again in my mind. Remember. Reflect. Retain. Keep all of it.

He said I would always remember my first EnRapture time, the essence of it, that it was with him.

What he hadn't said was how I would keep hungering for more. More with him. More... more...more.

But Draven would only give once. At least that's what he said.

But that just meant I had to get good enough so that he would want me again. Take his experience, make my own signature exchange, so others would want me, desire and wish for me, like I wished for Draven now. Another offering, one more exchange with him. I would work at this; I would become so good at this, everyone would want me—Draven especially.

I would not stop until I was the best.

Work. I had a lot of work ahead of me. I was at the bottom; no one wanted an exchange with me. But they would. I would go from a nobody, with a fake registry and a borrowed kit, until I found something.

I would build my mind into something—for Draven.

For another chance.

And then, he would want me as much as I wanted him.

He was so right—to be someone's first partner is a powerful position to be in. So wise. Draven. Wise, wise Draven.

I missed him.

Which is why I would keep waiting for him.

And another EnRapture pill, another hit to my mind, another wait, until Draven returned.

SEVENTEEN

LEILANI

Why hadn't Draven come back? I couldn't remember what he had said.

Something about needing time to detox. That this was a safe place.

I needed to be away from the city. People wanted me. So I was removed so I was not a temptation for me...no—a temptation for him. He wanted me out of the city, so I was not a temptation for him. Or for others.

That others don't discover me and turn me in. That was it.

Draven wasn't going to turn me in. Instead, he was taking me to this place. This cold, dirty, abandoned house so I could detox. Otherwise, he would turn me in.

But—

The words rattled in my head.

I asked Draven to stay. He said no.

I said I didn't want to go back to Ashyr.

He said the EnRapture pills were full strength, not the low dosage the trainees use. I had been thrown in.

If he stayed, we would have another exchange. Another. And another. Lots of exchanges. If he stayed, we would be together. Lots. And lots. And lots.

But then he would turn me in. I would be with him, but he would turn me in.

The thoughts cracked in my head, each crack a separate neuron, synapses not connecting, my mind hurting. My brain wasn't working right.

Not yet.

Draven said that was expected. That would happen with full-strength EnRapture pills. He apologized that we didn't use a lower dosage, that he hadn't treated me like a trainee. But I loved it. All of it. Every minute. The potency. Full strength. EnRapture. Desire.

EnRapture good.

Draven good.

Draven come back.

Come back to me.

He found me a house. A house for us. To live in. With its broken windows. The smell of cat urine. The brownish-bloody red stains on the counters.

We had traveled. I couldn't remember all of it. How we got here. It was far. Draven spoke of rules. Especially as I leaned into him. No touching. Only through the gloves. Only with EnRapture.

Time for EnRapture.

I reached for the bottle. I had asked him for more. More EnRapture. More. More. More.

He said no. No. No. No. I needed to detox.

But he left pills. A whole bottle of pills.

He said not to take them. Only when I found my next partner. And he left me a kit. For my next partner.

He said he made a mistake. Full strength EnRapture. Too much.

My brain too much.

Me. Not me.

I reached for the canister, the silver bullet, the kit. I pressed at the buttons, attempt after attempt until I remembered the code, and when I pressed it in right, the panels revealed the glove. How I loved sliding my hand into that glove. Such power as the nodes caressed my palm. If only I had a hand to connect with. A partner.

A Draven.

I took the glove off and put it back in the canister. I took the goggles out next. Always they reminded me of fly eyes, dark big eyes looking at me. Sharing nothing but darkness. Enough to hate without another person here. To share. To give images into the mind. I wanted fancy colors. A brightness like Draven had shown. High waves of light, of color, coming into my mind. I remembered that. My exchange with Draven.

I put the goggles back so I could pick up the pill bottle and shake it. I wanted more. But I couldn't waste them. When had I taken one again?

I needed them for the next partner that would walk through that door soon. Is that what Draven had said? Wait for the next partner to walk through the door. Draven. He would walk through that door. Again.

For an experience with me.

An exchange.

Another one.

Just with me.

Only with me.

He wanted another time with me. Another time with me.

No more pills.

I shook the bottle. I waited. Then shook the bottle again. It sounded like a rattle. A rattle with only a few rattle things rattling inside.

How many had I taken? I don't remember.

I have to save some pills. Save for the next EnRapture experience. With Draven.

No more pills.

I must wait.

Remember my exchange with Draven.

Remember it.

What he did to me.

And what I gave him in exchange.

My memory.

Sitting on the beach. Next to Dad. Talking with him. His arm around me. Us leaning together as we watched the waves drift over the sand. What were we talking about? Some science.

What if Draven found this boring? My memory. Dad and I lost in our talk about science. Everyone else grew bored when Dad and I talked about science. So did Draven. It's why he left. Why he said no more. No more EnRapture. Why he wouldn't do one more exchange.

One more.

Just one more.

Please Draven.

I closed my eyes. My mind still felt heavy. Neurons bounced around but they didn't seem to have a home. No place to go, to connect with.

But I could still see, quite clearly—the memory I shared with Draven. The beach. The sand. The breeze. Birds. The feeling of the island air. Nothing like the air here.

And Dad. His face, his eyes, the strength of his hug.

All would be well.

Dad.

My eyes stung.

My mouth began to tremble.

All would be well.

"I miss you Dad," I said.

EIGHTEEN

FOSTER

All Foster wanted to do was tear off his shirt and dive into the water. Let the waves wash away the strain he felt and soothe him, like so many times before.

Except—now Foster stared at the DNA scanner in his hand. He should be back at the lab. Taking in all the gathered data. Sending it through radio satellite over to Brody for his bots to analyze. One reading after the next, searching for the culprit, the source of what was still depleting their oxygen. Gathering and hoping, with no breakthrough returns. Time was running out.

Stuck in his pause, Foster stared out and embraced the water's soothing sequence, its harmonious flow to sustain him before his return to work.

Mariana deserved an update soon. Which was what? *No answers. The family was coming.* Unless today was the day for the breakthrough.

Brody had called this their unsolvable riddle— after building two islands, launching them into the sky, living in a balanced atmosphere for years, only for an undetectable microorganism to now undo them. Havoc in their biosphere—why could they not conquer this?

Small waves ran over Foster's feet, sinking him softly deeper into the sand. The past. The memories of the debates, years ago. He, Brody, Mariana, Sunny, other family members weighing in—attitudes, opinions, difficult decisions. For Foster, the benefits outweighed the risks. No intruders allowed. Otherwise, it put their entire ecosystems at risk. In the end, he won the persuasion. For both islands' protection. Foster and Brody ceased their family travels back and forth. No in-person visits. Each biosphere must stand alone.

Except Brody had an unsatisfied need to keep tinkering. And Foster's family longed for additional supplies beyond the island's reserve. Brody took the challenge to task. A purification system. Once it had been tested, and retested, and Foster was convinced it was safe, slowly, Foster allowed the possibilities of a supply run. On occasion, a few extra wants and needs could be met.

Limited exposure...only to lead them into all this.

Foster stepped backward in the sand, a few yards from the water, then he lowered down onto the beach. He let soft grains of sand sift through his hand while his mind went to Ashyr. Such terror at that moment, the island hemorrhaging oxygen, Brody believing Ashyr had the materials to stop the bleeding.

Ashyr came, chaos came, that awful day, right there on the beach, then one act leading to the next, until, at the time, the only solution—to ask Ashyr for his supplies. That awful trip, returning to Los Angeles after so long away, traveling with Ashyr, hating him, needing his help. Yuck, dread, fear, despair, lies, disgust—each mile, as the drone and trailer descended, Foster felt the weight.

As the city appeared, it quickly screamed of a foreign place. From the aerial view, Foster studied the walls created from the terrible earthquake. Like a bowl, the city exploded from the center. High-rise towers with specks of movement beckoned the drone to join in with the others. Little drones flying along with a monorail track below. The buildings—steel, plaster, cement, fiberglass, achromatic grays, from a dirty white to a thick, dark, nearly blackish gray—exploded around them. But as they descended lower, colors appeared. Teals, purples, neon blues, yellows, oranges, reds on capes, hats, hair, glasses, clothing. The vibrance of the city among the people.

The drone flew past the heart of the city to a warehouse district and landed in an open field. While Foster now watched the waves, he thought of Leilani there, in Ashyr's city. So often, within his memories, he had returned to that final moment with Ashyr. As they loaded the life-saving equipment into the trailer, Ashyr had said, "I hope this saves your island."

With desperation, Foster stretched out his hand. "Take care of her, please."

"Of course, mate."

Of all of Ashyr's tones, of all the mixed-up memories shared, this was the memory Foster held to. That sincere tone, the genuineness, the Ashyr who once befriended a broken Foster. In that moment, again, such a friend was there.

"The past is over," Foster said. "There was a time we invested in and challenged a lot of things, but it's over, Ashyr. Our differences are over."

"Agreed."

And the two shook hands. A loss for a loss, a struggling win for a win. Leilani in Ashyr's care. Ashyr providing the resources to stop the leakage.

And it had. Except they couldn't maintain the right levels. Even with the *Connect Four* device constantly working, the atmospheric readings never would balance. Each day, the overall percentages continued to slip back below the correct levels. And by nightfall, the oxygen level would remain a quarter of a percent below the previous day. Bit by bit they were still losing the war.

Foster arose. He turned away from the water, the sunset, the beauty of the island, to head toward his lab. With each step, as he moved farther from the sand, nearing the coarse gravel drive, he kept thinking of Ashyr.

On that day, as the drone's door lifted and Foster slid into his seat, Ashyr paused him one final time. "We will always have our differences," he said. "But I still say we work well together. We accomplish great things as a team."

"Take care of her," was all Foster could repeat before enclosing himself in the drone for the ascent home.

Now, as he gripped the DNA scanner, Foster turned back to the water, one more time, and watched the crest and fall of the waves as Leilani would do. "Please, Ashyr," he whispered. "Please take care of her."

The setting sun, reflecting against the water, announced another day had passed. Foster refocused to trudge back to his lab.

NINETEEN

YAM

It had been Aria's idea. Steal an airship. Head toward home. Blast a message using the airship's LED monitors to let Baba know that Leilani was gone.

To this, Yam had asked two questions. "Do you know how to fly one?" followed by "Do you think we actually could steal one?"

To both questions, she responded, "We figure it out one step at a time." Then she added, "Unless you have a better idea."

Finding Aria had been no small feat. At the third care center on the other side of the city, she spotted him before he recognized her.

"Hey, secret boy." Her hair was changed to thick, coarse lavender black waves with a pink bow resting in its wildness. Her eyes were hazel, her skin ebony. She wore a pink tank top and turquoise military-like pants with a small black seam running down to her matching turquoise rain boots lined with pink rubber trim. She kept flexing her biceps.

"Aria?" Yam stared, unsure.

"It's me." Her smile confirmed the truth.

Relief caught in his breath. He was tired of being without food, living on the streets, and being solicited for an EnRapture experience regularly. In time, he learned to deflect any approach with "no registry," which sent them walking past.

"Without your glasses, I didn't recognize you," he teased her over the extreme makeover.

She shrugged and said, "I was looking for a change." She pulled on a lavender-black curl. "Do you like it?"

He waited to find Aria in her smile before asking, "Do you?"

She shrugged as if the question were inconsequential. "I don't know. It's not me. But it is me. No matter how much we change, it's still us trapped inside."

The tone hit on a nerve. When he met her eyes, she gave a quick shake of the head. "Don't worry about it. This is just how it is here. Unless you want to fix that for me because you can, right, secret boy?" She folded her arms, cocked her head, and perched her leg on a mini-wall. The black trim on her military pants separated enough to reveal the line was stretchy fishnet. "Did you come back to pick me up?"

"Can we talk right now?" After the last time, getting accused of touching her, not engaging in EnRapture together, pairing up for other reasons, he didn't want to cause that kind of trouble again.

"You timed it well. It's our practice session. Ritual negotiations for EnRapture. Just keep your distance."

Yam looked around. Splitting off in two-by-two pairs, youth were everywhere talking. It appeared a three-foot distance was allowed. He followed form.

"So tell me," Aria said, "you came to offer me a ride out of here."

"Not exactly." Yam looked over his shoulder to make sure he matched what others were doing.

"You owe me!" Her tone brought his focus back. "You know that. I got a warning cause of you—my last one."

"What happens if you get another?"

"Why don't you take me with you, and we don't need to worry about that, do we?"

In a super low whisper, with his head leaning forward, within the approved three feet between them, he whispered, "Are we still negotiating?"

"Yes." She switched legs. Her arms remained folded.

"For how long?"

"For as long as it takes!" She sighed as if exasperated at him. "So what *is* it going to take, secret boy? I want to go where you're from." She stomped her foot to the ground and stood in a wide stance. Her arms never shifted.

He wanted to ask what to do next to stick with their charade, but her glare suggested she wasn't acting. "I need to talk to you," he whispered.

"Talk here. Tell me where you're from."

His voice could go no lower. "What if someone hears?"

She let out a sighing roar and threw her hands up. "First. Look." He did. "They're all busy with their negotiations. Didn't I say you timed it well?" Some youth were now giving each other mutual head nods, then breaking the approved distance between them to wave their rings over each other's. Soft chirping beeps sounded in various areas around the pavilion.

Aware of his own nakedness, Yam slid his right hand over his ringless finger. Although he despised going further into this charade, he went for it. "So... can we talk alone if we..." he nudged toward the most recent chirp.

"No." She lifted her hand and pointed at her ring. "Unless you have one of these."

He shrugged. "I forgot mine."

She rolled her eyes. "Liar. You wouldn't be in the pavilion at this time of day, for our training block, if you weren't planning to participate." This time it was she who leaned forward. "So where are you from?"

And then, as fewer couples surrounded them, Yam let his words come. He wasn't entirely sure what he could share, but he tried his best.

Each time he hesitated, she added, "Stop worrying. No one is listening. They don't care about our negotiations. Only theirs. And even if they did care, it all sounds the same. You are just trying to entice me with this *experience* you plan to share. This..." she imitated putting her words in quotes, "'special project with Ashyr' that you can't tell me about..." She gave him a mocking grin. "And this girl, Leilani—yeah, I've seen the *Missing* poster about her. Quite the story—you and her, huh? You come here on a secret mission and now you want to go home. And where exactly is home?"

He pulled in a breath and looked up.

"No way!" she hissed. "You're an alien."

He just gave a weak smile. "Not exactly."

"I'm wiping my whole month's training registry for this." She pressed on her ring. It flashed and then went dark. "Refiguring now." The soft chirp sounded. "Bring your hand near," she hissed. He obeyed. "Let's go to my dorm. We have under a half-hour for you to tell me more."

From there, Aria had plenty of questions. He shared all he could. Ultimately, he couldn't communicate with his home, and he needed help. Then she had one solution: Steal an airship. Blast a message to *this* home.

In desperation, Yam latched on, letting the idea take shape. Even if Baba couldn't see the full message, he would be notified of something within the skies. That would be enough to let him know there was trouble.

Before Yam hid his belongings in her dorm, the real negotiations began. *Steal an airship. Send a message home. Then Aria comes there to live with him.* That was the exchange. Her help for his home. Yam tried not to dwell on how Baba would respond to that.

While everyone zipped along the city streets, as advised, he stayed close but not too close to Aria.

The farther they progressed, the more far-fetched the plan seemed. To calm his worries, he chanted a supporting mantra: "*No plan* is worse than this plan." But after a few repeats, the emphasis shifted. "No plan is worse than *this plan*."

At the street corner, Aria turned and glared at him. Later, when they were on a quiet section, she turned back and walked at his side. "Do you *not* want to do this? You keep mumbling. Everybody can hear you." She waved a hand at the deserted street.

"Where is everybody?"

"We're almost to the district. If we time it right, we can talk more there." She took off again and he followed, until they reached the dull gray warehouse area. Here she confirmed what she'd already told him. They were entering the safe zone, a place where coworkers were allowed to pair up to get their jobs done. So they took the moment and walked next to each other. "You're not stressed over this plan?" he whispered.

"Of course, I'm stressed," she hissed back. "It's not every day you plan to go steal the leader of your everything's pride and joy."

"Shh." Yam held a finger to his lips. From what he understood, they still needed to not draw unnecessary attention to themselves within this region.

"Okay. Stick to the plan," she whispered. "Just keep walking."

He did, matching her stride while trying to sound confident over his own growing fears. "When you mentioned it...it seemed like a good idea."

"You said it was 'a brilliant plan.'" Her shoulders nearly touched her ears. "But seriously...we get caught and it's no longer brilliant. Do you follow?"

He rolled his shoulders back as if he could relax hers. "I gotcha."

"Good. Because if I get caught..." her words trailed off. She sped up her walk.

"We just don't get caught," he added.

"Exactly."

Suddenly, a bell chimed around them. Colorful workers moved past. Orange uniforms, green uniforms, brilliant blue uniforms. Aria just stood there and smiled.

Once all the workers were gone, her shoulders dropped. She started walking again. "We got this," she said lightly.

"What just happened?"

"It's lunchtime. Everyone will be busy now."

"So we are in the clear?"

She rolled her eyes at him. "Hardly. We haven't reached the hangar yet. Come on. Move fast."

*　*　*

The hangar was large, with a chain-link fence around it, followed by a little check-in station.

"Drat," Aria whispered as the guard at the window spotted her. "I was aiming to hit their shift change. Hey." She raised her head at the guard who stepped out to meet them. "Glad I caught you. Isn't this like *Happy-Whole-Hour*? I was worried we couldn't get in here."

The guard glared at her. "Nope. I'm still here."

"When do you get off?"

"Doesn't matter." He flipped his long ponytail around and stroked it. "Why are you here?"

"I forgot a hat during our center's field trip."

He eyed her closely. "You're in training."

"Two months to graduation."

He then dropped his ponytail and glared at Yam. "What are you doing here?"

When Yam was slow to respond, she flung a hand back at him. "Our shift leader sent him along, too; he forgot…" She turned around to eye him.

Whereas lies seemed to roll off her tongue, Yam couldn't keep up. "Uh…a hat. Too."

"Huh." The guard grunted as if not buying it. "You sure you two aren't *soloing* it?"

Even Yam knew the danger of this label. He let Aria work through this one.

"We're not *solo*. It's approved," she said.

Yam offered a mere head nod.

"By whom?"

"Ashyr," Yam volunteered, trying to help out the situation. Both the guard and Aria stared back at him.

"Mind if I check?"

She shrugged. "Go at it." Then she stepped closer to the guard and bent low, as if trying to shield something from Yam. "He's with the *Missing* girl. She left him. They were *solo*."

The guard pulled back and gave Yam a disapproving look. Then he spoke low to Aria. "Tell me his name."

"I have no idea." Aria turned around. "What *is* your name?"

Delaying, Yam struggled with a truth or a lie. One way or another, he was done with this. Ashyr owed him a way home. "Yam," he said quietly.

"Yam," Aria repeated it, as if trying his name out for the first time. Then she turned back, again lowering her voice as she spoke with the guard. "Look. I don't know him. I don't want him hanging around me. He doesn't even have a registry. He's not from here, and he is a problem. But our care center is babysitting him until they find that *Missing* girl. Nobody wants him, so even our shift leader passed him over; that's how I ended up with him. You can radio over and check, or I can put in a good word for you, and you can do us all a favor by keeping an eye on him while I go grab our hats."

The guard peered down close at Yam. "No registry. Solo," he whispered even lower.

"I know." Aria shrugged. "He's a problem."

A bell went off from the building behind them. "It's..." the guard glanced from Aria to Yam. "My Happy-*Half*-Hour." He gave her a grin.

"You only get a half, huh?"

He shrugged. "Too bad you're in training." His hand with his ring danced between them. "Otherwise... well...I need a bump to my registry right now. Can't volunteer my time to a trainee, and all that."

She pointed her thumb back at Yam. "Well, I've got a yuck chore for the full day. Group leader promised me some Golden Invites after this."

"Well…" He reached into a drawer and rummaged through it. Then he took a generic invite and scanned it over his ring before handing it to her. "Maybe another time."

"Yeah. Sure." She took it and gave him a modest grin.

Right then another guard walked out through the hangar doors. As he approached, Yam made eye contact. The magenta eyebrows raised. And the name badge confirmed it.

"You again?" Kit asked. "What are the chances?"

The first guard turned. "You know this kid?"

Kit rubbed at his wrist. "He's who landed me here. Here to stir up trouble again?"

"No." Yam stepped forward, feeling a tinge of confidence. "I saw our deal through. I kept my promise. Ashyr gave you what you asked."

A grin spread over Kit's face. "Yeah. He delivered. Thank you." Then his face shifted followed by a head shake. "But others complained you jumped the queue. Enough complaints and…I ended up here."

The first guard looked wide-eyed between the two. "So you *do* know Ashyr," he said to Yam, only to turn to Kit. "What work did you do for Ashyr?"

"Ran his penthouse security."

"Ever have an exchange with him?"

Kit flashed Yam a smile. "Sure did."

"Whoa." The guard rubbed his ring. "You on shift now? I got my *Happy-Half-Hour.* Any chance…?"

Kit met Yam's eyes. "You still owe me, kid, remember?" His eyebrows raised. "You were going to take a portion of my shift that night."

"Oh. Yeah. Definitely." Yam looked past the guards to give a grin to Aria, who was moving past the fence. "I can totally help you here."

"I'm just getting my hat," she said unobtrusively.

"Incredible!" the first guard said to Kit, then turned to Yam. "One of us will be back soon."

"No problem." Yam grinned at both. "Take your time. No rush here."

TWENTY

MARIANA

While Mariana sat on the bed, Sunny asked, "Can I get you anything?"

The meat and potato pie had been exactly the needed nutrients and now, with her belly full, the thin mattress screamed for Mariana to cocoon into it. After a day and a half of travel, from her island home to this bed in Australia's harsh wilderness, Mariana's body begged for the rest.

Dinner had been exceptional; between the much-needed food, watching the girls smile, and the sounds of laughter with their mother, it all gave Mariana's heart a pause for some happiness. But now the thought of her dust-covered body climbing under the rag-tied quilt bothered her enough to ask, "Could I take a shower before bed?" Sunny's soft smile, and delayed answer, left Mariana to fill in the gaps. "Limited water?"

"It doesn't mean you can't take one. It will just be your quota for the week."

Mariana nodded against the physically-taxing homesickness. She readjusted her position on the bed and avoided her friend's eyes.

Sunny pressed a fist to her lips. "I can still get you all set up for it though," she said apologetically.

Mariana delayed her nod. As much as she wanted it, to be clean and ready to fight the woes of tomorrow, she would accept delayed gratification. The promise of a future shower as she faced the next day would be needed. Besides, her heavy eyelids and the insistent quilt told her there were other satisfying alternatives. "Later works," Mariana said, noting the relief that seemed to fill Sunny's eyes at those words. Then, before she knew it, Sunny wrapped Mariana in a hug. Like rays of sunshine, a strange hope embraced; Mariana leaned into it.

When Sunny released her arms, she asked intently, "Are you going to be okay?"

Mariana tried to smile, but her words got in the way. "The right answer is 'yes', isn't it? It's..." her sentence trailed off.

"Give it time." With a courageous smile, Sunny reached for Mariana's hand and squeezed it as if saying, *You can do this—if this is required—you can do this.*

Against falling eyelids, Mariana wanted to say *I don't want to do this.* Instead, she asked, "You sure there isn't another—"

"There's Ashyr's life."

"I can't."

"I know."

Within their silence, laughter from the neighboring room filled the space. Young innocence, universal to a child who was immune to the cares of adulthood, answered all Mariana felt. For her grandchildren, Ashyr's way was not right for them.

When she met Sunny's eyes again, confidence surged past her exhaustion with the sound of hope. "The earth is a huge place! Surely there is another location for us."

Sunny's soft eyes brought back the memory of her recent hug. Then her head tilted toward the door. "Come with me."

The worn fibers of the rag-tied quilt beckoned Mariana to stay. Her hands caressed the softness, while she fought the desire to crawl under its warmth and leave all this talk for later. But to face what needed to be faced, she blinked against the thirty-six hours of travel and hoisted herself off the bed. She followed Sunny out, down the short hall, back into the humble living room, to be led through a discreet door, which opened into a short, narrow rectangular room. Two wooden folding chairs, a small round table, and a lamp lined the wall. At the far end of the room was an old, thick bookshelf. And there, covering the entire wall in front of them, was a giant world map.

Purple pushpins pressed into the landmasses, and, across all the regions, haunting bright red X marks. A large X through Africa. Through Europe. The Middle East. South America. North America. Central America. Even New Zealand. Small X marks were there too, through countries, states, islands. Soon all Mariana saw were red marks, large, medium, small, slashing all throughout the map. And then there were the two blue circles. One cut through half of Australia. The other much, much, smaller one was there around the southern California coastal region.

"This can't be real," she said. "It's a lie."

"While you and I've been living in our safe places in the sky, this is what scouts have found. And for now, this is all we have to go on."

"It's wrong." More words bubbled, ready to spew. Her tone mirrored that of one of her two-year-old granddaughter's blowups. If she didn't manage this sudden anger, she would burn her friend. Instead, she stepped back, controlling herself. Sleep would make everything better. So she walked out.

TWENTY-ONE

MARIANA

Sleep came quick under the knot-tied quilt, as did the dreams. Island life full of comfort, happiness, and ease. Subconscious sweetness. Safety while reality pulled at her mind. She awoke with a racing heart.

She sat up. The comforts of the island offered a danger now. Troubled and anxious, Mariana slipped socks on her feet and left the room.

Fortunately, the bright moon shined light through the dark little home. The brilliance led Mariana to a living room window to look out past the barren, worn-out houses and the dusty street, upward into the night's magnificence. An assurance was there, an answer, because that same moon shone down on Foster, who worked tirelessly on a solution. He would change the course. All would be well.

"Please, Foster," she whispered. "Please heal our home."

But if he could not...if the island could no longer be habitable...this was her responsibility, her stewardship—and she needed to be strong.

She stayed fixed on the moon, this connection with Foster. And...although it was a different time of day...this same moon looked down on Leilani.

What time was it where Leilani was? Seventeen hours? Nineteen hours? What was the time difference? Like an electric current, Mariana felt panic surge inside. She didn't even know what time it was for Leilani. Right now, was she asleep? Was she happy? Safe? Had Foster and Mariana made a mistake? Could they have stopped her?

Could they have? Could they have stopped Ashyr from intruding on their island? Could they have stopped any of this? She closed her eyes and pulled in a strong breath. At some point, such questions wasted energy.

It happened. All of it. Leilani in Los Angeles for Ashyr's science experiment. Chaos on the island because of Ashyr's carelessness. Foster and Mariana making decisions quickly. It now was what was it was.

She fixed her sight on the moon again. It had to fill her with hope—that Leilani would be okay—that being with Sunny meant Yam was with Leilani—and they would be okay. Brody was helping Foster. If there was a solution to be found, it would be found—all would be okay.

Such chants of *okay* encouraged Mariana to let go of the windowsill. But she kept her focus on the moon. Its light continued to reach down and touch her heart. It would be *okay, okay*...okay.

Quietly, she made her way to the rectangular side room. Darkness met her there as she stared at the map. When her eyes adjusted, a haunting shadow rested over it. The tips of the pushpins spoke of further darkness, more emptiness beneath them. The black holes of landmasses, the memory of the X's, the O's, the statement that there were no other options—Mariana pressed closer. So close she could barely make out the landmasses. Within her blindness, she wanted to reach out and touch the pushpins, use them like braille to read the map, to find the absence of their words, a gap somewhere that would lead them to their next new home...if needed.

What if they could just lower the island down? Like a parachute, soaring back to earth. Like the completed mission of a space shuttle. If needed, let it plummet down into the water, only to buoy back again like a beach ball resurfacing. Surely Foster could shatter the dome. Just their land on top of the water. The lid gone. And then, air. Air. Plenty of air, right there on the earth's surface.

As Mariana skimmed around the map, peering for spots where there were no pushpins, she admired her idea. The earth was full of water, and they just needed a small spot to settle down. Suddenly, a bright light glared overhead. Mariana jumped back. She spun around while her hand pressed against her chest.

"I didn't mean to startle you." Sunny hugged a robe that covered her light summer dressing gown. Her hair was pulled back into a night braid. Her feet were bare.

"No, no." Mariana stepped away from the map. "I didn't mean to wake you."

"There's a storm brewing inside you, Mariana." Sunny gave her a soft smile. "Even if it's a silent storm. The house feels it."

Mariana's eyes burned as she nodded back at the map. With an effort to keep that exact storm in check, she spoke with clear firmness. "There has to be another way."

Sunny joined her near the map. "I'd like to think so too." Her head now obstructed the view of the open ocean that Mariana had been staring at in the darkness.

"How is there not?" Mariana inched closer, pushing past Sunny to point at the exact space. "We set the islands down here. We live on the islands, on water, breathing in Earth's safe atmosphere."

Sunny shook her head. "Where is Earth's *safe* atmosphere?"

"I don't know." With her finger still on the spot, Mariana scanned the wider location. "What's wrong with finding a place in the Pacific Ocean? North or South, I don't care."

"Pollution. All of the oceans have been polluted."

Mariana took a step back. "How can you say that? How can you even know that?" The silent storm grew more turbulent, ready to strike. Surely she knew more about science, biology, marine life, than Sunny did. Even if she wasn't an expert, Foster was, and she had heard Foster speak science enough. Another option existed. An entire ocean could not be polluted.

"And we don't have the equipment to survive," Sunny said. "To make that transition. To build a boat to live on the waters."

"Not a boat. Build an island like we did before."

"With what resources?"

"We…"

"We don't have the same economic assets we did before. Not to mention a world that no longer exists. There is nowhere to buy the supplies we would need to build this."

"So we lower our islands down and make them work."

Sunny shook her head. "Brody says it's not possible."

"You've asked him?"

"I've been through this. Everything you are doing, what you are going through, I've been through this too."

Mariana let out a huge sigh. "There has to be another way."

"It's not the same world that we left when we became Air Island residents. The technology is gone. The communication. The order. It's over. We have slipped back in time, but we know too much. It's a difficult place to be, trying to properly exist while having the knowledge we have—but being unable to use it."

Mariana shook her head. Ever since they had come to Australia, Sunny seemed to talk in riddles. "Something's off." Mariana looked at her friend, trying again to pacify her inner storm while searching for the truth in Sunny's eyes. "There has to be another way."

"And if there is, we will find it." She put her arm around Mariana, breaking their eye contact. "Scouts are out looking for this. Risking their lives to find other options. But right now, this is what we have to work around. With the limited resources we have, with the number of people we have to transport, we first have to find a habitable place, make it a feasible option, and then we can start exploring where to go from there."

"The earth is huge!"

"Yes. It is. And it's been through a lot of abuse over these last few decades. It's tired and ill. And it shows as we try to find where we fit in it."

Mariana heaved out an exhausted sigh. "So only two options. I just can't fathom this."

"Los Angeles or here."

"What about New Zealand?" A red X shared the answer.

"It once was a beautiful place. But it's not anymore. I heard a bit of it was habitable, but the mafia runs it too. So...it's not for us. Not while they rule it."

"Tell me about the mafia." Mariana broke away from the comfort of Sunny's arm. "Tell me all the parts you aren't telling me."

Sunny's smile dropped. Sadness filled her eyes. She shrugged, then added, "It's not my story to tell."

Mariana shook her head. The riddles had grown old. "Who will tell me?"

"It's an ugly story with unnecessary weights, things separate from you. All I can say is some things are outside of our sphere of control, and this is one of them."

"Are you a prisoner here?"

"No."

"Are you slaves?"

"Perspective. It all comes down to perspective, especially here."

"This doesn't make sense. You. It. All of it. Things aren't adding up."

"Sometimes when the only choices are difficult ones, you can only do your best, even if it doesn't make sense. Even if it doesn't solve everything."

"Why won't you tell me what's going on?"

Sunny gave the softest of shrugs. "In time you will understand. Until then..." She put her arm around Mariana again and steered her toward the door. Mariana stepped out of the embrace but left the room. "You need your sleep." Sunny turned off the light then directed Mariana through the living room. The moon had lowered, its light spilling in through the window, making itself grander and more luminous than before. Sunny paused at the kitchen windowsill.

"When I can't sleep, when my worries and troubles get the best of me..." Sunny again placed an arm around her. Strong pressure was there, a deeper hug that pleaded at Mariana to feel her friend's care. "I think about the stories my nai nai would tell me, while she raised me until my baba

147

remarried...she would tell me about a Mother Goddess in the sky that watched me, that cared about me, that would always be there for me. So when I need her, I meditate. I commune. I reach out for divine help. And then I slip into sleep to find a reoccurring dream of a Mother Goddess who tells me all will be well. And I believe her. Because she seems to have the very best message that I can find through all this. She knows. Is aware. And is the only source I can hold to, to trust that eventually all will be well. And at some point," a softness filled her face, "you will know this too." The hug lessened.

"Now..." With her arm still around Mariana, Sunny steered her away from the window. "Try to get some more sleep. You need rest to deal with tomorrow. And..." In an exceptionally low, nearly inaudible voice, she added, "Trust me, for now, less is more. I'm protecting you; you don't need the extra weight, not right now."

TWENTY-TWO

LEILANI

I was stronger than this. Whatever had happened to me, I had to face it. I was in the gray zone. I think that was what Draven had called it. Or maybe we had passed the gray zone. But why was I still waiting there?

I tried to piece the details together. First, I had met Draven on the basketball court outside the youth center, right in the heart of L.A. Then he said we needed to go to the outskirts of the city to get me a registry. After that, he said we had to find a safe place for the exchange. And from there…what happened from there?

Before the exchange, he'd led me through the city, down streets where there weren't streetlamps. It was dark when we reached the gray zone. Or was that the gray zone? It was a district where people weren't as strict in following Ashyr's rules. Then what?

My head hurt. So much pounding inside. The neurons had settled down now. Synapses connecting. Brain working right. But it still felt disjointed inside.

I wanted my next EnRapture pill. But only two were left.

Draven still hadn't come back.

How much time had passed? Days?

And I was hungry. Tired. Weak.

I had slept a lot...and I felt like I could keep sleeping...for a very long time.

After we got to the gray zone—or maybe it wasn't the gray zone; it was the outskirts—Draven led me to the underground EnRapture bar, only for us to see that stupid *Missing* poster. Everything changed after that—the plan, the focus, Draven!

He led me out of the gray zone, past lots of old warehouse buildings, down railroad tracks, through a field, to a barn, and gave me an EnRapture experience...and that was like nothing else I ever knew.

And then, rather than turn me in like he had planned, like I had expected him to do, he didn't. And I didn't desert him either, as I had planned to.

What had happened? He had surprised me. And I had surprised myself.

From there, it all got cloudy. Draven led me through a ravine. A horrible, scary ravine—he talked about the earthquake that caused the earth to jut out like this. But it also divided Ashyr's world from the dead world beyond.

Down into the ravine, up the other side. My feet kept slipping. My mind didn't seem capable of telling my body how to work right. I scraped my wrist. Cut my elbow. Bit my lip to not complain.

I don't remember what we said to each other. I thought a lot about EnRapture. I followed him, and I think I asked Draven, five times, for another exchange.

He always said, "Keep walking."

My brain hurt and I couldn't quite make out all my steps, but I did keep walking. He stumbled some too.

Epicenter. That is what Draven had shared. The jutted rocks, the caverns—we were walking near the epicenter from the great earthquake years ago.

After we reached flat land again, Draven led the way to a house. The roof sagged. The wallpaper was peeled, and the house stank. Broken windows, broken porch, but not broken doors. Draven locked the doors and told me it would be my shelter. That seemed fine; I just wanted sleep. And EnRapture.

He did say I would be safe here. I remember that. I remember because I loved his words. How he said it. How he cared. For my safety. For me.

But then why had he not come back? And I didn't feel safe. In fact, it was the most unsafe I had ever felt. My eyes burned like they wanted to cry. But crying required too much effort. At some point, I had crawled to a corner of the room. Now I didn't want to crawl back to the mattress on the floor. So I hugged my knees...and waited.

One last meal.

Draven brought it for me. I don't remember when, or how he got it. But I figured he would bring more. More food. Clothes. EnRapture. A simple plan. Draven. Me. EnRapture.

But if he didn't come...I would need to hunt. Once I got hungry enough. And had energy.

How would I hunt? What would I...?

There were rats.

Lots of rats.

I had seen them run past. Once. Twice.

But now, in my corner, as I watched, I squeezed my knees and waited...and they didn't come.

There were cockroaches too. A black moving line came in when the rain fell.

I should get up off the floor. Get ready for the rats and the line of cockroaches. But I couldn't. I just stayed put and listened...waiting to hear the sounds of Draven. His footsteps. The clearing of his throat. His words.

He would come back because he wanted me to be safe. Because he didn't turn me in. He didn't get his reward from Ashyr. He wanted me safe. And more EnRapture too.

My head hurt, begging me for more, another pill, while I waited.

* * *

I blinked my eyes a few times, feeling the weight of sleep coming on again.

Draven found the old mattress for me. He set it up for me, for the nights, the days, whenever I needed it. Damp and smoky. I should go there now.

Instead, my head rested against my folded arms. Crouched and curled, I leaned against the wall.

Perhaps I should have stayed at Ashyr's odd castle, living like Rapunzel, trapped in his high-rise building looking out at all the life below. I should have been okay to be my own pincushion. I shouldn't have been bothered that I was taking pills to generate a high number of eggs like I was a seahorse.

One egg. Maybe two. That was normal. A normal cycle. I wanted to be a normal girl. A normal life. But, perhaps abnormal was better, being there, serving Ashyr, being ignored by Ashyr...maybe I should have stayed.

I didn't want to keep thinking. Instead, I opened my mind to the nothingness found in the air, so sleep could take over.

* * *

"Excuse me, miss."

My eyes opened. I drew the back of my hand against my mouth to stifle the scream. A large woman with stringy blonde hair stared into my shelter from a broken window.

"Are you alone?" she asked.

Quickly, I weighed the options while a loud chant formed in my head: *Lie. Lie. Lie!* I responded with, "My boyfriend will be back soon."

The woman cackled as if she were a witch. "Boyfriend. Antique term. You're cute."

I drew my body up against the dilapidated wall and felt the tips of ripped wallpaper curl around me.

153

The woman's head kept coming through the broken window.

"What do you want?" I asked sharply.

"What do you have to give?"

"I have nothing," I said strongly, but my words seemed to only encourage the woman.

With a hammer and force, the woman smashed away the remaining shards of glass around the window frame. Once the glass was gone, she used calloused and beefy hands to heft her frame through the opening.

"Wait!" I didn't move. I just sat and watched, using only my voice to stop her. "You can't come in here."

"It's not your place." She stood upright in the room. She wore short shorts, revealing legs with tawny skin that sagged like an elephant's, and a knit tank top with a high turtleneck—mauve, pink and orange stripes that ran nearly to her face.

Fright filled my breath. It was a cat face. Whiskers, round yellowish eyes, and cat ears poked out above her hair. The smile was a woman's. But the nose was a beast's.

"What do you want?" I sounded so weak.

"You're wanted. Aren't you?"

I had already trapped myself in a corner before the intruder came. Neurons couldn't keep up with my situation. I needed to formulate an escape.

Instead, I just remained vulnerable, hands wrapped around my knees. Before the intruder came, I foolishly placed myself in the corner. Now my brain ripped in pain. The neurons couldn't keep up. They couldn't think fast enough to formulate an escape plan.

"I'm not who you think I am." Air caught in my throat. If the tone of my voice didn't reveal me, the tears surfacing did.

"That's okay, pretty." The thing stepped closer. A burly, thick hand like a man's touched my hair. It patted me as if I were a dog.

I had to fight back, not just stay curled up. I had to present a façade that I was in control. That I could handle this.

Fight, flight, or freeze? The question rattled inside. Clearly, I was opting for freeze. My biggest face-off with danger, and I just froze! Cuddling there into a ball, my muscles only tightened. My eyes stared at the beast as if I could make it disappear; instead, the beast stared back, watching me.

I couldn't squeeze my knees any tighter. I wished for this *safe shelter* to swallow me up and send me back home.

Back on the island—the ache pierced me—while this...witch...petted my hair. Cooing sounds came from her mouth. "You're a pretty thing. Don't be scared. I have a place for you."

I gave in and closed my eyes. Against the darkness, I pictured home. The beach. The ocean. The waves. Counting the waves. Feeling the wind tangle itself through my hair. The lift and fall of it in the wind, not the witch's rough fingers pulling through it. I was home. Safe. Dad was close, up at the house. Ready to show me something new he'd made. Science. Talk. Inventions. Dad and me, together.

Even Mom.

I wanted Mom right now.

We could talk about whatever she wanted to talk about. And I'd be whatever Mom and Dad wanted me to be...just to be there with them. Why did I leave?

I opened my eyes only to see the witch had moved closer. Close enough I could see the long whiskers above her upper lip. "We have a den." The cooing words continued, hoarse, deep, and sugary. "For sweet ones like you."

I needed to think past the blaring thudding of my heart. I needed courage to shove the hand off my hair. To stand upright and dash out of the house.

"What do you want, pretty girl?" The voice spoke right near my ear. Arms wrapped around me.

"No!" Suddenly I did fight. I pushed at the hands, lashing at them to leave me, shoving at the face that breathed too close. "Leave me alone."

But as I fought, the muscular arms tightened. My elbows were forced down at my side. Wide hands wrapped around my neck, so I couldn't breathe. I tried to grab at my throat. I fought for air. Emptiness came until everything went black.

TWENTY-THREE

LEILANI

My nostrils revolted against the smell. It was unpleasant, but I couldn't place it. A bit rancid, sour and grassy, like goat's milk. My eyes batted against themselves. I tried to see the source of the smell, yet my eyes seemed to protest as if trying to protect me from the source, working against me not to open.

My body ached with a harsh tenseness, like I had been frozen in one position for too long. I lay on a bed, a hard wooden bed. And then I felt the gag in my mouth. Instinctively, my hands went to remove it, only to encounter their own restraint. Same with my feet.

While my eyes still fought my wish to open, my nose reminded me it was free. Openly it drew in the smells, again and again. There was manure. Mixed with vinegar. And moldy cheese. Another inhale of the stench and I felt I could vomit. Yet nothing came. My stomach was empty. I couldn't remember the last time I'd eaten. Dry, empty puke surged while I again met the gag in my mouth. The cottony texture and the dryness—I needed moisture. A bathroom too.

My eyes continued to fight me, refusing to open, as if certain whatever I'd find would be bleak. As I won the battle, the gag in my mouth stifled my scream. But inside, that scream reverberated back and forth, an echo that couldn't fade out.

A figure, hunched over like a man, faced me. He wore jeans. But his bare chest was reptilian with green scales. A snake-like tongue slithered out of his Adam's apple. No, it came from his mouth and traveled down to his Adam's apple. His face, like a human canvas, had been marred with gorilla cheeks and the sleekness of a greyhound dog.

"Squawk."

The noise from above startled me. My head lifted to find feathers encroaching against my face. Talons like fingers ripped at my cheek. The gag was torn off my face.

The feathers stepped back. A somewhat beautiful mismatch of part human and part bird stood above me. Talons for hands. Wings for a back. A beak for a nose. Eyes large and golden. The portions of human skin appeared extremely soft, absent of any blemishes. The chest, although human, pressed near me with a shape that resembled a chicken.

Leotard straps covered a portion of this creature's breast. The fabric, leopard print, also covered her torso and groin area. Flawless, dark, silken human legs traveled down to end with talon feet.

I lay on a bottom bed, with a top bunk feeling like some sort of protection against the oddities before me.

"Speak," the greyhound-gorilla face said as its serpent tongue curled around.

The talons pierced into my shoulder, shaking it roughly. "You," the winged creature said.

I tried to relax. This was a nightmare. The worst kind. Bizarre images that felt too real. Perhaps my last EnRapture pill had caused this, a psychedelic trip, my mind going too far. This would end.

My muddled mind knew enough. I had taken things too far. One last pill and I was done.

Then I'd find Draven. Then I would go home.

Or maybe this was an exchange with Draven right now. If so, I would let him know, next time I didn't want the extremes Ashyr had taught him to share. I wanted real world, not the unnatural. I wanted factual science, not tangential oddities.

Just an EnRapture trip. A disturbing one. An accident from Draven. It had to be from Draven because it felt too real. Far too real, and far too odd for my own mind's creation.

The talon pierced into my shoulder again. I felt blood emerging. Too real. It all felt too disturbingly real.

"She's going to be useless." The greyhound-gorilla-man pushed past the winged creature. The top of his jeans and his reptile torso were only a fraction away from my face.

He squatted down. The flurrying serpent tongue seemed so close, as if it might touch me. Against the restraints, I scooted back. Until I hit a brick wall. The wooden top bunk above, the bottom bunk beneath, and the brick wall closing me in like a box, I was prey in a hole while my predator hung near.

"Ah." Human eyes lowered, meeting mine. The serpent's tongue moved wildly. His arms folded to lean against my bunk. "She responds."

Green hands, close to human, yet with lizard-like fingernails, touched my cheek. Then with one black nail, he swirled a heart shape across it. "RexHera is right. She is a beauty. She'll go well with the den."

"Or the army." The winged creature scooped in closer too. Golden eyes blinked to meet mine.

"The den. Or the army." The lizard fingernail kept swirling around my cheek. I tried to focus on the cold brick against my back, but I felt too queasy. It seemed the more he kept touching me, the more I felt I was going to pass out.

And then, as if caught in a trance, I looked at his tongue. It circled in an infinity symbol, over and over again, stirring my eyelids to weaken, my body to soften, a darkness slipping in that carried me away from these creatures.

TWENTY-FOUR

YAM

In the hangar's quiet hallway, Yam hustled to catch up with Aria.

"Psst," she called from the shadows. "It's this way. Nicely played, by the way."

He just shrugged, too afraid to breathe, let alone speak.

She opened a door and Yam's mouth dropped. Huge airships of varying shapes and sizes welcomed them. Giant globes, smaller circles, rectangles, ovals, tear-shaped—Ashyr's fleet overwhelmed the expansive space.

"Which one?" He barely could make his question audible.

A bit louder, she said, "Whichever one will share the message best."

He stepped toward the largest; she stepped toward the widest.

"Freeze!"

Yam turned. Several feet away, Kit pointed a taser at him. "You really are trying to get me fired, aren't you, kid?"

Yam gave the faintest head shake.

"You run your games. We'll run ours." The other guard pointed his taser at Aria.

"How dense do you think we are?" Kit waved for Yam to move away from the airship.

"What group leader is going to approve a solo expedition for two youth? Never heard of such ridiculousness. I don't care who either of you are." With eyes still on Aria, the other guard threw a thumb in Yam's direction. Then he tilted his head toward the exit. "Let's go. Seems the council may have a few things to say to both of you."

* * *

The smells were intoxicating, more so than usual. So strong, like a mix of overpowering fragrance to cover up the smells of cleaning products, that were being used to cover up another smell. Cover-ups everywhere. All of the council sat on the benches in gray-colored robes. Gray turbans. Gray scarfs. Color was absent from the room like a death sentence. Only Aria's color shone, but each time Yam looked her way, a voice reprimanded him.

"Keep ahead."

The plan was to wait for as long as necessary for Ashyr to join them.

Yam closed his eyes and tried to listen for Aria's breathing. He would gauge her emotions through her breath. But all he could sense was the burn of his throat from the extreme chemically induced smells.

The more he strained the more important it became to know she was okay. A new item had been added to his to-do list. Sandwiched between *Find Leilani* and *Get home*, he now added *Save Aria*.

And then he heard it, the smallest whimper, like a scared, trapped animal, waiting for the attack ahead. Then it was gone.

In the room, silence hung, all waiting for Ashyr, for his justice to fall.

Finally, he arrived. Everyone stood as he entered the circular room and ascended the wide steps up to his marble throne to stare down at Aria and Yam, who were separated by two small tables. When motioned, they took their seats again on the slate-colored metal chairs.

He spoke to Aria first. "Of all the things my children have done, none have stooped this low. You tried to do what? You tried to steal from me. One of my airships!"

Through the council, a gasp flowed as if Aria must have affirmed with a nod.

"You have been given your warnings. Mercy's up. So…you know what this means. Don't you?"

The rumblings through the council made Yam close his eyes. He strained again to hear Aria's breaths.

But Ashyr spoke over it. "I love my airships almost as much as I love my own children. Do you understand that?"

"I'm sorry." Aria's voice was a soft cry.

But Ashyr already had moved on to face Yam. "And you've become a bit of fungus. I can't get rid of you, can I?"

Before Yam did anything, Ashyr was again speaking to Aria. "Should I send you there? Right into the heart of Australia?"

Another soft cry from Aria. "Please."

"You're a criminal now—you belong there." The intense blue eyes shifted. "How would that be for you, Yam?" He cleared his throat and rubbed his hands together. "Landing you in Australia, it would be me telling someone we both know that this is revenge, mate. From admiration to revenge—let them feel what they've done to me."

Yam drew in a breath, determined to steady himself. To let go of the fear and anger. He already felt enough coming from his right, without even looking at Aria. "You can send me," he said stoically. "But don't send her. I'm to blame, not Aria."

Ashyr gave Yam an amused smile. "I'm sure you are. But she knows the consequences. In fact... Aria...you made history today. You are the first of my children to ever try something so cruel and offensive to me—who gave you all that you have. And this is how you demonstrate such thanks. It's a sad case, child."

"No," Yam interrupted. "She was helping me reach home. Because we have to let them know. Ashyr, we need their help to find Leilani."

"Stop!" Ashyr raised his hand and one of the council members stood. A guard approached. Ashyr calmed both with his hand, sending them back into their positions. "I act in the name of the law. And justice is to punish you both for your wrongs. We are fair here, unlike your people. He's not from here." Ashyr raised a hand to the group. "He was invited here as a guest. And this is his thanks." He glared in such a way that Yam felt silenced. Then Ashyr shifted to her. "Aria, you come from people with a greater compass for fairness, and you are a child of ours who knows better than his lineage of traitors. You should have been the voice of reason."

"No—"

But Ashyr's hand silenced Yam and he continued speaking to Aria. "You exist because I gave you life. Do you understand that?" He waited until he got the response he sought. "Through all you have, I have offered you experiences, an extraordinary place to dwell, a good society, and you are going to throw it all away. I hope this little escapade was worth it."

She sniffed and then quietly said, "I won't do it again."

"It's a little late for that," a council member said.

Yam stood. "They will do terrible things to her. With EnRapture."

Ashyr pointed at the abandoned chair. "Sit." As the guard moved forward, Yam obeyed. "And they will not," Ashyr continued. "They don't use EnRapture there."

With panic, Yam shook his head, but the guard only stepped closer. Ashyr and Yam's eyes locked. Then Ashyr's tone softened. "I've never sent a child into the heart of Australia." He didn't look away from Yam. "But...I am fair. Be sure to tell them back at your home: *I am fair*." Then he turned to

Aria. "Because of that, because of your age, that you aren't yet an adult, I will soften the punishment."

A sigh slipped from Aria.

"I will send you to the coast, to the traditionalists. They will reform you into their ways." An amused look crossed Ashyr's face. "The cultural shock alone will be punishment enough. Not to mention the challenge of detoxing from EnRapture." Ashyr pressed his hands together as if sending Aria a blessing. "But you are young. And still in training. You will manage. The traditionalists will cure you of your destructive ways. Or they will cast you out to the center, where their criminals are. So I warn you, change your ways.

"Now, what to do with you?" He shifted to Yam. "What indeed? Mercy isn't as available for those who aren't my own. But...I am up for a trade. A youth for a youth. Do you understand me? Let's make Foster trade. That seems fair, doesn't it? Otherwise, if I were to drop you in Australia, I can't promise where you would land. Okay, then." Ashyr stood. "Looks like we're done here."

Aria stood too. "Send him home. That's all he wants."

The council gasped. Ashyr fingers folded into clenched fists. "Outbursts are not acceptable behavior." He stepped down from his platform and drew close to her. "And I will return him where I found him," he moved to Yam and spoke quietly, "and retrieve who should be with us now. Quite kind of me, isn't it?" But his face was gone, over to the council. "You are dismissed." He waved his hand at the group, who then filed out in whispers. "Next session," he said to them at the door, "I'll fill you in with more details about this ungrateful guest."

When he came back, he spoke to the guard. "I need something to clear my head. Reach out to my assistant. Have her move up my next experience."

As the door shut, Yam didn't turn around. The silence told him it was just Aria, him, and Ashyr.

"What does she know?" Ashyr stood in front of Yam.

"I know you need to send him home," she said.

Ashyr glared at Yam. "What is this *home* she keeps talking about?"

"She knows I live in the sky. That's it."

Ashyr shifted to Aria. "What else?"

"That you are looking for a girl named Leilani to help you with a special project. That's it."

"So…" Ashyr was back at Yam. "If we wanted to negotiate an exchange with them, you for Leilani, how would we do that?"

"Just send him home," Aria burst out.

Ashyr glared at her. "That would be lovely. Drop you off," he shifted back to Yam. "Pick her up. But your *baba* has banned me from entering. You were to contact them for pick-up when your project was complete."

Yam's chest heaved up and down. His eyes stayed on Ashyr while the girl stuck her hand out in front of Yam. "That's what we were trying to do.

To contact them. With your airship. Send them a message that they needed to come help."

"*Come help.*" Ashyr mocked the phrase. "Yes, come *help* us here. Like we had planned!" He glared again at Yam. "Right? Like the plan we already had!"

"We were just borrowing it," Aria continued. "Just to send a message to his family to tell them—"

"All right." Ashyr slapped his hands together, cutting the girl off. "Enough from you."

"Listen," Yam said, the fear suddenly gone, the fight for justice prevailing. "Aria's brilliant. So don't send her away. Listen to her plan. She knew what to do."

Ashyr laughed. "I'm not comfortable with her... her actions...what she still may know...but I might be understanding your plan. And...I like it. Send a message, with the airship. Not bad." He shot Aria a look. "We'll deal with you later." Then he motioned at Yam. "Come on, kid. You and I are going to send a message to *Baba Brody*."

TWENTY-FIVE

FOSTER

A voice came, "Hey."

Foster stirred at the noise. He lifted his head, which had been resting on his folded arms. He sat at the table in the little boardroom and couldn't remember how he had gotten there.

"Foster."

He blinked and tried to find the voice. There it was. Brody's tired face.

Foster rubbed at his eyes, only to confirm the aged look of his friend. His beard was longer, in need of a comb, a trim, or just a shower. Foster couldn't look much better.

"Good to see you, man." Foster scooted away from the table.

"Clark said you've been down here for hours. Where's the junk that needs to be fixed?"

The details came back: Foster pushing the *Connect Four* contraption's lever, yanking it, tugging, while it resisted until the handle broke off. Like a Jenga game, the pieces fell, exposing a complex scattering of tubes. The repair was beyond him.

This electrochemical contraption was what was saving them, splitting the molecules into oxygen and carbon monoxide, combing the oxygen molecules into O_2, then shooting pure, breathable oxygen back into the air. When it worked, it worked. But it couldn't keep up. Not until they stopped the overall leakage.

"What's your current reading?" Brody asked.

Foster shook away the tiredness and reached for the device he'd previously abandoned. "Sixty-five percent carbon."

"Still way too high. You look horrible by the way."

"You don't look much better."

Brody's nod made Foster's insides twist. "How is everyone?" he asked.

"Every time I buzz Clark on the radio, he thinks I'm announcing the exodus." Foster tried to shrug, but it took too much effort. "They're all just waiting for the word."

Again, Brody's nod confirmed what Foster already knew.

"The birds don't sing anymore." Foster tapped at the table. When he looked back this time, Brody didn't nod.

Instead, he slumped into a nearby chair. "How long have you been down here?"

"Or maybe they aren't singing because it's already too late. Bit by bit, they're dying. They're silencing themselves to tell us the island is no longer habitable."

"How long?" Brody repeated. "You need to take breaks."

Foster shook his head. He had no idea.

"Sleeping more?"

The question cued Foster into a yawn. "Just what's necessary."

"More intense headaches?"

"I have my share." His fingers already were at his temples noting the constant throbbing that always seemed there. "Nothing fatal, yet."

"No. Nothing serious yet," Brody said, only to quietly ask, "What about the others?"

Foster looked at the table again. "The same. Fatigue. Sleep apnea. Horrendous headaches. Our biggest concerns are the few with respiratory issues. The departure list is prioritized; they're just waiting for my word. You got any better news?"

"I wish. We should have found the source by now. But…" the words trailed off.

Foster glanced at him. "But instead, you come to repair our overworked bandage. It's in my lab." His head motioned toward the door, where down the long pathway through the belly of the island, and up the ladder, beyond the sandy road, was Ashyr's device, if only Foster had the energy to get there.

Brody's large hands gripped the table. He stood. "Okay. Let's go."

But Foster remained. "We can't sustain it much longer."

"Yep." Brody turned around. "What's this?" He looked at the whiteboard.

Foster looked at it too. At some point, he had created a design cycle on the board. In the center, he had written *Problem*. Then, using words and arrows, he had created the process circle: *Imagine, Plan, Create, Improve, Ask,* and then back to *Imagine*.

He slowly arose and stared at it. "I went back to the beginning." In the early days, the room had held so much creative energy—brainstorming, exploring, creating improvements, discussions, building on the shoulders of experts—but all that was gone. "The *problem* now is the island has expired." Foster pointed at the center. "And my *imagination* is absent. The *plan*... it's like Mariana said, the island was the plan. There is nothing to *create*. Nothing left to improve our situation. What we need is air. Healthy, sustainable air. Until we find the leak, or the microorganism, we keep losing more each day. So *ask* what? For the undetectable invader to reveal itself? And since all our efforts have found no answer, we are back to the beginning. I still *imagine* a paradise for my family, a place of peace for them to live their lives. But I got nothing, Brody. I've hit the end. No design ideas. No solutions."

"*Metanoia*. It's Greek. Know what it means?"

Foster slid back into his seat. "Nope."

"A change of mind, a reorientation. A fundamental transformation of outlook. It's the new vision of the world and one's self."

"I thought you were going to say it meant '*giving up*.'"

"No. It's time for us to change our direction."

Foster nodded toward the design circle on the whiteboard. "All right." He scooted his chair around to give Brody his full attention. "Give me what you got."

While studying the board, Brody crossed his arms. "The day before we launched the islands…" He picked up the blue marker and uncapped it. "That day I died inside. Because right then, either what we were about to do was going to kill us all or… if we didn't do what we did…we could have stayed and all died in some other form or fashion. Either way, we were going to die. So… I chose death."

"You died." Foster nodded toward the board, waiting for a better solution.

"I died," Brody repeated, the marker frozen in his hand as he still looked over the board. "So I could start living. We all did that day." With the blue marker, he wrote *Live* in the center, under *Problem*.

When Brody turned back, Foster opened his mouth, only to shut it again.

"Now," Brody waved the marker at him, "it's time to do it again. Think of yourself as dead. You have lived your life…. So now, take what's left… and live it properly." He nodded at Foster. "Words from the philosopher Marcus Aurelius." He leaned back and his large arms folded as if waiting for Foster to respond.

When Foster only gave the slightest of nods at the board, Brody accepted the challenge and turned back.

"I left that world a long time ago." Brody tapped the end of the marker against his beard and tilted his head from side to side as he looked over the design cycle. "I chose to leave it. The wars. The fears. The corruption. Ashyr. I just mentally stepped away one day...and I can't return. Not in the same way. None of us are the same. We left there and we changed."

"We built what we built for a clear reason, to not have to go back. But you've said it before...we may need to return...to what's left."

Brody shrugged. "Yes. You do. Temporarily. And yes, these islands were never home, forever. All of it's temporary."

Foster rubbed his temple and shook his head. "I had always hoped this was permanent. That we could make it work for our children, and their children, and we almost did."

"No. It's a pause," Brody said calmly, almost reverently. "Like an old Super Mario Brothers' level. The one where you jump through the trees. The islands have been that spot until we know the next place to jump."

Past the silence, the grumpy demeanor, the passionate frustrations with projects, there was this other side of Brody, which on rare occasions emerged—this dreamer at his most humble moments.

"There is a higher place, Foster." Intensity filled his voice. "Before all this...these delays, this current crisis we are dealing with...and other important issues that must be addressed...they're all slowing me down from what I really want to do."

At last, a genuine smile found its way onto Foster's face. "Aren't you always working on something big?"

"Well, I've had to pause *my* work, but when I was, the PIGS and I were building a contraption that can take us higher."

Foster laughed. "Like what? A spaceship?"

Brody tilted his head; no humor rested in his eyes. "It's the next holding place. One step at a time. One process after the next to get farther from the broken world we left behind…and to work at finding a way to connect with a higher plane of existence."

"Aliens?"

"Higher intelligence." Without a smile, Brody gave Foster a nod and then turned to the whiteboard. Against the black *Problem,* he used a red marker and wrote *No Return.*

Near *Imagine* he added, *Make contact.* Then he followed the circle along its path. At *Plan,* he wrote *Join a greater force. Evolve into more.*

"If you ever thought any of my ideas were crazy…" Foster tried to speak lightly.

Brody paused and gave him a light nod. "We wouldn't be where we are now."

"So…right now, would you say that whole crazy 'build an island in the sky' idea—what's the verdict—was that a good idea or a bad one?"

He turned back to the board. "Precisely."

"So let me get this straight." Foster maintained his light tone. "What you're proposing is a bit like the tower of Babel? Or more like building a tiered-level system to heaven?"

Brody shifted again to give a small grin. "Old Amway pyramid scheme—I'm going to multi-level-market my way there."

"Really!" The exchange of smiles felt so good. "Can I help?" A mischievousness was there, like a young boy playing with a childhood buddy, building something without supervision and hoping not to get caught.

But Brody's face didn't share that same grin. Instead, in full seriousness, he asked, "Do you want to come with me?"

Foster's light mood tempered. "How close are you?"

"I need time. That's been hard to come by, but if we make it a priority, close enough."

"So I have time to think on this?"

"As much time as your island holds breathable air." Through the beard, a mid-grin appeared.

Foster arose. "Sounds like we better go see if we can get a second life out of the *Connect Four* junk. It's going to be needed." As he headed toward the door, *Evolve more* caught his eye. "What was that quote again?"

"*You have lived your life.*" Brody dropped the marker onto the board's tray and slapped a hand on Foster's shoulder. "*Now take what's left and live it properly.*"

TWENTY-SIX

MARIANA

When Mariana had left the island in urgency for Australia, she had naively supposed there would be nightly conversations with Foster over the plan. Continuous communication. Instead of nothing.

Numerous times through the void, Sunny assured her that when Brody and Foster had news to share, they would be in contact.

But days turned to weeks.

The only message had been the first, relayed through Sunny from Brody. The contraption produced breathable oxygen. The focus now was to find the source of the leak and make the repair. Brody's instructions: Sit tight and hope for the best. From there, Mariana heard nothing more.

So she did just that—hoped for the best and went to work. She helped around Sunny's yard, gathered chicken eggs, cleaned up after the slaughtering of rabbits, weeded the garden, tended to the bareness of the area, hauled water from the well, and tried to pass the time while expecting each day would bring news that she could return home.

But as no word continued to come, Sunny must have taken pity on Mariana's struggle. "Talk to Misty," she said. "Ask her to help you get set up to connect with Foster."

With relief and gratitude, Mariana found Misty in the kitchen washing up lunch dishes. "I hear you can help me talk to Foster."

Misty kept her eyes on the dishes. "Talk—no. Connect—yes. And, if that's what Sunny said, then yeah, I guess I can help you." But Misty didn't stop her rhythm. Hands dipped into the small bin of soapy water. Then they dipped into the small bin of clean water.

"Want help drying?" Mariana asked.

"They can air dry." Misty scooted to block Mariana from the sink. Her hands dipped farther into the soapy bin. After a quick twist of her head, she said, "Can you grab those two cups on the table?"

Mariana tried to catch Misty's eyes, but the woman looked past her with that same aloofness that was always there. She didn't want Mariana's help. That had been clear on multiple tasks before. Each time Mariana offered, Misty cut her off mid-sentence or made an excuse to return to the chore at a later time.

After handing off the cups, Mariana watched Misty, her legs crossed at the ankle, her hips swaying slowly, as if a song were in her head. With impatience, Mariana pulled out a kitchen towel and approached the clean bin of dishes, only to brush against Misty's shoulder.

Misty stopped. Her lips pursed. Between her high cheekbones and broad forehead, her deep-set eyes gave Mariana a sharp look. With wet hands, she shifted her red headband back against her thick black hair. "Let's go," she said and left the sink.

"We can finish here first," Mariana called after the woman, who was already gone.

From the living room, at the map room door, Misty nodded at Mariana through the kitchen bar opening. "I will. After we get your message sent." Then she disappeared into the room.

Once Mariana joined her, Misty was at the bookshelf at the far wall. She punched at the spine of a book and the shelf unlatched, exposing a door. From there, a secret compartment emerged, a desk in an L-shape that held an antique-looking device, part typewriter, part old cash register. With the bookshelf fully out of the way, Misty grabbed a wooden folding chair and sat at the desk to fiddle with a knob.

Mariana just stared. "What is this?" she finally asked.

"What you need."

Mariana tried to find Brody in the strange device. As she approached it, Misty chided her look. "It may be archaic, but you should be grateful for it."

"I am." Then with extreme softness, she added, "Can you teach me how to use it?"

"No." Misty continued to fiddle with knobs.

"How did you learn to use it?"

No answer came.

Instead, Misty's head moved up and down, scanning the device. Hands, weathered and cracked, contrasting against the rest of her soft-looking bronze skin, pressed buttons and tightened gears. "What's the message?" she asked.

Get me out of here, Mariana thought. Instead, she rolled her shoulders back, squared her chin as if she were as tough as Misty, and reached for her confident voice. "'Hi Foster, dear, I just wanted to check in and see how things were going—"

"No!" Misty spun around. Impatience covered her face. "It needs to be short. No more than five words. Two is best."

Mariana stared back. She tried to nod, but the scowl that faced her made it hard, especially as she tried to formulate a concise message. Finally, she said, "'Any updates?'"

Misty turned back to the device. After several knobs were spun and a large collection of buttons were pushed, she arose. "Done."

Mesmerized by what she saw, Mariana's mouth had fallen open. "What did you just do?" The keys were labeled as 0 or 1, that was it. Otherwise, it was only knobs.

Misty's eyes finally met hers. "I sent your message."

"That's amazing. How?"

A smile crept over Misty's face. Her chest rose slightly. "A high-stakes poker game. We keep our cards close to us. We're cautious with each card we play." Then she walked past Mariana to the door.

"Wait." Mariana looked back and forth between the device and Misty. "Where are you going?"

She pointed out toward the living room. "To finish the dishes."

"No." Mariana waved her hand back at the device. "What about Foster's response?"

Amusement crossed Misty's face. "He has to get notified first."

"I thought we were..." Mariana looked back at the device, suddenly feeling quite frustrated by it.

Misty took a single step toward her. "It will go to the receiver. Brody's PIGS will pick it up. Once it's deciphered, Brody will share the message." Each time Misty said Brody's name, a softness filled her voice.

"So then what?"

"Once they have their message, it goes back through the PIGS to get scrambled. Then it'll be fielded through radio waves until it reaches us. And then I'll decode it."

Mariana couldn't look at her, or the device, nor could she roll her eyes. Instead, she looked at the map on the wall. "Who built this?"

"Brody."

Mariana laughed. "No. This is way too slow for Brody's taste."

"Oh, things go fast on Brody's end." Misty took another step back into the room. "You know, don't you?" Her eyes peered at Mariana.

"Know what?"

"What's happening here."

Mariana shrugged. "Act like I know nothing."

Misty tilted her head. "Sunny doesn't talk, does she?"

The smirk on Misty's face frustrated Mariana. "No," Mariana said quietly.

A scoff came, followed by Misty adding, "You think it was always like this…that these people lived like this?"

"No," Mariana said quickly, then she struggled with her words. "So…tell me…what was it like, before…"

"There was a need for us to safeguard our data usage. Keep it limited so as not to alert Tarthur of anything we are doing within the electromagnetic spectrum. Is that what you're trying to figure out?"

Mariana's brain hurt. She turned from Misty back to the device. "Low data usage. Coded messages. Under Tarthur's radar."

"Correct." Misty turned to leave again, only to shift back. "For the moment, be glad we have what we have."

"Since the fires? Is that when everything changed?"

"You don't know anything, do you?"

The statement caused Mariana's eyes to sting with tears. "No. I don't."

Misty's hands slid into the pockets of her lightweight jacket. "Why do you think I'm here?"

"Tell me."

Misty looked back to the door. "The dishes need to be finished."

"Then let me help you." Mariana moved forward, only for Misty to step narrowly in her way.

"No. I don't talk about it out there."

"Okay." As if her heart needed some loving protection, Mariana hugged herself. "Then tell me here."

As dark hair tousled back and forth, those deep-set eyes shifted toward a wild state. "You can't understand."

"Maybe not. But try me."

"So you can judge me?" Part child, part animal emerged in Misty's eyes—broken, scared, angry, wild. Mariana stepped back. But before Mariana could do anything, the child-portion in front of her broke. "I stayed. Sunny and Brody asked me to come. They didn't say where, just away. But I was young. So I stayed."

"Here?" Mariana asked in confusion.

"No. L.A. I stayed for the life Ashyr promised." Misty bit her lip and shook her head. "Forget it. You can't understand."

Mariana froze. Any movement seemed like a threat to Misty's state. But the silence wasn't enough either. With deep sincerity, she said, "Help me to understand."

"I'm going to go finish the dishes." And with that Misty was gone.

Mariana, alone in the room, stared at the map. Her eyes ran back and forth from L.A. to Australia.

The only two circled places within this vast world. What did Misty know? What would lead Sunny here?

Mariana's mind wandered back to that day when everything broke on the island, when Ashyr was going to take Leilani from her and Foster. What had Mariana said when she was alone with Foster, before it was too late? "Let's call Zane. Have him gather up the family." Put a call out. Gather thirty-three adults right there on the beach in twenty minutes or less. Use their family as an army to stop Ashyr... From what? From taking Leilani? Yes. Stop him from taking Leilani, from being there, from forming the catastrophe he brought with him.

But it was too late; when he first stepped on the island, he ruined them.

Why had this memory stirred in her like this?

Mariana reached out and touched the landmass of Australia, right in the center of it, right in the pit, feeling a fear beneath it. Did she want the answer, the truth around all this?

Within Misty, something reminded Mariana of Leilani. Perhaps the abruptness, the rudeness, the disconnect? The unhappiness?

She approached the odd communication device to touch the knobs and buttons. Familiar homesickness pierced her heart. Being unable to communicate with Leilani was brutal, nearly as bad as not being able to connect with Foster.

All Foster needed to say was *Come home*. That was it. Please, Foster. *Come back home*. She stared at the machine like it might send her plea, like it would deliver her out of this foreign life.

"You can't just wait for a message to come in," Misty spoke behind Mariana. "It's not going to boil with a response by you staring at it." Her voice was sharp. "It records the message. It can manage okay until I get back to it."

Slowly, Mariana turned around. "Do you want help drying the dishes?"

"No. I want you to sit." Before Mariana did, the wild eyes were back. "I want you to know why I stayed." Misty's hands pressed against her hips. Her mouth started to move fast. "I stayed in L.A. until I saw the ill side of it. And then I ended up here, okay?"

Ready to move past Misty's anger, Mariana gave her a safe nod. "Okay."

But Misty spread her legs out, taking a fair amount of space within the width of the room. Her height, accented by wedge-heeled shoes, towered over Mariana. "It was great," she said. "And fun. Exhilarating. Incredible. Until it wasn't. And all that freedom showed a new unfreedom. All Ashyr's professed fairness became unfair. The rankings?" Her eyes moved around the room as if speaking to others that weren't there. "How is that any different than the separation that once existed between genders, skin color, our outer appearances? All Ashyr did was shift it to our registries, which controlled our differences. It wasn't right. Or fair. And by pointing that out, when some of us wanted a change, we got our one-way ticket out of Ashyr's land to here. He dumped us right in the heart of the outback with the outlaws."

Mariana pressed her lips together and nodded again slowly, cautiously, so as not upset the unfolding story.

"You want to know the big secret, don't you?" She grabbed the other folding chair. It made a loud crash as it unfolded. Misty took her seat in the middle of the room. "What we don't discuss? You want to know it, don't you?"

"Sunny says it's not her story to tell," Mariana spoke soothingly. "So I take it, it's your story. And it's up to you what you wish to share."

Right then a beep sounded from the machine. Then a light blasted three sharp red blinks. Mariana jumped. Her heartbeat picked up in tempo.

"Move." Misty jumped from her chair, shooing Mariana out of hers. "Way under two hours. I'm impressed."

Leaning over Misty, Mariana watched a paper, like a printed receipt, emerge with 0s and 1s and spaces— that was it. "How long will it take to decode it?"

"Depends on how long it is." Then she waved an arm for Mariana to scoot back. "Just give me time." She shifted, leaning over the device while her fingers gracefully punched in numbers and rolled at a dial. Mariana's own fingers pulsed, dancing with anticipation as time slowly moved.

While Misty remained focused, Mariana heard a voice so low it didn't seem to be coming from Misty. "It's trafficking. That's what's going on here."

Mariana stepped forward. Leilani was always telling her she didn't hear well. She leaned closer and reshaped the heard word. "*Trafficking?*"

"Human trafficking. For EnRapture." Misty didn't look up. "They take and give nothing back. It's mind rape." Her voice held no emotion. "Control. Victims of all kinds. It's empty…and horrible."

Mariana saw the tremor in Misty's hands right as similar tremors hit Mariana's knees. She stepped toward the wall, leaning on it for support.

"No." Her voice sounded so weak. "No!" This was impossible. "Foster," she called out in a whisper. "Ashyr." Her mind was back in the lab, summoning them from so long ago to return there to their Em-Path days. When Foster had stopped the invention, Ashyr had gone forward. There were dangers with the invention, but not this. Ashyr had clearly told her that. She had one awful exchange with him, where he shared a fantasy with her. She vowed never to use Em-Path again. She hated it. But in the midst of all it's wrongs, he had explained no one could take control of another's mind…he had explained this. An exchange was consensual exchanges by both people. No one could…she tried to find her voice. "Um…" She rubbed at her forehead, ready to challenge Misty and discredit her words. "Ashyr said…it can't be…he wouldn't do this."

"No." Misty spun around. Her voice was hot and annoyed. "Ashyr sends anyone here if they abuse his EnRapture. There are rules there. Order. But where we're dumped—there's no order here."

"Here?"

Misty shook her head as if frustrated. "Not here now, here when it was their here...not our here...now."

"I don't understand. Explain. Please. I need to understand this."

But Misty just shook her head and turned back to the machine.

If Foster knew—the guilt. The horrible guilt! For so many years he had already carried it—the guilt and the fears that Mariana shrugged off. Because it hadn't mattered for them...they were in their paradise. They were okay. Safe. Their family was safe. *Human trafficking.* The words, like poison, formed in her head. "Slavery?" Mariana asked. "EnRapture slavery?"

Misty pressed a button down on the machine. "Correct." The voice was so hollow, so distant and terrifying.

Mariana wanted to keel over, or vomit—not think. One Em-Path experience so long ago and that was enough. Mind control. Abuse. Slavery. Along with her knees, her hands were trembling now. "How is here better than Ashyr's? Why would anyone come here?"

Misty twisted around in her chair. "You aren't listening to yourself." She stood. "Ashyr's world is fair as long as you all are in this together with him. As long as your views match his. Then it's fair. Then it's okay. Even if you have a low registry, you have a registry, so you can make it there. But contest Ashyr, and you lose your registry. You're dead there, so he sends you to the center." She turned back and moved the chair out of the way. Then she shifted the bookcase back into place, making the communication device disappear behind the wall.

"The center, as in *here*?" Mariana asked again as she left her wall and weakly approached Misty.

"The people are good here." Misty threw a fist against the spine of another book. A locking sound followed. "Pure." She waved an arm at the wall Mariana had left, signifying the town behind it. "Here," she said softly, her hands pressed inside her jacket pockets. "These people are good," she repeated. "The best people you will ever meet. They have turned this unwanted center into a home...and now, what you know...this doesn't apply to your family. They will be safe here."

"Will they?"

"Yes. It's only those who have used EnRapture."

"But Ashyr sends..." Mariana's words stalled. She tried again. "Not everyone's good here, are they?"

Misty shrugged as if deflecting the question. "Most are."

"The center which once was bad is now good." It all tangled into a horrible reality. "But they're not free."

"It's momentary freedom. For me. For others." Misty looked to the floor. "Brody, Sunny, Leif—they are working hard to also give others freedom, until all who are trapped have a way out."

"And bring them where?"

"Exactly." Misty's gaze shifted to the map. "Nothing can be done too quickly." Then she spun around and faced Mariana. "Here." From her pocket, she pulled out a receipt. "Your message is done." Like a slip from a giant fortune cookie, she handed off the paper and walked out.

Alone, Mariana read: *Does not appear repairable*

That was it. The message.

Mariana looked again at the map. Then, ever so slowly, she walked past it, past the sickness, the yuck, the numbness. Like Misty had said, there was plenty of work to do around here. And Sunny needed to explain that work.

TWENTY-SEVEN

MARIANA

She found Sunny at the well, drawing up water, whistling a light, happy song.

"I need to understand what's going on," Mariana said firmly.

But as soon as Sunny turned around, Mariana felt the fear again, its great paralyzing hand taking over. If this was true, what was she bringing her people to? This was wrong. Uncaring! How could Sunny do this to them?

"What does Foster know?" The questions fired out. "Will Brody tell him? Brody will tell him, won't he? Like you should have told me."

Slowly, gently, Sunny set the water jug down.

"No. He won't." Like a rock tumbling down the mountainside, Mariana felt it, her avalanche of anger rolling out. "Brody is the master compartmentalist. He won't think to tell Foster; somehow in all his other—"

"Worries," Sunny cut her off.

But Mariana rushed on. "He won't even mention it. He'll let Foster send them here! My family here—to what, Sunny? How could you not tell me what this is?"

Sunny stepped forward, reaching for Mariana. But Mariana backed away. "I want out. I want my home. We didn't sign up for this. They can't come here. None of them."

"They will be safe." Sunny still moved closer and gripped Mariana's arm. "And we can't talk here."

"No." Mariana tried to break the grip, but Sunny held it too tightly. "Enough of this. I want the truth—I want answers."

"Stop," Sunny said.

"You've taken your girls into this."

Sunny placed both hands on Mariana's arms and kept the words firm. "Reach for Mother Goddess and like large flakes in a snowfall, she will come."

Mariana broke out of the grasp, but the look in Sunny's eyes held her. Something intense and strong pacified Mariana's anger. With a tight chuckle, she said, "Sunny, I have never lived in snow. Never even seen it."

Slowly, powerfully, Sunny drew her into a half-hug. "Then you will need to imagine it. You need to reach for that image. Softness. Lightness. Temporary but peaceful. Reach for that moment of stillness, of quietness falling down. Now."

"I don't get—" But Mariana's words softened, fading out as Sunny carried on.

"There is a snow globe of a world that you get to be a part of. A magic that can fall around you, if you let it. If you truly witness the snowfall, you will see that She is there. And She will let you know this." Sunny released Mariana from the hug and stepped away.

Mariana stared back, feeling lost. Yet a strange calm had come from Sunny's hug. "I don't know what you're talking about," she said softly.

"Have you asked for it?"

"What?"

"For your Mother Goddess to come."

"No."

"Try. Don't lose hope. And she will come."

Mariana shook her head, feeling like Sunny had cast a spell on her. A strange solace, a peace over such uncertainty. Mariana hugged herself as Sunny picked up the water jug and moved away.

"Watch. She will come. And I will too. I won't be home tonight." The steps widened between them. "But early tomorrow morning, very early, before the moon sets, I will meet you in the map room."

* * *

Like a flashlight from the heavens, the full, luminous moon shone down on Mariana. Lying on her bed, Mariana twisted onto her side to block out the white rays. Her arm draped over her eyes, shielding them, determined to fight against the brightness, to not think about this Mother Goddess, or human trafficking, or Tarthur, or anything.

But the more Mariana fought the light, the more loneliness set in. The helplessness. The desperation. The realization of how horrid this plight was for her family.

Eventually, she gave in and twisted herself upright. Her feet draped over the bed. And the magnificent moon met her face, shining down as if in alert observation, watching her, waiting for her to make a move.

She wanted to scream at it. Her next move! Was she supposed to go to the mafia and put all this in motion? Playing the diplomat for her people while leading them into slavery? A fear, like a snake, wrapped its way around her ankles, knees, hips, torso, and chest. A horrific paralysis. And here she was supposed to be leading her people to safety!

Against the shining moon's trance, Mariana lifted herself out of the bed and headed to the dark map room. Black emptiness in the form of landmasses greeted her.

She must do the right thing—she just wasn't sure what that was. What choices were there for her people? In the darkness, she searched again for another option. Some other way with less pain.

With no direction, time passed until she heard the shuffle of feet near the door. Before Sunny turned on the light, Mariana greeted her with a whisper. "Don't let me scare you."

Sunny chuckled as the overhead brightness filled the room. "I could feel your restlessness before I even opened the door."

With eyes on Sunny, Mariana asked the tired old question again while her finger pointed to Australia on the map. "Why are you here?"

"Because of Misty." She nodded as if her response answered everything. "Because of Tarthur. Because this is where I need to be."

"I need to understand this. No riddles. Just the facts. No protecting me. No keeping others' stories from me. If I am bringing my people here, I need to understand all of it."

Sunny heaved out a sigh. "I'll do my best." She unfolded the chairs and set them next to each other. "Let's sit. It might be easier for both of us."

"Okay." As soon as she did, Mariana crossed her legs and placed her clutched hands over her knees. "Let's hear it."

Sunny nodded and then leaned back against the chair and closed her eyes. "Many months ago," her voice was tired, her face contorted in pain, "the takeover happened. At that point, through a device Brody had given Misty a long time ago, she was able to contact us."

"Why wasn't she able to contact you before then?"

"It required Internet transmission, which was only available along the coast. Only the traditionalists had access to the Internet. Until the rebels swapped places."

"Which is why you have such bad communication now." Mariana's head motioned toward the special bookshelf behind her.

"Correct. If we are in range of the mafia, we can communicate normally, but then all our messages are shared. Or we can go this other route."

"So Misty reached out…" The pieces slipped into place. "She had been living with the rebels, and after the takeover…"

"It'd been years since I'd last heard from her. We had said goodbye under strained terms. Brody didn't think she was being wise, choosing Ashyr's life over ours. But it was her choice. And in the end, we respected that."

"But now she's here."

Sunny nodded. "Now she's here. And Brody didn't take that news well either."

Mariana shook against the headache that was coming on, the shortness of breath that followed, the growing sickness over the news. "So what is Brody doing about it? Besides not telling Foster."

Sunny drew her head back and paused. When she spoke, kindness filled her voice. "Should we have told you both?"

"And ruined our paradise?" Mariana's own tone stung herself. "Funny, huh? We brought…Foster brought…us…" She struggled with her own words. "We were the ones who brought Ashyr to your island. Here I thought it was us who had ruined your paradise…but you had given it up long before now. Because of Ashyr?"

Sunny quickly shook her head. "Because as Brody says, humans aren't responsible enough to benefit from all that technology has to offer us. In the end, we will destroy ourselves."

"And that's why we left—in the beginning," Mariana said. "It's what I thought Brody wanted— to leave behind a broken world."

"It's far more complicated than that."

Mariana looked down at her hands. When she looked back, she spoke apologetically. "Then what is Brody doing?"

"Before saving the islands?" Sunny offered a humorous smirk.

Mariana smiled back. "Of course. Before now. What's his role in all this?"

Sunny's shoulders caved. A huge sigh came out, as if she had been Atlas carrying the weight of the world on those shoulders. She shook her head. Only to shake it again. Followed by a third time as if struggling, debating inside over the words she wished to share. Finally, she said, "He never wanted to use his AI inventions as weapons. But…" the head shaking was back. She wiped at an eye before adding, "Mariana, the more you know, the higher risk you will be in. You will be pulled into things you don't need right now—or maybe ever. There are things I don't even know, to protect me. Less is more around here. The less you know the safer you are."

"No." Mariana sat upright and protested with a headshake. "This is heavy on you. Clearly, this is heavy on you. You weren't even a part of Em-Path. If anything, Foster and I should be on the front lines with you and Brody. So share it with me. Help me lighten your load."

"It's not an invention that did this. It's humans. The corruption within us." Then her lips pressed together, followed by another light shake of the head, as if there was no more she would say.

"Please," Mariana begged. "Tell me."

The head shakes grew more violent. Sunny's body looked so fragile and small in her chair. She pushed herself forward, as if fighting the unrest inside. "I can't. I don't want to lie to you. I can't lie to you. But I can't share. You just need to leave it at that. Understood?" But the firmness in her voice broke, revealing her pain.

And Mariana latched onto that pain. "I need to help you. Foster will want to, too. Let us help."

Sunny seemed frozen in place. Her eyes pleaded with Mariana. "Are you sure?"

"Yes."

"Because once you know, you're right, you will want to help. You will feel compelled to help. But it's a high price. Horrible and high."

"Just tell me, Sunny."

"Your paradise will be gone. This will consume you and Foster. Like it consumed us."

"It's already gone." Mariana reached forward and touched her friend's hand, which was trembling. "Let me in, please."

With that, Sunny fell back into the chair. Her shoulders sank again over the weight she carried. "Brody rescued Misty through AI trading."

For a moment, Mariana didn't understand. Then her hands flew to her mouth. She tried to recover while more pieces slipped into place. Like a new puzzle box opened, parts scattered out in front of her, and the image slowly began to take shape. Mariana saw it: Brody, his life's work, Tarthur, Sunny's earlier sentence, AI inventions, weapons, Brody never wanting this.

As Mariana tried to lower her hand from her mouth, Sunny nodded then said, "You asked what Brody is up to. Brody is very much involved with all this. We had hoped to create some type of underground rescue for the victims."

Her hand was back over her mouth. As the picture formed, Mariana felt her heart break.

"But there are so many limitations we are up against," Sunny said. "So we are buying time. Over the course of these last months, we are slowly releasing, trading, negotiating."

While her hand dropped to her side, Mariana mumbled, "Brody. He would say he prefers the isolated life, and here he's…" She couldn't complete her words.

"Oh." Sunny waved a hand, her face showing a moment of carefree humor. "He likes being a hermit. Don't question that. Remember we, too, have had several years of just our little family on that island. But…" she sighed as if picking up the weight of the world again and hefting it back onto her shoulders. "He has to stay away from here. Tarthur would love to get Brody in his realm. But Brody has far too many AI secrets. And that is how this all works. The power struggle I mentioned that day, when you arrived—I usually have negotiation power, because Brody provides me with some AI tool to appease Tarthur, an AI trade for a release. But you weren't exactly that."

"I was the reason you didn't make a trade?"

"Oh, there were several things that went against Tarthur's wishes that day. Me coming in at an unplanned time. With another passenger. No trade. Throwing a new arrangement into the mix. Tarthur was mad and he was going to show me. That was the power struggle—who had more authority in our negotiations."

"I am sorry."

"For what? For being a refugee? For trying to save your people? We all are trying to do that."

Mariana drew her fists up to her lips. She gave Sunny the slightest nod. But this was different. Mariana's people were family. Sunny was taking more people, those in great need, and making them her family. She looked at her friend, sitting there, tired, real, and exhausted, and Mariana realized how very little she truly knew about Sunny.

"That day," Sunny said, "when you arrived with me, Tarthur, in his own way, threatened me. Had we not made it back by nightfall, they would have come for Misty again. Or…hurt someone else."

"Sunny! That's terrible!"

"Exactly." Her eyes said enough. "We worked hard to get them back and then…"

Mariana nodded, seeing that day entirely differently now.

"Leif saved my family that day. Him being there—it kept the peace. We need that, for right now...just as we buy time."

"For what?"

"Brody has something in the works. Designing to destroy. Designing to save. Designing to fight. Designing to win. He doesn't yet know for certain how it will all play out—just that he's building it. From there, we have options. So we can get us, our loved ones, our families, all of us, out of this."

"Protect the children." Mariana whispered words that the two had shared so many years ago while pregnant with Leilani and Yam—a time when they were ready to take risks, ready to take their families up into the skies. "Protect the next generation," she whispered. "Do whatever it takes."

"Protect the innocent...and protect those who want a second chance..." New words from Sunny. "Let them rebuild their lives." She gave Mariana a half-smile. Then her shoulders lifted, as did her breath, as if the break from holding up the world had done her a bit of good.

TWENTY-EIGHT

LEILANI

The cell smelled like urine. I wasn't sure if it was my own or just the floor around me. A cockroach ran across my knee. I needed to shoo it off until the next one came. But I felt too exhausted.

The large cat hissed. From the sound, I knew it was in my cell, a few feet away. Over the days, or weeks, or however long I'd been here in this cell, I'd learned to just keep my distance. If I didn't address it, if I didn't make eye contact, the wild and ferocious fighter would turn its attention to the rats that occasionally ran past. Then the feline would slip through my bars and disappear.

In the beginning, we clashed. With an arch of its back, it hissed and slashed its claws at me. I backed into the corner, my body shaking, while the feline went to work, finding its food.

Then, once satisfied, it left.

I learned to give it what it wanted. Let it eat. Then leave.

Same with the others who came to see me.

Sometimes they cleaned me up before they demanded their exchange with a hunger my lacking EnRapture skills never seemed to satisfy. They always wanted more. And always left me emptier than before.

After my fear left, I no longer cared. All I wanted was my memories of home, but it was what they wanted, too, leaving me with so much noise, so many extremes banging in my mind. At times, my grasp on the island seemed vague, like a fairytale I dreamed of often.

A bright light shone down on me, lying on the floor in my filthy clothes. The cool cement seeped through a hoody I think was once Draven's. I raised my head to see CasVaughna, a creature with mostly human female parts other than the nose that was flattened to resemble a bunny and her snow leopard's tail. She often wore costumes, her current one a maid uniform with scant fabric; she even carried a dust mop—a large feather one. I'd seen it before; she used it to trace up and down any figure she passed, then she would give a hop, a sway of her long tail, a scrunch of her bunny nose, and a pucker of her lips. Whenever I could, I tried to look away. What once all seemed ridiculous now just left me empty and tired inside.

I did what I always did when I saw CasVaughna. I drew myself up and tried to ignore the smells. She, over the others, offered a gentleness I appreciated. Whereas the others came with fanatic appetites, a demand for their obsession to be fed, CasVaughna talked with me a little before the exchange. Her eyes would look at me, as they did now, searching for something. Like she was requesting an allowance for the creature she had become.

She always asked for memories from the island, as if I had anything else to give. But more and more, my memories kept clouding up. Too many other EnRapture experiences intruded. Still, for her, I always tried to find Dad in my memories, wondering what he would say to all this. From him, would she feel the acceptance she sought?

But...it didn't matter Dad's response. It came down to survival. That was it.

I peeled the matted hair from my cheek. From my cheek, dirt smeared onto my hand that I then placed into CasVaughna's outstretched paw. A smile stirred over her lips. Her whiskers trembled.

"We have a special thing for you." The paw-like fingers pulled me to my feet. "A surprise." She chuckled. Her hips twisted. Her whiskers flickered. Her long tail swayed.

She let me press against her body, my dirty shoulder resting near her as if in a hug, my head leaning against her breast. Then her arms wrapped around me. I missed Mom. What I could remember of her.

Suddenly, the arms scooped me up, her strength far greater than I would have imagined. Never had she carried me out of the cell. I had always been led out.

I tried not to dwell on the differences. Tried not to think of CasVaughna but of Mom instead. How had things ended between us? I couldn't remember the different life I had once lived.

Down the hallway, she carried me, toward the entrance, out into the sunlight, where a dog man stood. Then CasVaughna transferred me into his arms.

I was so tired. And his arms felt strong, warm, and soothing. Like a little child, I pressed against the fur of his chest. Memories of Dad were there. Him carrying me. When I was so young. After we had played in the waves. The surf. The sand. I had been so little. I had told him I was too tired. Too exhausted from all our play. The trip back home was too far. If I just asked enough, he would scoop me in his arms and carry me just like this.

CasVaughna was right—a surprise indeed. I had not felt so much care since being here. Maybe I had earned it. No longer did I have to live in that cell. That was what they had promised me. Be good. Listen. Follow what they said. Give them what they wanted, and I could earn my place here.

At the start, I had fought. Just at the beginning. Until an EnRapture pill had been forced down my throat. A blindfold wrapped around my eyes. My body strapped down. A beast near me, the glove imposed over my hand. The hand locked down on mine, the tingling happening, the neurons firing fast, EnRapture working. After all the times before, when I had taken the pill solo with no partner there, now my mind worked fast, welcoming each partner, giving them, I assume, what they wanted to see.

Draven had told me part of an exchange required preparation, identifying a plan of what one would share. But I never had time to prepare. They came and left me with a mixture of fear, sadness, emptiness, and a horrible breaking inside. And I never knew for sure what I gave them, but they kept coming back.

Their leader, who they call RexHera, their goddess and queen, during my first exchange with her, had told me what they expected of me. "First," she said, "you will be shocked, my dear. Shock is what brought us here. Then you will find acceptance. And eventually, sweet one, you will find approval. Once you find approval, we will have a place for you here."

I remember that feeling, after she pulled away, leaving a strand of her baby blue cotton candy hair resting against my arm. I thought the sickness inside would never leave.

But over time, it lessened. I learned the rules. I began accepting the creatures' expectations. And now, something different was occurring. I leaned against the warm fur chest, my heartbeat in line with his steps. I had found their approval. I closed my eyes.

What if they offered me to become like them? Could I do it? Did they allow for choice? To say 'no'? To voice the uncomfortableness I once felt? To become like them. What would I choose?

If *no* was not an option, if to exist here, to no longer live in a cell with a feral cat and a colony of cockroaches as my companions, if my only way out was to become like them—would I?

*I've seen enough to see...*deep in the recesses of my mind, I heard snippets of a song.

Prepared as I am...

...I'll take care of you

The phrases were out of order.

Pulling me home...

...I've seen enough to see...

But it came like a lullaby.

The way I left last time...

...with my family...

Words that calmed my thoughts.

Home is where I want to be...

Against the rhythm of the strong steps, the drooping of my eyes, and the segments of a song playing through my head, I felt myself moving like a wave, in and out of consciousness. Other creatures stepped aside while the dog man carried me farther. They watched me, blowing me kisses. Smiling at me. Light clapping of their hands as if honoring me.

Then, like a cozy blanket wrapped around me, sleep settled in as *I've seen enough I want to see...* still played... *Pulling me home...with my family...* in my inner ears.

TWENTY-NINE

MARIANA

Somewhere far away an animal was crying. High-pitched yelps like grieving for a parent, lost, hurt, scared. Mariana listened, as her heart pleaded with her to arise and stop the pain.

Although her body wanted sleep, her mind wouldn't allow it. The entire day had been spent fighting to find some type of inner peace. How she wished she could talk to Foster. Unload all this, hear his thoughts, listen to his views of all that was happening here.

Tired of tossing, Mariana sought stillness in the bed. She worked to find a place for her mind to focus. There was so much she didn't understand. Right now, the only clarity was she needed to keep her people safe.

In sad desperation, Mariana's thoughts turned to what Sunny had said, to call out to this idea of a Mother Goddess. To speak freely to what Sunny believed in. *Please save us. Please.* As the words came so did the tears, until her mind began to soften, and sleep seeped in.

* * *

"Mariana." A knock at the bedroom door, followed by Ivy-Mai's voice. "You have to come."

Seconds earlier she had been on the beach, with Foster, wrapped in his arms, watching the grandchildren play in the water. The smile had run through Mariana's heart. Now, slowly, unwillingly, she shook the dream from her grasp. The knocking continued. "Something is here for you."

As Mariana pulled herself out of bed, she paused at the nightstand. The wind-up clock read 4 a.m.

Ivy-Mai's voice came again. "Your name is on it."

Mariana reached for yesterday's dusty, filthy clothes to replace her nightgown. As soon as she stepped out into the hall, Sunny, Misty, and Rani were there. Sunny was the only one not dressed in a nightgown. Instead, she wore a wide-brimmed hat, dark clothes, and the same hiking shoes she had worn that first day when Mariana had arrived in Australia. A curiosity now covered her face as she looked at Mariana.

"What?"

Sunny shrugged. "You tell me." She pointed at a box on the kitchen table.

The box was ceramic, glazed with a metallic blue, and wavy zebra pattern-like lines that had been drawn through the clay before its firing. A more pronounced zigzag line showed where the lid and box would separate.

"What is it?" Rani stood close, ready to open the box if Mariana didn't.

"We don't know." Misty's arms pulled Rani back into a loving but restraining hug.

"But it's addressed to you." Ivy-Mai joined the circle and handed Mariana a bit of torn linen fabric with her name on it, written in the same metallic blue color as the box.

Mariana stared at her name. "Where did you find this?" She brought the note up close to see the smallest of two joining circles in the far-right corner; otherwise, there was nothing more. When she looked to Sunny, she got a shrug.

Mariana used her eyes to question back. "Were you out?" hung on her lips, unsure if she should ask about Sunny's early hour comings and goings.

"I heard the knock," Misty volunteered.

"I just woke up." Rani grinned.

"And then you woke me up," Ivy-Mai added.

"It was on the porch," Misty said. "And I waited—"

"We all did," Rani interrupted.

"To see what we should do." Ivy-Mai nudged the box closer to Mariana.

"Aya's still asleep," Rani added.

"Mum thought we should wake you," Ivy-Mai gave the box another nudge.

"It's like Christmas," Rani said.

"Depends on what's inside," Ivy-Mai said to her sister.

"Open it," Sunny coaxed.

Mariana's fingers ran over the smooth glaze of the striped box. As she lifted the lid, the box, now with its jagged mouth, invited her to reach into its darkness.

Rani gathered close. "What is it?"

Sunny pulled Rani away. "Give her space."

"Do you know what it is?" Mariana looked to Sunny, feeling intrigued, while also nervous.

"I have no idea. But let's see." She nodded at the open box.

"We shook it." Rani volunteered. "We heard it. Something's in there."

Ivy-Mai playfully slugged her sister. "You make it sound like it's alive. It just rattled around."

"Not like a snake rattle," Rani said to Mariana. "Like a toy in a box."

Mariana smiled at the girls then reached in to pull out a shiny, metallic pyramid about the size of a mango.

"Oh!" Rani reached a hand out.

"It's pretty," Ivy-Mai said.

"Stop!" Misty's hands shot out. "You know what that is?" She looked to Sunny.

But Sunny calmly shook her head and reached for the pyramid. "May I?" After Mariana handed it over, Sunny ran her fingers against its edges.

"Be careful." Misty's eyes hinted at wildness. "That's from Tarthur."

"Same metal, yes?" Sunny licked a finger and smeared it down a triangular side. The wet mark became iridescently purple. "Or is it?" She turned the mark toward Misty.

But Misty only shook her head fiercely. "I would not trust it. Name on it. Pretty box. Looks dangerous to me."

Mariana reached for the pyramid to conduct her own investigation. The metal was cold and smooth, and although the item was small, it held a dense weight. There were no seams, just smooth texture, glossy beveled edges, and a pinhole at the top where the three triangle sides met. "Do you have a safety pin, a needle, something to see if it opens?"

"I'll get it." Rani wiggled out of Sunny's hold and ran down the hall.

When she returned, Mariana carefully, slowly, slid the sharp edge into the hole. But nothing happened.

"See." Misty threw her hands up. "I'm telling you. It's Tarthur's doing. I would chuck that as far as you can and pray he never comes looking to get it back."

"It doesn't do anything?" Ivy-Mai reached for it. She turned it over and over. Then she shook it. No noise came.

Rani took her turn inspecting it, shaking it several more times. "It's kind of a weird gift."

"It's dangerous," Misty said, pressing her hands into unmanaged hair. "Maybe it has a mic. Maybe Tarthur's spying on us right now." She waved a dismissive hand at Mariana. "Here we work hard to keep ourselves free from him, and now he sends his tricks right into our home."

Sunny took the object again. "I don't think so. If it's Tarthur's work, it would only be the shell. Brody's work is what would be inside. And it's not there. Whatever this is, it's unique."

"Chuck it," Misty said.

"I wouldn't yet," Sunny replied calmly, handing back the object.

Ivy-Mai was at the box now, flipping it over, reaching inside, then running her fingers over the open grooves. Rani mirrored her by tracing her fingers over the jagged lip of the lid. "There's nothing else here," Ivy-Mai reported.

"I'd hold on to it. At least for now." Sunny gave Mariana a light half-hug. "Someone knows you're here."

"Like Tarthur," said Misty.

"Or someone else." After Sunny offered Misty a kind smile, she turned to meet Mariana's eyes. "For right now, I sense it's something good. And, right now, we need that... don't we? Something good?"

With the coolness of the pyramid in her hand, Mariana brought it closer to her chest. "Yes."

"Then let it be that." Sunny turned to her girls. "Now let's head back to bed."

THIRTY

MARIANA

The pyramid found a home in her daypack or on the little dresser in Mariana's borrowed room. Each night she stared at it, wondering, feeling the curiosity, and a worry grow as her one-month revisit with Tarthur drew near.

The night before the scheduled trip, Mariana dreamed a strange dream, with Ivy-Mai knocking at her door. "Mariana, you have to come."

Mariana pulled herself from her bed. The wind-up clock read 4 a.m. Mariana slipped into the previous day's filthy clothes while Ivy-Mai called through the door, "They're asking for you."

As soon as she stepped out and into the hall, two people, a man and a woman, met her eyes from the living room. The man held a hat. The woman stretched out her hand. "Mariana."

But Mariana shifted to Sunny, who stood near the table, gripping a chair as if she needed its support. "I've already asked them. They won't say where they are from."

"Hello," Mariana said cautiously, still delaying the unknown guest's offered handshake.

"We want to know why you are here," the man said. His face studied her, so she studied him back. His dark complexion reminded her of Zane's dark island tan.

The woman kept her hand extended and gave Mariana a soft nod to shake it. As Mariana did, she felt light pressure squeeze around her fingers. The grip felt soothing, in a protective way. She looked into the woman's eyes to briefly find safety there.

"Who are you?" she asked.

"We are here on assignment." The woman released her grip.

"Yet you know my name."

"Call me Point 1." The man, continuing to hold his hat, nodded at her. "And you can call her Dot 2."

"I'm usually Dot 1, and he's Point 2." The woman had soft eyes and fair-colored hair. "But he's had a bad day." A hint of a smile was there, and she playfully jabbed an elbow toward the man.

"Point 1 and Dot 2." Sunny folded her arms. "You sound like you're out of a children's book."

"We aren't," the man said.

"So where are you from?" Sunny placed her hands on her hips. "I know pretty much everyone from this village, and you aren't from here."

"We are not." Point 1 nodded his head. "And we apologize for the intrusion." He kept running his fingers across the brim of his hat. "Our time is different than yours."

"You're not with Tarthur, are you?" Sunny's voice raised as if it were Misty's. "Are you checking up on Mariana? She'll keep her appointment. So you don't need to be here."

"It's okay." Dot 2 reached out and touched Sunny's shoulder. Sunny's arms unfolded and fell to her side. Sunny stepped back, out of the touch. Her eyes held a look of shock, almost disbelief.

With a soft smile, Dot 2 stayed focused on Sunny.

"We came to check on you," Point 1 said, his fingers still rubbing his hat. Mariana felt torn as to whether to meet his eyes or watch the scene happening with Sunny.

Her eyes finally settled on him. "Who sent you?"

Point 1 looked at Dot 2, who shook her head. "Not yet." Dot 2 made eye contact with Mariana. "You should have lots of questions. Questions are good. And answers will be coming, so keep finding your questions. At the right time, we will return with your answers."

While Mariana felt frustration, she also met Dot 2's smile with a strange sense of peace.

"Your question: Are you ready to change?" Point 1 asked, tapping the brim of his hat against his knee.

"Depending on what you choose to do," Dot 2 said calmly, "nothing will stay the same."

The dream seemed almost to break as Mariana struggled with her laugh. "Right now, nothing is the same. I can't go back."

"What about Foster?" Dot 2's eyebrows raised as if challenging her. "Isn't that what he's doing? Making it so you can go back?"

The question stung in an unclear way. Still, she found she could answer Dot 2's tender eyes. "I don't know if Foster can make things right. There may be no 'going back.'"

Dot 2 nodded. "You speak wisely. So what will you do now?"

"What are my choices?"

The woman grinned as if pleased with Mariana's response. "Find your choices, and you will find your answers."

Point 1 placed his hat on his head and turned to the other. "We need to go."

Dot 2 kept her eyes on Mariana. "Make your choice. Depending on your choice, we will help you through what happens next."

Sunny and Mariana walked the guests to the door. As reality tapped Mariana out of her dream, she heard the whispered tones still inside it. "What just happened?" she asked Sunny as they watched Point 1 and Dot 2 walk away from the town.

"Something good," Sunny whispered. "Something good."

* * *

A stomping of feet, a sway of arms as Tarthur's crooked back propelled him forward. Soon, in the wide, empty warehouse, he stood in front of Sunny and Mariana. His forehead seemed pronounced as it grew closer to Mariana's. She drew in a breath, waiting for the conversation to begin, determined that she would be okay and handle this beast correctly for her people.

With those dark eyes, he raised his head at Mariana. "Follow me." Then he was off again, his crooked back swaying with the arms, his thin legs stomping in precision. They entered a room with an oval table in the center and an old vending machine in the back with a dusty water dispenser next to it. The vending machine was empty; the water dispenser was full.

With an index finger and a middle finger that was cut off at the second knuckle, Tarthur pointed at Mariana. Then he pointed at the three o'clock spot at the table. Next, he pointed at Sunny, followed by a point to the six o'clock spot. At the twelve o'clock, Tarthur took his place. The last chair, at the nine o' clock, was taken up by one of his muscle escorts. The other escort, like a blockade, stood at the door.

"Sit," he ordered. Then Tarthur's head nodded around the circle as if completing a quality check of everyone's positions. From there, he placed his elbows on the table, clutched his hands together, and looked at her. "All right, Mariana Grady. Your time is up. Tell me the real reason you're here."

"Yes," She pulled in a breath and grabbed at the strength she had taken days to build. Sunny was only there for support this time. Today it was Mariana's turn to speak. "My people need refuge."

"So no wedding?"

She shook her head. "No wedding."

He did a jerk of the head as if the statement carried no surprise. "Refuge from what?"

"An island in the sky."

A snort sounded from Tarthur. Amusement covered his face. "A sci-fi project, huh?" He shot Sunny a look. "Brody?"

Sunny nodded. He returned the nod and grinned. "Refuge from an island in the sky that Brody built." He turned again to Mariana. "What else?"

Mariana shifted to look at Sunny. The original island plans had been Foster's; he was the master builder, yet a strange protectiveness emerged, as if in agreement with Sunny, Foster's name did not belong here.

"Focus!" Tarthur's fist hit the table and Mariana jumped. He tilted his head, and with a minuscule shake gave her a swift scolding. He turned and nodded to the muscular man on his left. Under his sport coat, from the holster, the man retrieved a gun and set it on the table.

She despised the moment, him trying to intimidate her and it having an effect. Slowly, she raised her head, challenged her trembling heart to settle back down. "Yes, um. Well..." She was losing control. Her heart only beat more rapidly. She pressed her back against the chair. "We need help." She was determined to remain strong. "We are one hundred and ninety people who need refuge here."

Tarthur raised an eyebrow high. "That's a lot of people."

"It is."

"And why should we let them come?"

She kept her head lifted. "Because we have nowhere else to go."

He pressed his palms together and rested his chin on the top of his index fingers. "Awful place to be, isn't it? No place to go." With his hands still poised under his chin, his face leaned further down. The grin he offered seemed amused and mischievous. "Which is why you've come here. To bargain with me, correct?"

More wild racing of the heart—her mind was so tired of this question, yet there it was again: *Had they really exhausted all of their options?* "To make a bargain," she said smoothly.

He lowered his interlaced hands onto the table and straightened himself to glance at Sunny. "I'm always up for a bargain. Right, Sunshine?"

Mariana wanted to shift back and meet Sunny's eyes, but she kept her focus on Tarthur while he stayed focused on Sunny. A wait emerged, as if he were waiting for Sunny to give him the correct facial response. Eventually, with a pleased smile, he returned to Mariana. "So...why not Ashyr's world of fun?"

Mariana had to close her eyes and keep her head still to answer; otherwise, the burn in her eyes would make her voice unsteady. "I don't consider that an option." When she opened her eyes, Tarthur's grin expressed a great deal of pleasure in her reply. He jutted his chin at her. "Tell me why not."

There were too many reasons, reasons this gorilla monster could not understand. Reasons for Mariana and Foster hating Ashyr for the last twenty years. Reasons that Ashyr's actions had put her family in this current difficult situation. Plus, Ashyr had taken her baby for his own fouled-up science experiment. Everything "Ashyr" meant death to her and her family. Instead, she said, "We don't like EnRapture."

"You don't like EnRapture?" He tilted his head to the side. "Or you don't like the rules Ashyr has put in place around it?"

Mariana felt a need to look at Sunny, as if the question placed before her were a trap, something the gorilla man intended for her to step into. Yet she also watched, across from her, the muscular escort's fingers tap against his gun.

And then an idea struck for how to answer his question. "I don't like EnRapture for the same reason Sunny and others who opted not to stay with Ashyr don't like EnRapture."

He raised his head in acceptance. He approved of her wit enough that he shifted his eyes toward Sunny. "Want to remind me what that is?" He gave Sunny a grin, as if he knew the answer, but liked hearing her say it.

"I would rather..." Sunny's voice sounded weak. "Rather choose habitat confinement with our dwellings than be placed in the moral confinements of EnRapture."

A pleased smirk spread across Tarthur's face. Mariana couldn't quite make out if it was mockery or a pride that they would choose his awful option over Ashyr's. Mariana had dissected such an answer multiple times in the past few days. It seemed crazy under certain microscopes: the life Ashyr promised versus the choice before them. Yet this was the choice Mariana was making. A moral choice for her people.

She released a huge exhale and Tarthur eyed her closely. "So," he said, "all one-hundred and ninety of your people will come here instead of Ashyr's playground?"

"She will need to give them the choice," Sunny inserted.

The standing bodyguard's fingers wrapped around the gun. Tarthur waved him back. "She's fine," he said.

Then he nodded at Sunny. "Fair enough. Each of your people," he looked back at Mariana, "must choose. One choice. No turning back. It's what Ashyr will require. It's what I require too. Here or there. But once a decision is made, they remain. Understood?"

"Unless they choose Ashyr..." the bodyguard at the door spoke with a trill, "and then end up becoming exiles here anyway."

Tarthur raised a hand as if to silence the guard. "If they're exiled from Ashyr's place, then we will welcome them under our conditions. Our oaths here." He looked again at Mariana. "We will find them their place, where they belong among us."

Tarthur turned around and gave the guard at the door a strong nod, which was returned. Mariana disliked everything about this moment, which she knew she would. Such a difficult choice ahead for her children and grandchildren. But who would dare choose Ashyr's world? Yet this place also held such evil, such heartache, and challenges. No options were good. Everything was temporary. The requirement to find a home for her people had led her here; she had to remain strong.

With a wide grin he looked back at her and then past her. "All right, Sunshine, let's work out the arrangements then."

THIRTY-ONE

YAM

With a travel mug in hand, Ashyr slipped into the captain's chair opposite Yam. "Lovely morning, isn't it?"

For the past forty-five minutes, Yam had been waiting in the airship, with his temporary handler close at hand. It had been explained that Ashyr needed to freshen up for his trip. Now as Ashyr rolled his neck, Yam felt the hunger for his own morning stretches.

While Yam had slept on an uncomfortable couch-like seat in a holding room at the detention center, Ashyr had been completing his rounds of EnRapture appointments. Yam had no shower, and his breakfast had been stale toast and a sulfuric-smelling hard-boiled egg. When Ashyr had entered the hanger, his hair was brightly bleached and slicked down, except for his new raspberry tips, which arched like a wave. He wore a paisley baby blue tuxedo jacket with white cuffs and lapels and underneath a richly colored purple lightweight linen. Several gold chains adorned his exposed neck and chest area.

As soon as the airship lifted into the sky, he turned to Yam with a vibrant grin. "See, in some ways, we aren't that different." He paused to take a drink of his morning beverage. "You and me, we both carry heavy secrets." He set his travel mug in its holder then leaned toward Yam. "Today's it's your turn to share some of yours. So what are the coordinates?" He turned the console toward Yam and with polished nails pointed at the keypad.

With folded arms and pressed lips, Yam nestled farther into his seat.

"Such irony!" Ashyr rubbed his palms together. "When you first led me to Foster's island, I used my best ship, with a clear goal of invisibility. And now what do we have here? This little jewel, my flying cereal box, updated last night with a few modifications to reach our desired destination." He waved his hand toward the window in front of them. "It's going to light up a section of their sky like a giant billboard. Great call, kid—let's hope he gets the message."

"It was Aria's idea," Yam said, breaking his own vow of silence.

"Well, great call, Aria." Ashyr shrugged as if passing praise around was inconsequential.

"So you can thank her by not sending her away."

"I still haven't determined if I like you or not," Ashyr said. "What I understand is you both were trying to steal an airship. Did you have a plan on which one? Because had I not come along, this one would have never made it up into your skies. And this is one of two that don't require a certified pilot. But since you're no stranger up yonder, I figure you could manage this one fine. So let's see what you got. Navigate us to your home."

He couldn't look at Ashyr, but Yam managed the smallest headshake. His only plan was to oppose Ashyr, who, at the moment, seemed unbothered by Yam.

The unprogrammed airship floated upward into the sky. Ashyr looked out the window to the shrinking city below. "I don't care much for traveling. I prefer all that I find within *The City of Angels*."

Yam didn't need to glance out. He knew what he would see. But Ashyr kept talking as if they were conversing. "Once, a disoriented visitor tracked into our city. He was covered in ash dust. Soot all over him other than the whites of his eyes. He said Yellowstone erupted. For a month ash fell from the sky. No other humans for miles. It disrupted everything, that wet ash. Destroyed electronic components, telephone equipment, cell phone services, clogged engines, destroyed vehicles. Aircraft in flight failed. Buildings collapsed from the weight of the ash. Computers were damaged. Air systems overheated. Agriculture ruined. Livestock dead from dehydration, starvation, poison. Breathing was impossible. Yet that one man survived.

"Remarkable, isn't it?" Ashyr waited for no answer. "My city..." he leaned again to look out below, "like a rose, blooming above the rubble and destruction, was fine."

A gray rose, but Yam kept his words silent.

"That soot-covered man visited with one of our doctors, but a short while later he died. That season, we all stayed indoors as the rains fell. Then a colder aura set in around the city, but other than that, the experts all said we would get by okay. Safe from the effects of the nuclear events on the other side of the world, or the tragic natural disasters all over the globe, and we were fine. One theorist claimed we were safe due to the decades of smog that created an inversion of protection. A dense solution of gases that became our protective blanket. No idea if that's true—doesn't matter—we are good. We lay in a safety chasm, our own utopian society, and with EnRapture—new sights, new experiences, new adventures. Why do we need to leave?

"Yet, on a rare day like today, here we are." Ashyr swiveled his chair to face Yam directly. "Are you ready to put in the coordinates?"

This was about to be the longest ride of Yam's life. For the second portion of Ashyr's story, the airship had stopped moving and just hung in the sky. Sitting here in nothingness, in blank space, listening to Ashyr's tales of his city, Yam debated his options before volunteering in an even tone, "I don't have the exact coordinates. It's all programmed into my helipod."

"We don't need exact. Just your quadrant of sky." Ashyr's stern face said enough. "Get us close so they can't miss our message."

"I can't help."

Ashyr raised his eyebrows. "Because your FID is missing?"

Yam pressed his lips together and nodded.

Their eyes remained locked. Then Ashyr leaned forward. His necklaces hung loosely down while his chest nearly touched the navigation device. "Stop the game. You already were planning to head this way, so—" he slapped the console. "Go with what you would have done had you succeeded."

"This was Aria's idea," Yam repeated as he punched in the coordinates, resigning that he just needed this horrible ride over with. "She was helping *all of us*." He spun the console back to face Ashyr. "Remember that. Okay?"

"Sure. Sure. I'll remember that just like I remember how I almost got to see this FID device for myself. So why don't you fill me in now? We have some time. Coordinates are in. Let's lean back and talk about it."

"I already did."

"Did you? I've been thinking about your pap, your baba, Mr. Brody Daniels. His name, his duties, his job title—what would you call his profession? A farmer of technology? A farmer seeking to harvest a possible myth? Or...is a treasure hunter? A modern-day Alan Turing, a Ray Kurzweil, on the programming path to the AI holy grail? And has he found it? Has he achieved what he is seeking? There are things about your pap, your baba, that you may not know. Things that I understand about him from way back. And you, his offspring, you stir a kind of hope in me because I see it in you too. A part of your father, where you, too, understand certain things."

Yam's fingers had been tapping nervously against his knee. Ashyr looked at the hand. Yam curled his fingers and tried to stop the movement.

"This trip is turning out to be a bit of fun. Isn't it?" Ashyr grinned.

Yam twisted to look out below. The city was barely visible now in its little spot that rose above the sunken valleys, the slabs of earth jutting out, crafting a haphazard protection, as if it, too, had a bubble covering it.

"Your baba, my Brody, that kid had huge potential," Ashyr continued. "He was so young, about your age, ready to change the world. In huge ways. Like you…Yam, are you like that? Doing big, important, world-altering things?" Only a short pause occurred before Ashyr carried on. "Well…that was us. Your baba and I…and Foster…Mariana… we were changing the world. Until…why did your baba leave?"

"You lack morals," Yam volunteered. "And that killed his career goals."

"I lack morals, huh?"

Yam couldn't resist turning back to meet Ashyr's face. But the eye contact only encouraged Ashyr further.

"Comic how Brody and Foster raise their children. Fill you with fibs so you can serve as traitors."

"I don't serve you."

Ashyr waved a hand, as if anything Yam said held no impact, leaving Yam, instead, to be lost in the word *traitor*. If Yam was a traitor, he certainly was being punished now.

"I believe your baba was bitter that the world was not what he thought it was supposed to be. He had his view of reality and when life didn't match those views, he couldn't manage it. His great mistake was leaving when he did...he should have stuck it out. Your baba built an amazing thing."

"He did not build EnRapture."

"He had his part. Tragic he never participated in its final state. But you could."

Yam looked to the window again. A blue void was below. He spoke quietly. "His work was to help others understand humanity better."

"Oh, it has...empathy, right? You think I'm not familiar with Foster's buzz words? I speak *Foster*. I speak *Brody*. The problem is none of you speak *Ashyr*. So let me teach you a few things. As far back as we homo sapiens decided to keep a written record, there's been a problem with our people, differences among us because of a hierarchy system that created resistance to fairness. That was until I came. Think on that. Think what your baba was a part of...but when he left...it came down to me. Empathy? Yes. I saw a problem and I fixed it. No family differences. No set gender. No discrimination over skin color. No longer do we have obstacles our society can't solve. Instead, we have a united environment for all.

So let's fix it and get back to living in a better place of existence."

"You isolate people." Yam stared ahead, his fingers again tapping loosely against his knee. "You aren't connecting them."

As if Yam's words held no value, Ashyr shook his head. "You need to think past what you don't understand."

Yam's breathing picked up in tempo. "You feed people what to think."

Ashyr raised a finger to silence him. "We each feed people the experiences they want to have."

"No." Yam wouldn't be silenced. "You claim unity, but you divide your people."

"You clearly don't understand." Ashyr gave him a small sympathetic headshake. "You with no experiences. You need to try EnRapture."

"Never."

"You'll become more knowledgeable. Your baba would understand that. It's called *research*."

"No."

"Fine." Ashyr shrugged. "But...did I mention... I'm offering a one-time opportunity for an exchange with me?"

Yam stared back in disbelief.

Ashyr folded his arms and mirrored Yam's posture. "Your loss." In unison, he drew in a breath at the same time Yam did. Then released it in tandem with Yam. The imitating was not helping the situation, Yam leaned back in his chair and looked down, only to look back.

"You need to understand something, kid. What is here is good and eventually, you need to see that. And we need to become a team. We leave this message for Foster and Brody. And then we go back and we—"

"Find her."

Ashyr cocked his head to the side. "Fine. Let's agree to disagree, okay? I see EnRapture as beautiful. But you haven't yet. So let's agree that we have different views. And let's move to something else. Like...your secrets, your baba's work." A grin broke over Ashyr's face.

The look was so pathetic, Yam couldn't help but grin back. "His secrets...as in his life work that he specifically doesn't want you to know about—that's what you want me to talk about?" He angled his head to suggest his own imitation of Ashyr.

"Ah, you look just like your father now." Ashyr straightened and the cocky grin lessened. "Yes. That work."

Yam's eyes rose. "The Top Secret work?"

"That would be it."

Then Yam casually shrugged. "I don't know anything."

A laugh burst from Ashyr. Approval filled his eyes, which made Yam smile in return.

"Hmm." Ashyr pressed against the headrest. "Right then, it was like old times. Me sitting across from Brody. A time long ago when we would daydream together. Lots of hopes and aspirations. He was your age when I met him. Didn't have a father, and I became that for him for a while. An adult male who cared about him, a lot. So if you don't want to share, fine. But just…humor me a little longer. Let me in enough to see that Brody again, the one who now is raising *his* next generation. For instance, what's your job? How do you help your pop out?"

Yam looked down and shook his head. "My job is to protect Baba."

"And you do it well."

"I don't know a lot of what he's working on. But what I do know is enough, and I'm supposed to guard what I know."

"All right." Ashyr rested an elbow on the console and pressed a fist against his chin. "Then tease me. When we were looking through Leilani's things, share exactly what we were looking for. What would you have showed me, had it not *disappeared?*"

"I already told you, a communication device."

"Yes. A device to talk with others using AI."

"Yep." Yam shrugged as if the information was inconsequential now.

"So how is it different from what's already existed?"

He shrugged again.

"Okay." Ashyr kept watching. "Why did he design it?"

"I can't speak for him."

"How do you use it?"

"Lots of ways."

"Well, this is fun…like a little question game between us…how am I doing?" Ashyr leaned back in his chair, no longer looking at Yam, and rubbed his hands together. He stared straight ahead into the blue skies. "Seems a little unfair...you had planned to show it to me...and now you won't even share simple answers." His voice remained level. "I don't care for unfairness. I tolerate lots. But not unfairness."

"I communicate with Baba," Yam said quietly, tiredly.

"How?"

"It's simple..." But it wasn't. The words that spilled out felt complicated, like Yam was indeed a traitor.

"Simple in what way?"

"Once you know how to use it..."

"Which is how?"

"I think..."

"You think..." A smile spread across Ashyr's face. He kept his eyes focused ahead. Then he spoke quietly as if directing his words elsewhere. "And Brody hears you."

The airship hummed back, letting the silence between them lift the corners of Ashyr's mouth further.

"The pieces align," he said at last. "Yes. So much more than a communication device." Yam hunted for something to stop the unraveling, but Ashyr was already at work. "It's everything, isn't it? Your search engine. Your navigation device. Your communication tool for reaching out to Brody— or whomever—wherever you are. Distance—no obstacle."

Yam nodded slowly. His words came out meekly. "It hasn't been yet."

"Ha." Ashyr shot him a glance. "I'm back in your spell, Brody." He looked away, then back, his eyes meeting Yam's but not focusing on him. "As you said before, it could do a lot of good. Couldn't it? Let me guess...remove language barriers...give anyone...maybe anything...the ability to speak...to be heard."

Yam's breathing paused. His fingers froze in place. All he could do was meet Ashyr's eyes, as he kept talking to him without focusing on his face.

"I know what you would say, Brody. If it got in the hands of the wrong people... I know. They could control your thoughts. Your mom told me when you were seven years old you wanted to 'save the world' by helping all the humans communicate with animals. You said as a result, we would eat less meat. We would make a difference with climate change." He closed his eyes, and his grin spread. "You didn't think I remembered that, did you?"

Yam still couldn't speak. No loud breaths. No twitching of muscles. No verbal corrections. Just somber eyes on Ashyr, waiting for him to correct himself, to open his eyes and put Yam back in the airship, not his father.

"Even back then..." Ashyr settled farther into his captain chair, spinning it straight ahead. "Even as a child, you were trying, Brody..." His head swayed with the airship's rhythm. "Trying to change the world through your work."

"Ah." He paused. All of his movements stopped. His eyes softened. He spoke calmly, slow and drowsy. "I need time…kid…lock all this in my mind. I'll call this a fair trade. In place of my afternoon EnRapture, you gave me a memorable experience. I need a nap now. A little time to consider what all this means. What Brody could do for us."

While Ashyr's breathing slipped into steady beats of meditative sleep, Yam focused on his deep, loud, heavy exhales. Traitor indeed.

THIRTY-TWO

FOSTER

Sweat clung to his forehead. Foster had expected the barn to be freezing; instead, it was far warmer than room temperature. From the ceiling, like elegant chandeliers, quantum computers surrounded them. Copper tubes and wires, superconducting chips, qubits, chessboard patterns—under any other circumstance, Foster would have been full of questions, entranced and eager to explore the mysticism around him. Instead, inside the supercomputer lair, he felt restless. The feeling had begun well before he had arrived on Brody's island, before the new round of readings on Brody's terrain. For days, this anxiety had been heightening.

Like a computer superhero, Brody plucked away at an old keyboard hooked up to an ancient-looking laptop. Two large monitors displayed program codes that Brody altered while he muttered to himself, leaving Foster alone with his recent memory of pulling all his family together, the entire island, right in the center of town. And his words, masking optimism, telling them the next steps were all precautionary. His role was to keep hope alive, to not feed a frenzy of panic. An organized departure. Their next steps.

Brody kept mumbling as he hunched over the keyboard. "Input. Output." After some time, he left his seat to circle the barn and tug at his beard. Meanwhile, Foster fought his own processing.

"Ingredients in. Ongoing investigation," Brody said. "Results. No results. Where are the results—real, accurate, correct results?"

At least here Foster was on the front lines of their last effort. Even if all Foster was doing was listening to Brody curse under his breath, bang at the hardware, pound a fist against his forehead, or pull at his wild auburn curls.

Another drop of sweat rolled from Foster's face down his chest. He had expected it to be like a cool refrigerator, not a hot sauna. "I have to get some air," Foster called to Brody, only to receive an absent nod. Brody's fingers attacked the keyboard again; more large, unreadable codes became modified on the large monitor. "I'll be outside," Foster added, swiping at more sweat.

"Same air outside," Brody said. "Same damn air. It's not breathable inside, not breathable outside."

Foster paused at the door. He could almost see the exhausted cloud that swirled around Brody. "You need a break. If Sunny were here, or Yam, what would they tell you?" Brody didn't answer, so Foster did for him. "Let's pause. Get some space to come at this with a fresh mind."

"Breaks aren't going to fix this."

"Neither is exhaustion beyond repair. Come on."

Brody wiped an arm across his glistening forehead. "Weeks on this and nothing sustainable. No leads. None of this is getting us anywhere. If I sit here, or if I don't, it's all the same." With an exasperated sigh, he slammed the laptop closed and joined Foster.

Outside, deteriorating plants greeted them. With too much carbon dioxide, bugs hunted for more nutrients by consuming the leaves, leaving no flowers, just a sickening sign that this island was dying too. Foster took a seat on an iron bench directly outside the metal barn. Brody took a pewter yard chair and shifted it to face the door.

"Why's it so hot in there?" Foster wiped the residual sweat from his face.

"Too much is going on. Everything's overloaded. In addition to this island time bomb, I have a high-priority item for Sunny. Plus, my Mario leap. Systems are all maxed out."

"Including yours." Foster pointed at Brody's mind. "How long is it going to be safe to be doing this?"

But Brody's flushed face only grimaced back. "What? Overrunning the systems? Or being here?"

"Both."

"It's still safe."

"For how much longer?"

"For as long as it takes." The two stared at each other until Brody added, "You need to get your group to leave. All of you—you included. But for me, not yet. I still have time. Still need it. It all just requires more time."

"Your air is just as heavy as mine."

"I'm fine. I use less."

Foster looked at Brody's serious face and debated the option of contesting further. Finally, he settled on, "Makes you wonder when it's all going to die."

"You keep talking like that, and I'm headed back in there." He placed a hand on the pewter armrest as if he needed the support to arise. "There's no time to start planning funerals for anything. We keep fighting. Otherwise, everything we've been working on is pointless. None of this will have meaning." As if he found a surplus of breathable air, he stomped toward the barn. "We're either nothing, or we're part of something bigger. I'd rather be part of something bigger than nothing at all."

"Nothing or something," Foster said as Brody passed and disappeared into the barn. "The paradox of our existence," Foster added. "What we are or what we are not...with wrong data in wrong results come out."

Brody resurfaced. A large finger pointed at Foster as if accusing him of something. "What did you say?"

"Um..." Foster had no idea, just the ramblings of a spent mind.

"That's it." Brody's eyes appeared crazed. "It's what's broke."

"I have no idea what I said...but I'm glad it could help."

"It's basic. Common sense. Garbage in, garbage out. Flawed input produces flawed output."

Foster shook his head. Brody spoke computer science basics. Nothing useful. "And that's why we continuously feed in the data. The more input we share, the more likely we'll get an answer."

"No. That's the whole problem. If that's what we give it to work with...wrong info in... wrong data out. We can't build an accurate algorithm from that."

Foster clasped a hand on the other armrest. His lips pressed together. His mind felt hot, like he was reaching for something in the oven without the proper mitt. Something stinging, fervently glowing. He couldn't quite reach it, but the eagerness in his chest told him he needed to grab it.

Brody's face told him the same. The answer felt close but unreachable, like the air around them. "Okay," Foster said slowly, cautiously. "Wrong info in."

"Wrong info out." Brody nodded, gripping the armrest next to Foster. "It totally makes sense."

"Of course it does...but what's the wrong data?"

"No." Brody waved a finger at him. "All we are feeding in is wrong data—lies—and we don't have time for lies. We need truth—the right info in. We feed in accuracy, and we will get somewhere. So where do we find that?"

"Pretty sure if we knew that, we wouldn't be here right now."

"Where have we not scanned?"

"We've scanned everything."

"We have to be missing something. Some organism we haven't checked, something we've overlooked. We figure out what we haven't considered, and we find our invader."

"Underground?"

Brody shook his head. "What would it be feeding on?"

Foster felt an inner laugh at his suggestion. The man-made workings of the island, the metal pipes, the transportation dock, the concrete dwellings below—the menace would be feeding on nothing!

"Or..." Brody pointed a finger at Foster. "Unless..."

"No." Foster shook his head adamantly. "It's a micro-*organism*." It required organic materials to consume.

"We've just accepted it was..."

The two just stared at each other.

"The solution may be down, not up," Brody said.

"In the technosphere?" Foster could scarcely believe it. "If that's true...what's it consuming?"

"Wrong info in will give wrong results out."

Together they raced into the barn. Each grabbed a DNA scanner. As if in a sprint, they moved quickly, rounding corners, crushing along the gravel path, through a grove of trees, toward an open field, only for Foster to raise a hand. "I have to catch my breath."

"Hurry," Brody said, just as much out of breath. As if the air was lighter beneath him, Brody leaned his large torso down. His chest heaved up and down.

"Okay, I'm ready," Foster said, only for Brody to raise a finger, delaying them further. While Foster took in another raspy breath, Brody cocked an ear to the side, like a dog hearing an inaudible sound.

When Brody stood upright, he looked to the sky. "There's an alert."

Foster scanned around, straining to hear what Brody heard. "How do you know?"

"A PIGS' sending me an incoming notification. It's above us."

Foster looked up, but there was nothing. Just clear brilliant blue skies.

"Stay here," Brody called back as his lumberjack body pounded harshly along a trail. Foster wasn't sure he could obey. His heart kept racing. Hope, if only the slightest sliver, was there. He looked at the dirt. Beneath it might hold their answers. A man-made world, hardly anything organic to sustain life, yet new data to feed into the system. If this worked, they could finally build out an accurate algorithm. From there, the AI system could run the scenarios to find the solution. The idea felt so far-reaching, yet it was a glorious hope!

Correct info in. Correct info out.

And then Foster saw it. A black dot in the sky.

"Here." Brody was back, pushing binoculars into his hands. "See what you can see."

At first nothing. Just a vast field of rich blueness.

"Oh, Foster!" Brody's tone made Foster's stomach turn. "Here." His voice was tender, broken. Softly, he touched Foster's shoulder. "Use these." With hands frozen in place, Brody led Foster to swap binoculars. "You need to see this."

Foster slipped into the place where Brody had stood, letting his eyes settle into where Brody's had been. Slowly, his eyes adjusted, until he made it out. A lit-up billboard, puncturing through the blueness, blaring in contrasting letters, *Leilani Lost?*

Foster couldn't breathe.

Ready to trade for Yam.

"I don't…"

"Understand," Brody completed the sentence while taking back the binoculars. "I can't reach Yam," he added. "I've been trying right now."

"I'm taking the drone," Foster said, moving toward the underground with new urgency.

"Go."

THIRTY-THREE

MARIANA

Mariana sat in the back of the Land Rover and tried to make peace with what she had done. After Sunny and Tarthur met privately for an uncomfortable half-hour, Mariana then had to endure her negotiation time with Tarthur. In the end, the settled price tag was 70% tax on her people in exchange for immediate jobs in the mines, with Tarthur also providing her people food.

No current structures existed. Building supplies were limited. Nevertheless, Tarthur said they would find an abandoned town near Sunny's area where they could take residence there. There would be no running water, no electricity, no sewer system. It would be a move back in time. From living on an island in the clouds to a nomad regression, such devolution, such devastation.

But all Mariana could do now was move forward.

On the ride back, as Sunny and the driver remained silent, Mariana processed what was next.

Clean water. That would require a well.

Food. Tarthur said he would provide.

Labor. Hard physical labor—Mariana's people would supply.

Miners.

Only Misty had shared the purpose of the mining: natural resources used to build out the EnRapture kits, those tubes that held the goggles, the gloves, the earbuds, and pills. Once Sunny had implied more was being mined only to follow up with, "And just leave it at that."

Mariana didn't dare ask Sunny or Misty how Tarthur got the rest of the items. Still, the thought of her family mining for equipment tied in with EnRapture nauseated Mariana. They still couldn't get away from Ashyr's corrupt existence.

Among all the wrongs and broken options, Mariana had done her best and made a choice on behalf of her people.

* * *

The Land Rover pulled into town and Mariana wiped the silent tears from her cheek. She had nearly pulled herself together right as Sunny's home came into view. Ivy-Mai waited on the porch steps. She waved at her mom, but no smile was there. She ran up the porch and called inside, "They are here."

Right as Sunny and Mariana got out, Misty appeared and walked straight to Mariana. Then she pulled out a long receipt. "From Brody," she said grimly. "On behalf of Foster."

Mariana ran to the paper, skimming past the coding to reach the translation.

Leilani's missing.

She gasped, searching further as the horrid truth took shape.

Leaving island now to find her.

"I need to go," Mariana looked behind her at the dust settling in the distance from the Rover that had disappeared. Still, she would find a way back. She would negotiate with Tarthur, join Foster, and find Leilani.

But Misty's hands were there, unfolding the long receipt, displaying more that Mariana had not seen.

Best for you to stay.

With a hand wrapping around Mariana's shoulder, Misty's other hand pointed farther down the translation.

Liam and Zane left this morning.

Mariana's breathing stalled. The first group. It was beginning. To have those sons here, Foster had chosen wisely.

She found the rest of the message.

Exodus is underway.

Had Misty's arm not been there supporting her, Mariana felt her knees collapsing. A breaking heart over Leilani, the vagueness of this message—but warmth to know Zane and Liam would be joining her.

At the very end of the slip, there was one last line.

Caroline orchestrating the details.

"Bless you, Foster," she whispered.

As Mariana leaned into Misty's hug, Misty handed her one final slip, a much smaller scroll where Mariana skimmed to find *Kate will be coming next, and Olivia.*

Mariana's breath caught. Little granddaughter-Liv. This was happening. She needed to be strong and focused. Her boys were coming. The men. The women. And the children. Protect them fiercely. Two at a time, they would come, growing, until the little negotiated plot of space held all her people. All one hundred and ninety, with the last two being Foster and Leilani.

Sunny's arm was there, too, holding her up, these women supporting her, helping her know she was not alone.

Foster's job had shifted to what he needed to do. Leave the island. Find Leilani and bring her to their new home. And Foster would.

She had her own critical task to focus on. One day at a time. A drone voyage at a time, bringing her family here soon.

THIRTY-FOUR

LEILANI

I awoke to long, talon-like hands cradling my head. The rest of my body was submerged in a bath of warm water and bubbles touched my chin. I remained still against the talons as if their purpose was to keep my head upright, but their firmness also reminded me that with one twist they could break my neck.

Still, the moment felt joyous. Dirt was leaving me. The talons shifted ever so slightly, allowing another creature with a washcloth to dab at my chin.

Bubbles clung to the human-like arm that scrubbed at my face, a bit too rough over my eyes. When the cloth lifted, I fluttered open my eyes, feeling relaxed and clear-headed.

Around the bathtub, two creatures worked on me, plus the one at my head. I looked upward to meet large bird-like eyes. She blinked back, followed by a human smile. I smiled too.

The one with the washcloth was a squirrel-like female who now scrubbed at my shoulder and elbow. The tenderness was not there, but the warmth of the cloth, the removal of the dirt, couldn't stop me from smiling at her either.

And at the end of the tub, a kitten-like female used a pumice stone to work at my feet. As she scrubbed against the calluses, her kitten-like tongue moved up and down like a rhythmic part of her own cleaning ritual.

The washcloth moved down my arm, sometimes pausing in softness, sometimes picking up the tempo, until it reached my wrist and hand. Then the squirrel creature scurried to the other arm. Starting at the shoulder again, she worked her way down.

Straight ahead, above the kitten female at my feet, I met the gaze of RexHera. She sat in a tall chair, a cross between a lifeguard tower and a throne. Her fingers pointed at the creatures then pointed at different parts of me, overseeing, ruling, guiding, and instructing their movements.

"Ah, you wake," she said. Her lips curled in satisfaction. She looked like a goddess dressed in a large golden gown. Her chin jutted out. I couldn't place the animal it belonged to, but there was a reptile-like quality to its shape and a pronouncement of authority as it drew down toward me.

I had seen her many times before. Never spoken to her. But she spoke to me plenty. She was a regular for EnRapture time with me. Whenever she left, I always felt sick, like I needed to vomit. But she always told me she adored me.

"A special moment for you, my dear." Again, the chin drew down toward me, drawing my eyes toward her. "The day of your approval."

I felt a need to nod, like an indicator of my approval was needed, but the talons around my head did not allow it. So I kept looking ahead, toward the chin, which led me up into her intensely strong dark eyes. I tried not to flinch as the pumice stone rubbed harshly against my left heel.

"There, there," RexHera's chin moved toward the kitten creature, who abandoned the pumice stone and replaced it with her nails that pressed against the arch of my foot. As little nails danced across my feet, I felt my muscles soften. The squirrel creature lifted my other leg and pressed the warm cloth softly against my calf muscle.

The bird creature breathed out a long sigh of release. The air that filtered down smelt of peppermint and seemed to settle around me. The other creatures followed suit, leaving my legs and feet to huddle around me, breathing down. Lavender. Rosemary. More peppermint. I breathed in an entanglement of smells. Another breath and I felt a connection to these creatures.

"It's going to be sensational today," RexHera said. "The weather is most accepting of you." With the other creatures' faces breathing down on me, I couldn't see her, but I could hear the warmth in her voice. "You will look lovely today; a fine specimen for your duty."

The kitten's hand applied a thick cream over my face and jaw. I closed my eyes. The three creatures' closeness stirred a suffocating feel, yet I drew in another breath. More peppermint, lavender, rosemary.

The kitty's chest leaned down close, her paws now wrapped in gloves as she worked to smooth a mud-like substance over my right cheek. My face turned into the arm of the bird creature.

"Enjoy this time, adorable one," RexHera said sweetly. "Your moment of great honor nears."

THIRTY-FIVE

LEILANI

Crimson chiffon and lace with a sweeping train—I couldn't help but smile at the princess who twirled in the mirror. I ran my hands from the lacy top that started near my neck to the V-line chiffon beneath. Metal boning and the lace-up corset gave my shape a mature beauty. My arms were covered to the wrists with see-through lace. Beaded embellishments, along with ropes of beads, crossed like X's over my upper arms. Three shiny beaded ropes looped across my back. The lace disappeared down the skirt, replaced with gold and silver threads, like vines, dancing around the chiffon fabric, accented with rhinestones and silver specks like falling stars.

A tiara crowned my head, my hair looped in an elaborate do. In the reflection of the mirror, three creatures shared happy eyes, smiles, and clutched hands of admiration over their accomplishment.

"Pretty. Pretty," the kitten purred.

"A unique specimen," the eagle stated.

"One last finishing touch." The squirrel approached me with baby's breath in her hand.

She signaled and I obeyed, curtsey down, lowering my head so her little fingers could slip them into place.

"Fine. Fine." From the dressing chambers doorway, RexHera appeared. "You are ready. And the altar is nearly ready for you. The ceremony will begin within the hour."

Then her reptile-like chin motioned toward the creatures. "She's complete. Come conclude the final preparations. We need petals prepared for the walk." Then, in her own olive green gown, her fabric swooshed away as she left.

The kitten purred near me. "The sacrificial walk." Her hand rubbed at my shoulder, against the dress's elaborate embroidery as she passed.

"Yes," the eagle breathed near my face, leaving soothing peppermint behind as she also left the room.

"See you soon." The squirrel turned back, our eyes meeting again before her fingers clutched together and pressed against her chest.

It was the eagle who shut the door, leaving me along with the lovely girl in the mirror.

I stared for a long time, trying to see myself in the image that stared back. I smiled. I swayed the long princess gown back and forth. I touched my hair and felt its slick spray that kept every strand in place. I tried to avoid the eyes, because when I did, what replaced the girl image before me was RexHera, their queen. The smile she gave me, the pleased look of approval.

The kitten's pat. The word *sacrificial*...The altar. Ceremony. *Sacrificial*...The locking sound when the door shut.

I was a fool.

The gown swooshed loudly while my feet in their simple ballet-like slippers scurried over to the far wall of the dressing chamber to the one small window.

Two stories down, in the twilight, I saw them. Human-beasts circling the building. The line, long and sweeping, two to three creatures deep. Then siphoning to a single line as they entered the building. My breath caught as I listened to their chants. Cheers, happy hollers, and...I strained to hear it. *Happiness to the gods.*

My hand, so manicured, so perfect, polished, and smooth, ran up toward my ear, directing the noise even closer. *A fit offering.*

I closed my eyes and pressed forward, my cheek touching the cool windowpane. *Prayers to the gods that our sacrifice is accepted.*

RexHera's earlier words returned, that which she had said to me right before starting her exchange, "My dear, first a bit of shock. Then acceptance. Then approval. You want approval, then you have your place here."

What had become of me?

Against the confines of my gown, I stumbled in haste back to the mirror. My eyes looked wild now with the urgency that filled them. A me—from long ago—screamed at my face. I had to get out.

Those flawless hands scraped at the gown, trying to reach the tie in the back that bound me. The corset—I clawed at the fabric, my nails scraping against lace, against rhinestones. I flailed my arms, trying to tug on the bow that was double-knotted against my back.

I grabbed for the lace at the top of my neck. Tight against my skin. The boning was deep against my ribs as I forced my fingers underneath the fabric. I ripped, I tore, I worked at holes until the first layer of fabric began to give way. I yanked at the ropes of beads around my arms, against my back; I peeled off the long, lacy sleeves. Then I worked at the chiffon portion, right at the V-neckline; each valiant tug, each fight against the fabric made the smallest indentation toward my release.

Bit by bit, I made it work until I could shimmy out of the horrid dress. In front of the mirror, I stood in a black spandex slip. I wanted it off. All of it off! But a desperate spin around the room showed me no other options existed.

No clothes. A barred wardrobe. A window with a crowd below. And a locked door with a doorknob that was turning.

THIRTY-SIX

ASHYR

The intensity of the alarm shook the entire airship. Shrill beeps, three in succession, caused Ashyr and Yam to jump. Twenty minutes after sharing the *Leilani* message with both islands a tip came in, a description matching Leilani, spotted with an underage youth. While Yam's grin suggested pleasure over the tip, Ashyr educated him. "It's from a disreputable part of the city."

The kid's grin only grew. "I thought you didn't have any *rough* parts."

"I didn't say it was rough."

"Then what did you say?"

"Just not as reliable."

"So you have people you can't trust in your city?"

Time to be done with this kid. Still, Ashyr punched in the new coordinates. "We're wasting our time," he said as the airship flew straight from their high-altitude travels down into the outskirts of the city.

* * *

The children at the care center were neatly dressed. Perfectly posed in their chairs, waiting to hear his words. Such innocence on their faces, such trust.

The care center director ran through the announcements: tomorrow's schedule, their upcoming camp, and their special spontaneous guest. What an honor it was that President Ashyr Harmon had chosen to speak to their group.

Hard to actually fathom why he was there. The tip from that deplorable and illegal EnRapture bar still seemed too far-fetched.

At least now, the bar was under investigation. As for the tip, Ashyr questioned its legitimacy; it seemed suspicious. More likely a struggling registry seeking a boost through unreliable tips in hopes of the reward. Even his people could be tempted beyond their ability to resist. Yam needed to understand that.

Still, Ashyr came, with Yam in tow, to offer the appearance of an investigation. But this was outrageous. Abominable. None of Ashyr's people would do this. Certainly not his children.

The youth...if the tip held any credibility... had tried to scramble his identity during his illegal exchange to acquire a kit and a fake registry. This unreliable source, from the Southern Exposure's EnRapture bar, said it took some time to unscramble enough details to offer a tip and did so only with a clear expectation of a reward. The mere idea was a raging insult to these children. Ludicrous and insulting.

As the director presented the mic to Ashyr, his final seconds were used to scan the group. Last time he had been here was for graduation, welcoming the first batch on to adulthood and integration into his society.

Ashyr ran his hand through his recently bleached hair, brushing away the pained thoughts that this batch hadn't been integrated at all. Rather he was paying extreme fees, in medical attention, as well as silencing potential blackmail, ensuring that no words slipped out to panic his people.

"Hello, my children." He shared a grin with his audience. "I wish to share with you a special story." He took in all their smiles and let his shoulders and jaw relax. They adored him. Together, he would take them to a happy place, a memory he loved dearly.

"I call you my bicycle group. Do you know that? You may have never heard me say that to you, but to me, you are my bicycle group. So what does that mean?" He paused for effect, giving those beautiful faces one of his grand parental smiles.

"All of you have your very own bicycle. I make certain of that. But a long time ago, before there were those bicycles, before there was you, I didn't know what it was like to give such a gift to a child. Before there was EnRapture, before all this…" Ashyr waved his hand across the auditorium, taking in the wide eyes that followed his every move. "Before any of this, my very first exchange—remember, you will never forget your first one—well, let me tell you about mine. A man by the name of Foster gave me that first exchange, not from EnRapture but from its origins, Em-Path." Ashyr paused at the memory, the moment, the happiness he still felt as he held to that inaugural exchange. "Foster showed me what it was like to experience a child's joy." To feel parental love. To experience approval in their eyes. "He showed me the joys of having you," he said. "And I have given and cared for you. I have done so much for you. Shared epics beyond bicycles. I love all of you the same. I have built our society around your happiness. This world is for every single one of you."

For a brief moment, a flash of their future— so full of pain—crossed Ashyr's mind. He held no love for Leilani. She could have set all things right; instead, she delayed saving them.

He arched his shoulders back, and he embarked on his stern parental role. "I've been involved in something extraordinarily important for all of you. I've been dedicating my efforts to giving you the brightest future. So many resources, time, care, and attention for your upcoming needs, but there's a rumor in place that one of you might have taken something you shouldn't have."

Quickly, he raised a finger. "Like I said, just a rumor. I scarcely believe it myself. But I am here to ask…if any of you have seen this girl?" He didn't need to look back; he could feel her presence appearing in the projector behind him. Using the photo from the *Missing* flyers, he sensed her eyes staring out at them.

Hands shot up all over. Within the youngest group attending, a boy was jumping up and down. His red hair bounced with his rhythm. "I know her."

"We saw her," another from his group called out.

From across the room, a child yelled louder than the others, "She was here."

Looking at their young faces, Ashyr recalled the field trip. His fist pounded lightly against the podium which caused the noise to cease. Kindly, he said, "I know. She came here." If…there was a skunk among his pure children…, it would indeed be here.

While all waited, and watched him, he surveyed their faces, alit from the Leilani photo behind him. "Have any of you seen this person, not here at the center, but away from here?" While the question hung, he searched the audience.

It was difficult to meet their eyes; he could hardly do it. But each face told him nothing…or they told him everything—what he already knew! These children knew *nothing*.

Still, he finished out this pointless witch hunt. "I won't be angry with you. If you know something, you need to tell me." He shifted his parenting voice into deep, compassionate care. "If you have anything to share, please come and talk with me." Mutual trust with these children. That was the proper way to parent them. "I offer a Golden Invite in exchange for any reliable, true, real tips on this girl." Then he shared a final smile, a nod, and started to leave, only to turn back and blow them kisses. They stood and applauded, cheering him along as he made his way off the stand. As he moved down the aisleway, he pumped his fist and blew kisses to those he passed near the aisle.

Unfortunately, at the end of his walk, Yam's tall frame leaned near the door. With fingers shoved into pant pockets, and with a face that mocked in only a way his father could, it was if Brody were there in Yam's place.

While the director led the children in their unity chants, Ashyr walked past Yam into the foyer. "Come," he commanded. "What are we going to do with you?"

"Would you take my help?" a voice came from behind.

Ashyr turned to see a youth with silver hair, one he recognized as a favorite. "Draven." He smiled, motioned him closer, and placed one of his own between him and Yam. "One of my future leaders. How are you?"

"I want to help you find her. That girl," Draven said.

Such a beautiful child. "I like your attitude." Ashyr reached into his inner suit coat pocket. "Just for your offer, I give you this." He handed him a Golden Invite.

"The experience will be with you." It wasn't a question, but rather a statement from the youth.

Ashyr laughed over the method. "I've heard about your negotiating skills. You have a reputation. I also recall you have great standings. Solid rankings in your training. When you graduate, those traits will position you well."

Draven nodded confidently. "I'd like that exchange now."

Amusement filled Ashyr. Past the youth, Ashyr made eye contact with Yam, finding joy at this moment. Yam was there to witness the love his youth had for EnRapture, and for him. These were children who appreciated what they had.

But Yam only rolled his eyes.

Ashyr heaved out some disappointment. "Unfortunately, I have an issue I need to take care of." He waved a palm at Yam. Then he ensured the ticket had his seal on it before handing it over to Draven. "Be sure to get in touch with my assistant. We will get it scheduled on my calendar. Soon."

"No. I think it should be now." The ticket disappeared into a pocket and the youth folded his arms.

He really knew what he wanted. Ashyr fumbled, feeling his own hunger surge. His afternoon appointments had already been rescheduled.

"I've got nowhere to be." Yam raised a hand. "Just waiting for my ride *home*." That emphasis on home, as if Yam wanted to alienate himself from Ashyr's youth.

Draven turned around. "You're from somewhere else, too, aren't you?"

That was it. Ashyr was done with Yam. His hands circled in an anxious manner while his lips pursed. The thirst. The hunger. The need for his next fix. Yam, and now seeing Brody emerge within his son. Certainly, Ashyr needed a break, a short rest from the trouble and stress of having to deal with Yam.

"Hey Draven." Ashyr motioned him closer. "You know what?" He glanced down at his ring and pressed the button. It lit green. "Green light means go. I've an opening right now."

Draven's face suddenly fell. "Okay." It was like the youth was in shock. "Um...that's good...but...I don't have my case on me."

Ashyr shrugged. "Don't worry. I always carry a spare."

"I also don't have my registry."

Ashyr's eyebrows shot up. Scolding filled his voice. "Draven. Never. Ever. Go without your ring if you're going to be soliciting an exchange. That's like indecent exposure. Nakedness. It can hurt you. But today, I'll let it pass. Just remember, when you graduate, harsh penalties, missed opportunities, no identity, you are not a person without it."

Like a good son, Draven nodded, taking the scolding with the intended delivery to learn. Yet, from the corner of his eye, Ashyr spotted Yam and practically heard the rumble of Brody's mockery.

Such disrespect. "Let's go find a training room." Ashyr motioned Draven toward a hallway. "And you," he looked back at Yam. "Any chance you could stay out of trouble until I return?"

Yam shrugged. "I'll try my best."

The assembly was set to run for an hour. The children would all be contained. As long as Yam stayed put, he would be harmless. "Don't leave this spot."

Had this command gone to his youth, they would obey. But with this unwelcomed one, he had no assurance. Instead, he got a raised eyebrow, like another mocking look from Brody, which only pushed Ashyr further. If he had to keep dealing with Brody's disrespectful offspring, he needed an EnRapture experience now. The opportunity was worth the risk. "I'll be back soon."

* * *

Inside the training room, his shoulders softened. With control, he gave Draven a parental pep talk. "Without your registry, normally, I'd say you'd be better off to make an appointment. It's not every day you get an experience with the founder of all this. And if we go forward, you are giving up your chance for this exchange to be recorded. Are you really okay with that?"

"Yes." Such clarity, almost an urgency, in the youth.

"Well…" Ashyr felt his own urgency stir for some momentary relief from his current problems. "I just want to make sure you've thought it through."

"I have."

Ashyr closed his eyes. A promise of calmness reached his breath. "Okay." He opened his eyes. "Let's proceed then." He retrieved his spare case and extended it to Draven, only for Draven to reel back. Pain filled his eyes. "Are you all right?" Ashyr asked.

"I...I don't know." His arms wrapped around himself.

"Is something troubling you?"

Fear took over those eyes.

Ashyr examined him. "Are you dealing with a heavy secret?"

"I'm fine." The youth shook away the look. "I just need to do this...then I'll be okay."

"Are you well?" Ashyr asked slowly.

Sudden tears pooled in the youth's eyes.

"You're in pain. Aren't you?"

It was there, clear, difficult pain, making Ashyr wish he had a gift, like a bicycle, that could stop this moment. Instead, he retreated to the bench near them. "Sit. Let's talk first."

Draven pressed against his back. With a soft exhale he lowered himself down.

Ashyr's own body tensed. The sound, the posture, the memory, the hidden hospital, the beds filled with the first batch of the new adult generation—the concerning issue screamed at Ashyr. "Which group are you in, Draven?"

"Second batch. Your order."

"Huh?" Ashyr eyed him closely. "You sure? I kind of think you might be part of the first batch."

"I've always been with the second batch."

Ashyr rubbed a knuckle over his chin. Inside, his heart beat wildly. He released a weighty exhale.

"I need to check your file. Make double sure that's right."

To assist the moment, Ashyr extended the spare silver kit again and slid it into Draven's hand. When the kid looked up, a lightness filled his eyes. A bicycle moment for sure. "EnRapture helps, doesn't it?" Ashyr owned the moment.

The youth gave a firm nod.

Within his inner suit coat pocket, Ashyr produced his own platinum blue case. "Had you graduated, we would be breaking code, not logging an exchange in your registry. I know you know that, so let's not let the word out, okay? You are still in training, and heaven knows, sometimes, when you're having a hard day, an EnRapture moment can certainly clear those blues. So let's do this, Draven. What kind of experience are you in the mood for?"

The youth swayed his head as if unsure, while Ashyr leaned over and placed his thumbprint on the spare kit to unlock it.

With his case open, Ashyr slipped on the glove, positioned his goggles overhead, and dispensed the pills. "As soon as you give me an indicator of what you want, I'm good to go."

Draven finished his prep, then, with a gloved hand, reached for the pill. "Let's do this." He sounded firm and determined.

"Great. What are you looking for today?" Ashyr asked again.

"The *why.*"

"The *why* of what?" Ashyr swallowed his pill. Draven did the same then slid the goggles over his eyes. Ashyr followed. With an outstretched hand, he felt the youth's glove lock against his. In the darkness, Ashyr said, "You have to answer me, Draven. It's about to begin."

"I want to see why you got rid of family units." The grip around Ashyr's hand tightened.

The tingling of the brain had begun. Ashyr tried to make sense of the request. What was Draven asking? Such a strange wish. Was this about the abundance Ashyr had given him? The bicycle life he enjoyed? "I'm not sure...I understand your request."

"Why is every adult my parent? Why do I not have *one* father and *one* mother?"

The words felt like profanity. They hit with intensity, leaving Ashyr in shock, throwing him off his game. While neurons fired out into their new route, Ashyr felt strange. He hadn't felt this way in decades. Like an amateur, his inner mind, a bit out of control, stretched toward a genuine, unaltered memory, one that was not for the taking. Yet here he was sending it out, not calling it back, letting it go forward to Draven.

Like a computer, Ashyr's past was being downloaded. He couldn't pull it back. This would become a virus, it would go, it would spread. Shared. Like the Internet of the past, Ashyr would lose all control. War waged within his thoughts. Information fought to break through. Draven's exchange was incoming; the neurons stacking up, firing intensely, wanting their place in Ashyr's consciousness. Yet Ashyr now wanted to firewall his thoughts. Stop what was being sent to Draven.

If this came out, it would be catastrophic! Like a safe, Ashyr tried to lock his mind. Yet at the same time, Ashyr saw the transfer, Draven's exchange coming through, Ashyr now within Draven's point of view, seeing Leilani's face, as he saw her.

His mental door cracked, his thoughts slipped away, nothing sugar-coated, straight to Draven, while Draven's hand locked against Leilani's, breaking her into her first EnRapture experience.

Raw.

Hot.

A strange anger brewed from Draven. Fiery thoughts, red blasts of color.

A glimpse of Foster. On the beach. The Air Island.

Leilani next to him.

The exchange carried a strange aura, like an intentional disruption. Like Draven wanted Ashyr to see this. There were no modifications. Nothing flowery. No details altered. He was feeding Ashyr what Leilani had fed him. Undiluted. Fresh. And recent.

Father. Daughter.

The touch of a parent's hug.

A surge of calm safety.

The beach.

A breeze. And birds.

Care. And concern.

What was Draven doing?

Foster's eyes. This love for Leilani. This exchange coming in from his own youth. This was obscene. Such longing. Love and longing for Foster.

This was no EnRapture ecstasy!

Nothing thrilling. No entertaining. No heightened arousal. No daredevil stunts. No fulfillment!

This was horrid longing.

Homesickness. From a girl who was destroying him.

She and her father.

Ashyr felt a twitching in his left hand. Despite all the mental noise, Ashyr couldn't sort through it. One muscle wanted to pull away, to release himself from this repulsive exchange. But he was locked in place.

Sick. Home. Family. Island. Foster.

Leilani the deserter.

And Draven, a deserter in himself. Why would he share this with Ashyr?

What did Draven hope to gain from all this?

Certainly not any accolades!

And here he had forgotten his registry.

He'd been played. In a horrific way, Ashyr had been played by one of his own.

While the final minutes ticked on, Ashyr fought to stop the series of images. The feelings. The sounds. The dangers if this were to be logged into his long-term memory. But like a hammer, the neural images banged on his mind.

No matter what he tried, all Ashyr could see was Foster. Not just Foster from this Draven-Leilani catastrophe, but Foster through the ages, Foster the friend who haunted him in his sleep. Foster who lived on his shoulder. Foster who ruined all that Ashyr had ever wanted.

Foster.

The glove nodes unlocked. Ashyr drew his hand back and clasped it against his chest. He rested his head against the wall, afraid, angry, confused, unready to look at his youth, unsure what to say, how to say anything.

How to even process what Draven had just put Ashyr through. How wrong! How evil. How divisive. A traitor in his own midst.

But while Ashyr waited for his neurons to start firing properly again, he heard the thump. While the EnRapture drug lessened, footsteps fell, and the door opened.

With great mental effort, Ashyr pulled off the goggles to see Draven in the doorway. His head rolled around in small circles. His hand braced against the door frame. He seemed ready to run. His feet even twitched as if waiting to get the full command from his head.

His eyes met Ashyr's.

Neither said a word.

They only stared.

He needed to stop the kid. Punish him for all this. Instead, he couldn't seem to do anything.

"You're killing all of us," the black-tattooed lips said. "Bit by bit, we all will be dead." As Draven disappeared, Ashyr tried to process the hard words. Uneven, staggered steps clamored down the hallway.

Ashyr wanted to throw up.

He tried to take inventory of his incoming and outgoing thoughts. What had he shared? What did Draven know? What had Draven just shared with him? What exactly did it mean?

Against his own will, a folder slipped into Ashyr's mental file of exchanges. Leilani. Foster. Air Island. Beach. Comfort. Safety. Love. Harmony.

That new file, from that horrific exchange, was where Ashyr's mental door had cracked. His children's future, the deadly disease, and the fear to follow had been exposed.

It was over. No more options ahead. Leilani. If full-strength EnRapture—sterile. Draven. If exposed to the issue—then Ashyr's people—exposed to a state of emergency. The End.

THIRTY-SEVEN

YAM

From the assembly room, Yam kept hearing the chants, the cheers, like parrots repeating the words of their masters. *For today. For the moment. Our future is free and undetermined.* The duplicated phrases felt like Yam's sister's fingernails running down the antique washboard Baba acquired during one of their joint junkyard salvage runs. *We are content to learn. To be where we are, in the present...* Rani had found a thrill in annoying Yam with that sound. *Learning to live in the moment...so we can truly channel our focuses...* Now it was like she was there, watching him cringe over and over again. *Our energies.* The memory almost made him miss her. *Our minds into the ultimate exchange.* He let a mini smile form, focusing on the Rani memory to block out the other noise.

A stumbling sound broke through the auditorium chants. Yam turned to see the silver-haired kid emerging from the hallway. Their eyes met. Then Draven reversed his steps. A wobbly, yet swift move toward a side exit, only for him to disappear.

Like a bolt of lightning, the moment registered for Yam. He took off toward the same door, down the steps and over the gravel lawn, keeping his eyes firmly on the boy, who had shifted into an awkward run.

In no time, Yam overtook him and without second-guessing himself, Yam toppled Draven to the ground. As the scared face looked at him, Yam practically yelled, "Where is she?"

The boy's fists clenched up near his lips. "Don't touch me."

"But you know! Where is she?"

"I know nothing." The fear in the boy's eyes shared enough to contradict that statement.

"Did you take her?"

"Ashyr…" Draven's voice broke like he was about to cry. "Do you know…" he looked into Yam's face, "Ashyr's secret…about us?"

"Did you take her?" Yam repeated.

"She wanted to be taken," came the weak reply.

It was too late—no amount of meditation, no breathing exercises, no channeling thoughts of love, like Mum had taught him, could stop Yam from hurting this boy trapped between his legs that crouched into the ground like a terrified animal.

"Where is she?" The sound roared as if it came from outside him.

"I don't know." The boy's head cowered further. "Why are you here? With Ashyr? Because he thinks we're going to die?"

All those years of working to control his emotions and now the rage begged for explosion. He would hurt this face that spoke of weakness.

And with this explosion, with this fight that pounded in Yam for release, what was he then...a failure? A bad person? Did he care?

He was a seventeen-year-old boy who could splatter his enemy. They were nearly the same height, looked to be the same age, but the face that stared back was so broken, confused, and terrified.

Yam clenched his fist, preparing for his attack, calculating his rage, while his mouth delayed his act. "Where did you take her? Where is she?"

The boy began to scoot, right out from under Yam. "I planned to go back..." Another scoot. Hands crab-crawling backward. "I wanted to."

Eyes intent on his prey, Yam stepped forward and closed the distance. "And...you left her."

"No. I was going back." The boy whimpered. "But I got sick...and so...I was just waiting until..." Elbows and hands kept working, dragging him farther from Yam. But Yam kept following.

"I was going to turn her in...I think...I don't know...I got confused." A wrist buckled under. He staggered. "She messed me up. Everything I knew." He moved again, hastening to widen the distance between them. "I don't understand my life anymore."

Yam stomped and the boy scrambled across the gravel, his eyes never leaving Yam's. "I was going back," he said weakly, "I am going back. I wasn't leaving her there."

Yam heard it, the *me-centric* voice, the complete focus on self, the boy stuck in his own universe. With his steps, Yam guided the boy's scoots directly toward a tree. "How do you know she is safe? Why didn't you tell someone?"

The crawl sped up.

"She's been missing for weeks. Do you even know what you've done?"

"I'm going to die."

"You could have lived."

While Draven shook his head, his fingers tripped over some gravel. An elbow crashed to the ground. Quickly, he twisted into a baby crawl. Then with a swift look behind, he leapt up and started to run.

But Yam caught his shoulder. With one martial arts sweep, the boy was back on the ground, staring into Yam's eyes, sharing the terror inside.

"Did she use EnRapture?"

The boy didn't move.

Yam stepped back. He wanted Draven to stand up, so he could knock him down again. When he didn't move, Yam took care of the desire himself. He grabbed at the boy's purple silk shirt. Air blasted in and out of Yam's lungs. "Did she use EnRapture?"

Still no answer. One swipe of the hand and Yam could break the boy's nose. A kick in the stomach and the boy would crouch in pain. Or...there were so many ideas...so many options that would be much worse.

Instead, while gripping the boy's shirt, Yam slowed his breathing, one round of clear breaths. Then he dropped the kid to the earth.

To not touch Draven again, Yam held his wrists. A wrestling match erupted, left hand holding right fist, right hand twisting to hold left fist. For if one went free, the pretty boy's face might get smashed. A busted lip. A purpleness around those terrified eyes. "I don't want to die," the boy whimpered.

With a hold on his right fist, Yam froze, holding even his tight breaths. The boy only knew of Ashyr's ways, recognizing what served himself. Yam exhaled while taking a fraction of a step back.

As if the small distance had now turned Yam into a possible ally, Draven looked up with pleading eyes. "I tried to help her. I wanted to. I did. And…I… when I got extra sick…I didn't know what to do…I didn't know…I don't know anything…anymore."

"You never should have left her." Both hands dropped to Yam's side. Slowly, he unclenched his fists. "You should have never taken her away, to begin with."

"Ouch!" Draven suddenly crouched in pain. "Ouch," he cried again as if Yam had actually hit him. As he rolled further into a ball, Draven's eyes met Yam's.

"What's wrong with you?"

"I understand now." Great pleading was there. "That's what this is. The pain. It's not a bad muscle that won't heal. You came to save us." Then his face softened as if the pain had left as quickly as it came.

"Didn't you?" Although his body uncurled, fear still filled his face.

Yam drew a hand to his lips. This was a difficult moment. He released an exhale into the curve of his fingers.

"I'm only going to get sicker." Draven looked to the sky.

In a defining moment, Yam stepped forward. A chance to be a better person than he wanted to be. He extended his hand. "We came to help you. We need to find her...and then see what we still can do."

THIRTY-EIGHT

LEILANI

The abandoned dress lay between me and the slowly opening door.

I met the eyes of the kitty. "Ha." A grin spread over her lips. "You lost your pretty dress."

I backed closer toward the window. She stepped in and relocked the door. My hands reached for the bobby pins in my hair, as if I could pick the window lock in time. But her eyes trailed me, staring me into a place of terror, telling me I had no way out.

Soon she was beside me, a claw running along my slip's spaghetti strap. "You don't belong here." With a swipe of the claw, she cut the strap and scraped my skin. "So let's have some fun with you."

A red line emerged above my collarbone. While the kitty licked at the blood, I froze near the window. "Pretty, pretty," she said, purring near my ear. The crowd's chants outside were fading.

Her paws rested on my shoulders, pressing me down onto the ground. Furry fingers ran along my skin. I closed my eyes and focused on a sunset breaking over the island. Light rose colors over a cliff. Gray blues emerging. Palm trees waving at the morning. A bird flying across the sky, as if just discovering the beauty of the day.

The pill was at my lips. The kitty's fingers shoved it in; I swallowed. The paw pressed firmly over my eyes. Whiskers tickled at my ear. "Had you stayed in the dress, you could have been honored by us. Instead, now, you're going to learn how to run. Put on the glove."

With my eyes still covered by her paw, I felt a glove press into my hand. I obeyed. The cool touch of the fabric covered my skin. The nodes locked into place as the other glove pressed against mine. Then the neurons scattered as new input pounded into my mind.

THIRTY-NINE

MARIANA

Mariana approached the plot of land with a strange sense of broken acceptance. This was happening. Outside of her wants, outside of her control, this would serve as her family's temporary home.

As expected, the deserted town Tarthur offered was filthy. She stepped into one of the dilapidated houses to find, amid the dust and debris, broken windows, busted doors, a mouse that scurried across the floor.

Mariana hugged herself. She would get through this.

Mayor Leif and Sunny, who had joined her, were talking, trying to cheer Mariana on, but she only heard a portion of the words. *Ice chest provided to each home. A bus each week to pick up the workers. Shuttled to the mines. When they returned, crates of food for their village.*

Village—Mariana played with the word. She squinted to see this abstract image blend into something comprehensible. One eye saw the past, the island, the barefoot children running through the streets, laughing, the palm trees swaying, her grown children parenting with a smile and carefreeness. Her other eye strained harder to see the future, children running on hot dirt, the weathered porches shielding her grown children as they parented with hands worn from the day's work. The sun beating down. No children shoeless. Instead, thick boots of protection from the snakes, the critters, the rodents, the harshness of the land.

But they could do it.

While Sunny spoke of her town helping, sharing supplies, laboring together on their days away from the mines, Leif retrieved a map from the borrowed Land Rover.

"I've been told there's a spring within a decent walk," he said.

"Tarthur wouldn't have recommended this place if it wasn't livable," Sunny added like her statement was there to bring comfort; that somehow *kind Tarthur* had really been looking out for the refugees he would be housing under his care.

Mariana tried to smile, but the muscles around her mouth didn't work. Instead, a burning behind her eyes told her she might break soon. Big ugly sobs, the kind that she wanted no one to see.

"Are we in any rush?" she managed to say.

"We are here for you." Leif gave her a warm smile.

"All day if you need," Sunny added.

"I think I need to go see it, the spring." Mariana looked in the direction the map pointed. "Alone," she quickly added as she heard Sunny's feet approach.

"Are you sure?" Sunny's eyes were there, searching Mariana's face.

"Yes."

"Take your time," Leif said as he stepped away. "Take *all* the time you need. We are in no rush to leave."

As Mariana set out to find the water for her new home, she heard Leif speaking to Sunny. "This is the moment we need. Let's use it well."

FORTY

LEILANI

I waited, but no noise came. I fluttered my eyes open, but the room around me was dark. I lay on the floor, the wardrobe across from me.

My shoulder burned slightly. I turned my head to see a thin red cut and a torn slip strap. With unsteady hands, I tied the loose ends into a knot.

My head fell back, pressing into the floor. Slowly, I arose.

The window was now open.

Although I could still hear crowd noises, they seemed to be coming from inside. The streets, hardly visible in the darkness, appeared bare.

Move slow at first. Then you can move fast.

As if I had already seen this, I knew what to do. Climb out the window, steadily, slowly. A ledge would be there. It was.

Press against the wall. I did, confirming no one could see me while I followed the next round of clear instructions.

Climb the wall.

My body struggled with a pained slowness. The muscle commands from my brain seemed less alert.

The temperature was cool but bearable. The slip I wore, while not ideal, was a heavy spandex, giving me a vague sense of warmth.

Focus on the building's wall. There are jagged spots in the bricks. These are your handholds and footholds. I checked my first placement. Then my next. The slip covered what needed to be covered yet let me do what needed to be done. Steadily, I climbed. Soon in a rhythm, my muscles worked with a robotic precision up toward the roof.

Quicker now. I sped up, my breath feeding into the race.

As instructed, I reached for the next brick, only for it to pull loose and tumble past me.

Smash!

To survive, I couldn't look below. I focused up. One task at a time.

At the rooftop, I caught lights and sounds below.

"What was that?" a voice asked.

I lay low, waiting, catching my breath, letting the clamor die down.

"Look!"

"The window."

"An escapee," a voice yelled into the building.

Pounding feet. Gasps. Grunts.

"The hunt is on! Wo-hoo!"

A wolf's howl followed.

Obey the next task. It was all I could do.

Jump to the next building.

But in the darkness, I couldn't.

More images came, a clarity emerging from the kitty's exchange. The action order: *Run and leap*!

I tried, only to retreat. Noise grew below.

In my dance slippers, I tried again. But again, the darkness stopped me. Several feet across and down, a landing spot waited.

The noise seemed to swarm like flies. So I gave in. As fast as I could, I ran, pausing only slightly, right at the edge, and leapt.

From what the kitty had shared, I was to land on all fours. Instead, I crashed down, hurting my knee.

But I was alive.

Next task: *Jump again to another building.*

I ran to the edge. And stopped. *Land. Run. To the next*…until…I wouldn't. Not this next command. This was all part of the kitty's plan. After the buildings, scale the wall. Run like a terrified animal. While the beasts followed. To hunt me. Their prey. To devour me.

My chest heaved up and down with great force. I fought against the incoming messages. Break the code. Fight against the firing neurons.

There were two ladders, one on my building, one on the next. New commands came, my commands. *Climb down the ladder, a few rungs. Outstretch my hand. Swing. Catch the other ladder. Land there.*

Fighting against the pounding in my head, I pressed through. My hands gripped the ladder, my lungs chugged through terrified breaths. I swung, not as graceful as the neuron command. Clumsily, with the misfire of a muscle command, I barely caught the other ladder's rung. But I did, just as my body crashed against the ladder's wall.

With noise coming in all directions, I scaled the brick wall until I reached a tight balcony. Then my fingers took on a life of their own, clawing, tearing at the corners of a window screen, while I pleaded with my lips that the window was unlocked. As the screen ripped away, the pane screeched upward. Without a second thought, I tumbled into the darkness below.

FORTY-ONE

MARIANA

The path to the spring saved Mariana from deep sobbing. It wasn't treacherous. Or overly long. In fact, the sound of the flowing water seemed to speak comfort to her hurting heart. With each step, she worked through the future, the job of hauling water. It would get tiresome, but they would build a well. And hauling water was a safe job, better than mining. There were other jobs too. Maintaining the village, caring for the families, educating the children, building new homes—there was so much work to be done!

But seventy percent of all adults were required at the mines, five days a week, staggered shifts, leaving only a small percentage of adults behind for the village needs. Her sobbing ramped up again.

She worked to calm herself by listening to the continuous flow, the refreshment, the clean, fresh sound of water. As the spring moved, she thought of her people, moving, too. This all was temporary.

At the bank, she cupped her hands. The coolness washed through her. She wanted to bathe in it. The last time she had had a real shower was beyond recollection. While they worked on the well, and Foster provided a filtering system, they would also create bathing schedules. The rough wilderness would not undo them. They would conquer this.

She scooped more water up and let her tongue lick at its coolness. A chime sounded. She paused. Water seeped from her hands as she listened. The strange sound came again from her pack.

She opened her pack to see a light, a lavender purple glow. She dug past her canteen, her bandana, and jacket. The pyramid, after days of keeping it with her, now chimed and glowed.

On the pyramid's base, the metallic coloring shifted to a white shiny screen. Words appeared. *One who drinks with her tongue.* She nearly dropped the object. Scrambling backward from the bank, she surveyed the area. "Hello," she said weakly.

The pyramid chimed again. Timidly, she looked at it clutched in her hand. *We didn't mean to startle you.*

Mariana tried to breathe but her heart wouldn't stop racing. "Who are you?" she called out.

As the chime sounded again, she stared at the base. The pixels on the letters scrambled to form new words. *We come with information.*

Mariana paused, waiting, scared to breathe. Finally, the chime and the pixels changed again. *Set it down.*

She looked around. Other than the flowing spring and the breeze through a little grove of trees near the water bank, there was nothing.

Slowly, cautiously, she set the pyramid down on a neighboring rock, keeping the base still in view. Then she waited, straining for a chime and watching for more words to come.

The wind around her picked up. The water rushed with more urgency. A cloud floated above, moving over the bright sun overhead.

"Don't let us startle you."

A thin light projected across the bank from the pyramid's top, creating a hologram of three bodies. Mariana could hardly breathe. "You are…"

"Dot 2." Within the hologram, the woman's blond hair flowed under her wide-brimmed hat. "I also go by Eta. And you remember Point 1. Also known as Tau."

"And today," Tau said, "we bring Pi." He pointed at the third person, a young teenager. Inside the three-dimensional image, all three wore hats, long-sleeved shirts, and khaki work pants.

"You made a choice," Eta said softly.

With an unwillingness to blink, Mariana's eyes burned. "Was it the right choice?" she sent her question across the bank.

"With the information you have access to," Tau nodded somberly, "you did what you needed to do."

"So did I choose wrong?"

"We're here to help you," young Pi said. "That should be a good sign." He had bright white teeth that contrasted warmly against his dark skin. Something about his smile stirred a flickering smile in her heart.

"We have a message for you." Tau lifted his hat off then held it in his hand. The cloud was shifting; lighting was throwing off the hologram. The sound of water grew louder. Mariana inched forward, straining to hear. "You are not alone," he said.

Pi lifted his head and gave her another one of his bright smiles. "More are helping than you understand."

Mariana headed closer, almost stepping into the spring. "I need to hear you."

Tau placed a hand on Pi's shoulder. "For now, that's all we're allowed to speak."

"For now," Pi repeated.

"For now," Eta said, "share this with no one. Guard this. Keep this moment safe. You will need this memory for later." As the cloud shifted from its place, the sun blasted light around Mariana. The hologram was gone but their last words lingered in her ears. "You are stronger than you think."

Tau's words repeated too. "You are not alone."

The pyramid base blinked the words at her. *Goodbye, Mariana.* The screen turned back to its glossy metallic color. The purple glow was gone. Reverently, Mariana picked up the pyramid and held it near her chest. A smile deep from within emerged.

As she returned to her new village, a strange lightness accompanied her, a great contrast to the earlier heavy despair. While she shared her report about the spring with Sunny and Leif, she felt like she held a floating soap bubble in her hands. She didn't share anything about the pyramid, or the hologram, but she looked at Sunny as if hunting for an indication that she, too, had angels watching over her, and that such a gift extended beyond Mariana's needs.

But needs Mariana certainly had. This floating bubble, the hope, felt so delicate in Mariana's heart. She needed to shield it, protect it so it didn't pop.

Of course, she wanted to keep peeking at it, wishing to confirm its iridescent color, its invisible ways, its floating wonder. Because she needed to know once the fears set in again, and the doubts about all this returned, she could still remember the bubble which had floated in her care.

"We need to tell you something," Sunny said after Mariana finished her report.

Leif led them toward the Land Rover. "We thought it would be important that you know."

Sunny draped an arm around Mariana and gave her shoulder a firm squeeze. "There are two things actually." Sunny's breathing stilled. Already the moment was there, the anticipation that if Mariana wasn't careful the bubble was about to pop.

Sunny looked around as if she needed to watch her words. After a long inhale, Mariana saw it again, the weight of the world back on Sunny's shoulders. "Tarthur takes people, like he took Misty, only if they are familiar with EnRapture."

Leif cleared his throat and took over for Sunny. "What that means is your people are safe. Tarthur won't harm them, not in that way."

Mariana slowly nodded, feeling the awful yuck around the words *human trafficking* that no one shared. But Misty and Sunny had hinted at this, that her people were safe in that regard, which Mariana had held to this.

"It's thanks to the training period," Leif said quietly.

"Tarthur's people crave those who have gone through the process," Sunny added.

"So since your people have never used EnRapture, they will carry no draw for Tarthur."

"This is good," Mariana said to Leif, only to look to Sunny, whose face still bore a weight.

"For the others," she said, "those who Tarthur does keep...we ask that you share this with no one—do you understand?"

Leif took over again. "None of your people, at this time...should know what we are about to tell you...but...we need to trust you. Can we?"

With her heart still around her hope bubble, Mariana gave a firm nod.

Sunny picked up the words again. "Brody, myself, Leif, and some others are working on something..."

"A weapon if you will, that will..." He didn't finish.

So Mariana did. "For Tarthur."

"It's all about timing," Sunny said.

"It will be our war," Leif said. "But when it hits, it will be to finish him and his operations here."

"That we will help with." The words shot out of Mariana before she even acknowledged them.

"At the right time," Sunny spoke cautiously, "when we are ready...perhaps those of your people who wish to join..." she shared her next words very slowly, "would join us...in this war."

Mariana nodded, but her eyes looked past Sunny toward the old, hurting town. A strange resolve, beyond herself, came out of her. With the memory of the spring bank, the hologram so clear, a new Mariana spoke. "Please know...my family will do whatever we need to do, whatever must be done."

Sunny heaved out a breath. "We'll see. Thank you."

PART THREE

FORTY-TWO

LEILANI

With my eyes closed, I was six years old again. Back on the island, on my little bicycle, riding with Violet. I was zipping around her mom, Stella, who ran in her bikini top, pushing a stroller with Violet's brothers, born nine months apart.

I had first heard the term "too fertile" from Stella. It was an adult term, shared in the adult circle, while us young ones were out playing. As I rode my little bike, I played with those words "too fertile," not sure what they meant, as I watched Stella run with her stroller of boys.

I opened my eyes. The island was gone. I was back in the old worn-down house where Draven had left me. How I made it back mystified me.

The loose sheet was wrapped around my naked body as I lay on the mattress on the floor. I stared at the sticky table across the room. The finish had worn away ages ago. The surface shared a story of many lives. A burnt iron mark in one corner. A chunk missing from another. There were black streaks, pen marks, colorful scribbles, dents from knives cutting into it.

Off to the side, there was a graveyard of busted-up chairs. Had I had the right tools, I could construct a suitable one from the different parts.

But my hands, as I looked at them, were trembling, unsuitable to pick up any tools. The pale fingernail polish was gone. My nails were scratched from ripping the fancy gown; sliced and jagged from digging to lift the screen; chipped as I pried a window open to fall into a neighboring building to escape.

Pulling from my memory, the world stood still as I leaped. From one building to the next, such a grand exit I made. Brilliant colors in the shape of clouds behind me.

But there had been no brilliant clouds. Only darkness.

I closed my eyes to shut out the dissonant thoughts. Instead, I went back to the island. Six years old again while Clark was tattling on me to Mom. Something I had done. Someplace I shouldn't have been.

That's how it always was...my older siblings—later their spouses—lecturing me over something, sharing their reports with Mom, landing me in a round of her endless scolding and swift punishments.

My eyes opened. Against the sheet, I rubbed at my ribs. As I fell, I must have broken something. Six feet. I bet it was six feet down. No—more than that.

I pulled at my memories. Why had I fallen? The plan had been to climb down a tree. Or had it been a building? Or a wall?

There had been a jump. A twist. Freefall. Horizontally. It all came like an EnRapture experience. Some moment, descending, but...I tried to shove thoughts away. How far had I fallen?

Yes, my ribs were surely broken.

I closed my eyes. With force, I pushed out the memories, the sounds, the extremeness of the fall. I rubbed at the painful area and grabbed for another memory. But like a black box, my mind shut me out.

I opened my eyes. The old house. I was still there.

My stomach worked up and down as my arms stayed wrapped around the sheet. Breathing hurt.

At the corner of the ceiling and wall, black spots ran down. Before, when Draven had been here, there had been rain. And mold. Foul air, not like the good, fresh air back home.

I should have stayed on the island.

I wished I had.

But dishonesty...

It was Ashyr. He said he would treat me like royalty if I came. But he didn't.

If Ashyr...my entire body hurt...if he had not lied, things would be different.

My head ached like I needed another EnRapture pill...none were left.

My only choice was to fight it, block it out, this hunger. *Dig. Go deep.* I told my mind I was tired of EnRapture, of the confusion, the uncertainty over what was real, and the headaches that came, screaming louder as I fought against the call for EnRapture.

I breathed in, past the broken rib, the moldy air, the dampness all around me, and felt the cold sheet against my dirty skin. I shut my eyes again.

I told myself I could either miss home, miss Dad, try to remember our last hug, our last talk, and all the things he didn't share with me; miss Mom, and all the times she didn't listen to me; miss Huck, how at the wrong times he wanted my attention; miss my brothers and sisters, how some treated me better than others; miss Violet and Grace, how they never talked about anything useful...and how happy and content they were living on the island; or I could remember I found a way off the island.

I made a choice to leave...and now I missed them all...terribly!

Outside, birds called each other. Birds...and Dad. Right then, I wanted to call, to beckon, to cry out for my family too. Had Dad just told me what was happening, instead of leaving without a goodbye...things could have been different. If he'd shared what was real on the island...I wouldn't have wanted to leave.

He could have told me of so many things!

I opened my eyes, looking again at the ugly house. A chip from last night, a slice of memory came, my escape wearing a black slip whose straps ripped along the way.

More chips. Crazy chips. Like I was losing my mind. My eyes batted open and closed. Too much confusion inside. The first part was fine. I had snuck out a window. *Clink. Clink.* My memory reset. I focused again on last night, this time running across the roof, jumping to another building, prying a window open to another building, tumbling inside.

My mind hurt. A concoction swirled inside—EnRapture experiences, real experiences, a blend melding into my signature exchange.

A wall. Me running on it. Humans chasing me. Beasts chasing me. Tree. Climb. Fall. Run. Scrape knee. Another tree. Climb. Branches scratch. Slip strap caught. Rip.

I fluttered my eyes open to stare at my shoulder. A scrape was there.

I wanted to move, lift myself off this bed, leave the memories, my escape, how I wrapped the slip, once the second strap ripped from a branch, around my hurt body like a towel, the faint light of the quarter moon. The house. The cloud that covered the moon. The momentary darkness. The dropped slip. The run, the hobbled run. In the house. Shooing away the little animals. No longer afraid. Wrapping the sheet to cover myself. The collapse. The mattress. The daylight shining at me now.

The cracked mirror was placed over the broken window. When had I moved it? But I had, because I had a memory of me staring into it, not seeing me but a girl with a bloody lip, a blackened eye, matted hair, and the stained, discolored sheet entangled around her. Through the dirty glass, the eyes that looked back belonged to a stranger.

The wind roared outside. Something kept whipping against the roof like loose shingles. The wind was so different here, compared to the island. More violent. More demanding.

From my place on the floor, lying there on the mattress, I twisted to let my eyes continue tracking around the room to spot...in the corner...I paused. My eyes burned. My overnight pack! Draven had placed it there. Inside—clean clothes from Ashyr's place!

My eyes kept burning. I twisted my body up, the sheet still tangled around me. I moved slowly toward it. But as soon as I touched the pack, I saw Yam's jacket inside. My jagged nails hovered over it. Yam. He tried to help me. During our long days together, he even tried to talk science with me. Not for him, for me.

But his talk led to the "why," why we were doing what we were doing. Talk I didn't want to hear. So what did I do instead? As I dressed, I lifted my knee into my leggings and felt the large bruise as it bent. I couldn't recall how this injury had come. It didn't matter.

Once I was dressed, the warmth and fresh clothes cuddled me even against my scrapes and damaged skin. I closed my eyes to hold onto this moment.

A new memory came, Yam and I heading to L.A. in the airship, that first day together. There in the lounge, he strummed his guitar and sang. I pulled his jacket around me now as if I could hear his deep, beautiful voice.

Pulling me home...

...is where I want to be...

I stole his jacket to stay warm. To come back. To promise me—I would return.

Home ...is where I want to be...

I hadn't meant to be gone so long.

Pulling me home, with my family.

I was always coming back.

Pulling me home...is where I want to be...

...where I need to be.

Yam. Dad. Mom. Family. Home. It was time to find my way back.

FORTY-THREE

FOSTER

As the drone settled into the gray skies of Los Angeles, EnRapture billboards surrounded Foster. How he hated it! Like EnRapture even needed to be advertised among these people. That which he had given seed to, his invention that had led to his most magnificent failure, and now his daughter was lost in all this.

The moment the drone landed, Foster was out, his feet heading straight to the doors, only to find access denied for him to enter. An automated voice instructed him to leave the roof entrance and head to the ground floor. His feet pounded down the endless stairs, hitting the streets to become lost in a maze of loud hairstyles, bright clothes, and skin alterations of extreme design.

Foster stopped one with peach and tan swirl patterns across their cheek lines. "I need to find Ashyr."

Small round, opaque sunglasses with neon green frames stared back. "Good luck." Then the face shifted as if to point at the rotating doors behind Foster.

Turning so quickly, Foster nearly ran into a man resembling a grandma in a brilliant orange dress with navy blue polka dots. "I'm hoping for an autograph." Under a large-brimmed, orange-colored straw hat, gray hair wrapped in curlers appeared. "What brings you here?" The grandma man did a little jig in front of Foster, blocking his entrance into the building.

Foster just shook his head then waved a hand at the rotating doors, inviting the roadblock into the building so he might quickly follow.

"I hear we probably have a *long* wait ahead." The man raised his handbag. "Want to have an exchange before we go in?"

Again, Foster shook his head and then worked his way around the grandma man to step inside the rotating doors. Against his wishes, he felt the other person enter close behind. "Want to take a look at my registry?" The voice teased with excitement. "I might have something you want."

As soon as the opening came, Foster bolted out the doors straight to the receptionist desk. "I'm here to see Ashyr!"

With two-inch-long eyelashes and a headband with antennas that bounced above her head, the woman stared back. Her skin resembled the pattern of dragonfly wings. She tilted her head then swayed it toward the entire lobby behind him. "You and everybody else. Share your registry code." She waved a hand at a nearby electronic reader. "If you are lucky, maybe you'll win his lottery."

"No!" Foster pounded against the counter. "I need to see him now. It's urgent."

Her antennas waved around. "I'm sure it is."

Foster heaved out an exhale, a long burst of oxygen-balanced air. "I will see Ashyr now."

"Sure. Sure." She pointed again at the electronic reader. "Share your registry. And...I'll see what I can do."

With clenched hands to control himself, Foster scanned the room. One large guard blocked the entrance that led farther into the building. He watched the rest of the lobby with its isolated, obscenely dressed, misplaced groupies, hoping for some Ashyr love.

"I am not here...like the others..." He looked back at the receptionist. "I have no registry. But Ashyr will be waiting to see me. Tell him Foster Grady needs to see him now."

"Sure. Sure." The antennas kept waving around. "Take a seat until you get called."

He met the receptionist's eyes. With inaudible force, he tried to communicate with his eyes that he would not leave until she made a move. Seconds creaked on. Finally, the dancing antennas froze. With a scowl, she punched in a number. "Message to be relayed to President Harmon. A Foster Grady for him. He claims no registry." She ended her transmission to glare at him. "Now." She pointed behind him. "Be good like everybody else and sit."

* * *

In all his life, Foster had never felt more fury. Ashyr had done many things, complicated Foster's life in horrible ways, but this—waiting in the lobby until Ashyr was ready to see him—this had taken Foster's fury to an entirely new level.

Five times he'd been approached for an EnRapture experience: a man with dreadlocks sweeping to his knees, another with thick grayish-blue hair that extended out like a dandelion weed, a woman with pink and purple hearts tattooed all across her body, a man with skin that looked like red leather, and a youth around Leilani's age with large gaping holes throughout his attire—all solicited Foster. Each time, every cell in Foster's body screamed over the outcome of his invention.

To stop the soliciting, Foster kept his eyes down and watched his feet tap against the marble tile, swirls of dark gray and white with dizzy patterns of unclarity, breath after breath, as if this place owed him every particle of oxygen offered.

Leilani Lost—Ashyr owed some clarification!

How long had his daughter been missing? Instead, Ashyr tortured Foster with this unmerciful wait.

A loud rush occurred around him. Every person in the room crowded toward the entrance doors that led into the rest of the building. The security guard was calling people back, yelling out threats to hits on registries if they didn't give him room.

And then, across the lobby, Foster saw those clear blue eyes approach him. The rest of Ashyr was unrecognizable. No smile. No cocky grin. No flowing words. While the blue eyes stayed on Foster, no explanation came. No speech at all.

The blond hair, with raspberry-colored tips, was a wild mess on top of his head. The face was flushed with a harrowing sadness around the eyes. There was no suit coat, and the purple linen shirt was unpressed.

Foster was stunned into silence. Still, he moved past the crowd to meet Ashyr face-to-face. "Where is she?" he managed to get out.

The blue eyes dropped. "I don't know."

The guard pressed in close, nearly stepping between them.

"What does that mean?" Foster asked.

Another person looped his way close to the guard, pressing in front of Foster. "For three days, I've been here, waiting, hoping for this moment. An exchange with you, Mr. Ashyr Harmon."

"Hello Ashyr!" A turquoise boa skirted past Foster's arm, another person pressing between them.

More and more people. "Can I get your autograph?" along with "Before I die, I just wanted to see you once."

The security guard roared, pushing the crowd away. "Give President Harmon some space."

The crowd broke around him, and there were the blue eyes again, meeting Foster with an extreme blankness.

"You don't generally come down here." Fascination held in the guard's tone. His eyes lit up over the celebrity he spoke to, except this celebrity seemed only to see Foster. "What can I help you with?" he asked Ashyr.

"Me." Foster broke forward, pushing his way to stand next to the guard, who according to his shirt tag was called *Pattie*. "He came down to escort me..." Foster glanced at the hungry crowd with bodies fighting to remain in place. "Ashyr, I assume you want to take our conversation upstairs?" While this Pattie eyed him, Foster placed a firm grip on Ashyr's arm. The crowd gasped over the touch. But Ashyr didn't move.

Pattie pulled Foster's hand away, tossing it as if it were hot. "President Harmon!" he called out. "What would you like me to do with this person?"

But Ashyr didn't say anything, only moved toward the elevator, nodding his head like an obedient child. Foster waved a hand after Ashyr. "I've been summoned." Then he walked right past the guard. More gasps erupted from behind.

When they reached the elevator, Ashyr just stared at the buttons before them.

"We can talk right here." Foster pressed closer against him. "If that's what you want?"

Automatically, Ashyr raised a thumbprint and pressed against the scanner. The doors opened, but as soon as they both stepped inside, Ashyr stopped moving as the doors closed them in.

Foster nodded at the buttons. "I assume we are heading to the top floor."

Like a robot, Ashyr inched forward. Again, he used his thumbprint to activate the elevator box.

As soon as they were in motion, the windows out displayed a rising city full of colored specks moving along the streets. Foster watched the actions below, trying to delay his fury for as long as he could. "Where is she?"

When he turned back, he met the brokenness. *Empathy.* Foster could almost laugh at the word. An awareness of one's past pain, present enough to allow one to recognize the pain of another.

The elevator beeped. The motion stopped. Ashyr stepped out, then down the hall. Foster followed, past another security guard, whose mouth gaped open as Ashyr passed. Foster gave the guard a friendly nod, as if following this icon, who moved like a zombie, was completely natural.

Ashyr led the way into a grand, ornate, colorful room. Large paintings of blooming flowers decked the walls. From the expansive desk to the cream suede sofa, a palette of hot reds, pinks, and purples ran across a high-end rug.

Ashyr toppled into the sofa. Then, like a child, he curled up into a ball. He tucked his legs inward and wrapped his arms around his chest. He stared at the glass coffee table in front of him. "I don't understand what happened."

His neck twisted in such a way that the *EnRapture* tattoo ran down the open portion of his shirt to stare back at Foster.

"Tell me what did happen."

Ashyr's hand reached for his head. The bangles danced down his wrist. "I don't know. She left us."

Like a hurt animal, pain came from his lips. "One of my children...my youth...they did this to me." He pressed a finger with a large ring to his lips. He bit on the finger, then looked at Foster.

"Did what exactly?"

"Ruined the plan. Made her one of us. It's over, Foster. It's all over. I no longer can save my people."

"I'm here to take her home!" Foster's voice cracked over the word *home*.

"We've been looking for her." Ashyr kept shaking his head. "Flyers are posted all over. They're supposed to turn her in. Not take her. Not do this to me."

The fear in Foster broke through. He grabbed at Ashyr's arms, forcing him to come close. "Where is she? Tell me everything."

The scrunched-up face fed Foster's dread and terror. He shoved Ashyr away, pushing him back into the couch. "I'm here and I'm taking her home," he repeated as if his words could command control over the situation.

"She was safe, in my care. But..." Ashyr crouched lower into the sofa. "She ran away—ran away with that kid."

Foster's hands burst forward, yanking Ashyr up. Huge explosions of air shot out. A strong, overpowering smell of aftershave caught Foster off guard. A cough broke to counter the odor. Foster had to drop his grip on Ashyr as he fought to breathe. He stepped away, trying to recover, only to hear, weakly, "His name is Draven."

Firmly, Foster walked a path across the brightly colored rug. "Well, where is he?" When he reached the end, he retraced his steps. "Where can I find him?"

"They went together...he and Yam..." The eyes looked past Foster. "They'll bring her back."

"Did Yam run away too?"

"No."

"Then what...explain this to me...where did they go?"

"Draven left her. Outside the city."

Foster bolted back to Ashyr. Hands pressed firmly against his shoulders. Then Foster stepped back, grasping at clear air, working to soften the fury that raged him. Fists pounded against thighs. How he wanted to hit the man. "Why aren't you with them?" A yell burst out. "Why aren't you protecting her, as if you were me?" He turned to a wall. "How did you let this happen?" His fist hit a wall, right beneath the large peony flower. Pain shot up his arm.

He closed his eyes and folded his torso down, toward his knees. He drew in breath after breath, breathing hard so as not to feel, not to think. "Help me find her." He lifted his body to meet the broken man's nods. "You will do that. We find her, you understand that, Ashyr?"

FORTY-FOUR

YAM

Before they reached the crevice-like incline, Yam's breathing rose and fell like he already had expended the necessary exertion. In a way, he already had. Parts of his body had been immensely taxed: ears that tried not to listen too closely as Draven kept talking; a mouth forced to not retort all the things Yam wanted to say; strained brain focus as he tried to just keep putting one foot in front of the other. Clear, precise steps dedicated to the goal at hand. Find Leilani. Bring her back. That was all.

No need to preach to Draven over the damage he had done. All that was required of Yam was to keep moving.

However, Draven wanted more. Question after question: *Tell me what it's like where you live. You have a family too? A traditional one, with a mom, a dad? Three sisters? What else can you tell me? Share what it's like to live with each one. Please.*

Such an obsession, like Draven had this hunger, this appetite that could only be satisfied by exploring Yam's world.

Whereas Yam wanted none of it. "Let's just keep moving. We can talk later." Words repeated at least three times.

At one point, Draven said, "So...we find her, and she'll make it right. She'll stop me from dying, right?"

The things Yam could say: mean things, spiteful things, concerning things. Instead, all Yam did was shrug. That was enough to keep the boy moving.

At least four times they had to stop to let Draven rest. The pain came like a sudden stab, causing Draven to clutch at his side, then he curled forward like a hurt animal. Each time he arose, the Air Island questions came with more urgency, specific inquiries into Baba, Mum, Ivy-Mai, Aya, and Rani. Like he needed this specific focus to keep moving.

But for Yam, each question fed homesickness, seasoning his eagerness to do what was required— and get home!

At the ravine, Draven struggled. This limited his talk, making him fall well behind—and Yam kept going, through the climb and fall, scampering around the chunks of earth and the jagged slabs around them. Once he reached flat land, Yam saw no sign of Draven within the chasm.

The wide-open field beckoned Yam to continue forward, but the weak cries of a human, coming faint from the chasm, held him. Yam, reluctantly, turned back to do what he didn't want to do.

Help Draven.

* * *

"You need to back up," Yam said for the third time to Draven, who had led himself to the ledge of a perilous drop-off.

"I can't."

"You're going to have to."

"There's a cliff behind me too."

And indeed there was.

"How did you get there?"

"I don't know."

Yam pressed his hands against his eyes. It seemed unfathomable to think Draven had done this climb before with Leilani. For a rescue mission to find her, Yam would have done better going at this alone. Still, he now couldn't leave Draven stuck. So again, Yam retraced his steps, up, down, and around, trailblazing a way through the rocky incline.

"Here." Across a four-foot chasm, Yam reached out his hand. "You need to jump."

"What if I fall?"

"It's the only solution I have for you. Trust me. My hand is right here. Reach for it and jump."

Draven breathed in a long breath. He looked down toward the crevice then looked back at Yam with a face full of fear.

"Stay focused on me. On where you need to be. Not on that."

Draven gulped and nodded his head. "Okay."

"Okay, let's go."

Draven shook his head. "Not yet. I'm not ready."

Yam wanted to inquire how Draven even got to this spot in the first place, but his tone would certainly not help the current, perilous moment.

"You count and I'll go," Draven said.

"How about you count, and I'll be ready," Yam said, sounding far kinder than he felt.

"All right." Draven drew in a deep breath. "One." He closed his eyes. "Two." He opened them. "Three." He reached for Yam's hand and jumped.

"Whoa!" His chest rose up and down. "That was intense. Way wilder than what it felt like with EnRapture jumps. Like this was real. Crazy!" Draven kept looking back at his jump. At the dead-end path he had just left. "Wow! That was—"

"Let's keep going." Yam again paved the way ahead.

*　*　*

Once they left the ravine, they traveled through the open field for nearly a mile. The afternoon sun reminded them that limited daylight remained. "There." Draven pointed to some black dots off in the horizon. "We went there."

"What are they?"

"Houses. I mean old ones. Nobody lives out here. They did before the quake. But not since."

Ready to put distance between them again, Yam picked up his pace, only to see a black dot moving. As it grew, it seemed to be heading toward them.

And then Yam started to run.

Thick, long hair swayed back and forth. Her thin body ran toward them. Joy! After these long weeks, there she was. Nothing but relief and joy swelled in Yam's heart. They had found her.

Or she had found them.

As she neared, her arms were outstretched. He stopped. His chest rose and fell with gulps of relief.

And Draven sprinted past, right into her arms.

Going against Ashyr's laws, Draven wrapped her in a hug. "You are safe."

Yam just watched, too frozen to move.

When she released Draven, her arms remained outstretched as she rushed toward Yam. But he couldn't do it. He took a step back.

She was alive. She had been found. She was well. That was it.

As his arms crossed over his chest, and his fingers curled into fists, his legs took on a martial arts stance. She dropped her arms to her side. Her feet stopped in front of him. He exhaled a protective sigh. "Hey." His voice reflected his caution.

With so much gratitude on her face, her eyes felt like a machine gun firing at his heart. "Hi."

And then he spotted it, his jacket interlaced and tied to the pack on her back. He pointed at it. "I need that."

"Uh," she spun around, the pack moving with her. "Yeah. I'm sorry…" She fumbled with her gear.

He thought of helping to detach the jacket but doing so placed him too close.

"Here." She handed it over, and even though she was saying something to him, he jetted away, jacket clutched in his hands, straight to some trees, off in the distance.

With each stomp against the ground, he played his mantra: *She's found. She's safe. Alive. All is well.* They could go home. This was all over now.

At a tree, Yam's fingers flew into the inside pocket. With deep relief, he felt the small FID stickers. It was there.

With a confirming glance to assure it was safe, he slipped one sticker behind an ear, only to catch Leilani pulling at her hair while Draven stood nearby, looking like an idiot trying to wrap his arms around her as if trying to replicate Leilani's earlier hug.

Such hypocrisy.

It didn't matter. Draven was an idiot. Leilani was too if this was what she wanted.

He didn't want to keep watching, but he did while slipping the other sticker into place. As Leilani and Draven talked, he began the long-awaited conversation through his mind.

Baba. Baba. I'm here.

Leilani's hand combed at tangled hair. Her body looked thin and unhealthy.

Baba. Please hear me.

Yam closed his eyes and pictured home.

There working alongside Baba, helping with the PIGS, looking through the recent junkyard treasures, listening to Baba's enthusiastic talk about programming a new system while Yam tried to understand.

Baba.

And then the clear response back: *I'm here, son.*

*   *   *

The trip back through the ravine was just as treacherous as going in; still, Yam remained determined to stay ahead. Leilani could help Draven through, because Yam was finished listening to Draven explain himself over and over again. On the mile back toward the ravine, while they all walked close. Draven dominated the conversation with, "I got really confused. And things just got more confusing when I got back." He threw in a pause, but when Leilani didn't volunteer anything, he just kept on talking. "I didn't know what to think anymore. What to believe."

Yam tried to shut out the words, but they still came in.

"What you showed me through EnRapture was like nothing I'd seen or felt before. It was amazing, Leilani. Like really amazing. Like I want to feel that again. I want that. Like what you have."

At this point, Leilani did offer, "I'm done with EnRapture."

That caused Yam, a few strides ahead, to look back. But as their eyes met, Yam's heart and foot stumbled.

"You okay?" she called out, but he was back on his feet, moving to stay ahead.

"Now that you're back with us," Draven continued, "you can take care of this, and heal us."

Yam wanted to jog ahead and miss her response. Instead, part of him strained to hear, to listen past the weak sound in her voice, past the other words she shared: "We came to help...Ashyr had a plan...All would be okay." He searched for it, some indicator, some uncertainty. But it was not there. Rather, she spoke as if she was unaware of what she had done, as if she still was Draven's solution.

Yam just kept on moving, setting a quickened pace for the rest to follow, determined to reach the chasm and put some distance between them. But even in the up and downs of the rocky path, Yam couldn't escape the echoes of Draven's words.

"I took the experience you gave me, and I shared it...with Ashyr. Direct. Undiluted. I gave it right back to him. It floored him. I walked out from the experience like I had told him off. And you know what? Had I known what I know now, I never would have...I wouldn't have hidden you from him. Or left you."

Like a mountain goat, Yam climbed up and down, weaving his way to get space from the chatter. Once he cleared the chasm, the plan was to head straight back, leaving them behind. However when the city loomed ahead in the distance, he was disoriented, unsure of where to enter.

Eventually, Leilani emerged. Silence followed while she stood several paces behind him. Until

Draven came, then Yam made the mistake of looking back. Draven reached for Leilani's hand, and she let him hold it.

So much for any of Ashyr's rules.

Yam picked up walking again, unwilling to face the hand-holding couple, even though he was unsure of his direction. Shortly after, the footsteps came from behind. Soon she was beside him, with no Draven in immediate view.

"Where are we going?" she asked.

"Back."

"Back to Ashyr's?"

The question made him cringe. It was over. Her and full-strength EnRapture—Ashyr was done with her. Their time in L.A. was a bust. The only thing needed now was to go home. But all he did was shake his head. He didn't need to reprimand her. Ashyr would do that.

Still, he scratched at his neck, only to look down as he released the good news. "I talked with my father..." Just a mention of the recent conversation and Yam choked up. "He says your dad is on his way. He should be arriving soon."

"Really?" Her feet shuffled closer.

He paused. "Yeah." He picked up the walk, hoping he was headed correctly. "It's already decided. I'll take the drone back. But you, with your dad, and Ashyr...you can figure out what happens next."

Her sigh was so loud, deep, and intense, Yam failed in his efforts and turned to his side. And even further against his will, he met her eyes. They looked so different from before.

"Wrong way," Draven called from a few yards behind. He waved in a different diagonal direction. "It's this way."

Yam couldn't bear to walk past her, so he faced forward and waited, straining to hear her footsteps. When they didn't come, he turned and braced himself.

Their eyes met again. She spoke in a whisper. "I'm sorry."

He walked past, leaving behind her words, her eyes, her uncleaned face. He couldn't dismiss the pity and the sorrow he felt. Determinedly, he just kept moving.

Soon he passed Draven, too, only to hear Draven pick up his conversation again with Leilani. "I don't know what's going to happen with me when Ashyr sees me, you know? I mean I did something really bad. A couple of bad things. Helping you. Hiding you. Touching you." He let out a laugh.

Yam pressed a palm against his head. Just keep the feet moving. It was the only viable option.

"You know how I was going to turn you in, but then I didn't. 'Cause I thought about keeping you for myself, like an *us* thing, a *solo* thing, but we'd have to keep it all quiet. We wouldn't let others find out, but you could have shown me more of all the stuff you know that I don't. I just know there's so much you could show me. It was going to be amazing. If

I dared. I just wasn't sure. I planned to come back, but I got sick after that. But now that you're back... it's all going to be okay."

The fool was a broken record. Yam lengthened his pace, only to hear Leilani's lighter feet move faster, as if trying to catch up with him.

Draven's words sped up too. "You know, there's a point, with a choice, where you can't turn back. Like once you do something, you can't take it back. Like helping you. I didn't know at first, but meeting you has changed my whole life. That's why I took you where I did, so I could figure things out. And I wanted the reward Ashyr offered, but I wanted you to show me more stuff too."

Yam strained to hear Leilani's response, but she said nothing. There was certainly plenty Yam could have said on her behalf. But as the city drew closer, Yam didn't delay. He wanted to be gone. Let Draven navigate her back. Let the traitor have the rescuer's victory party...whatever that might look like...with Ashyr.

It didn't matter. All Yam wanted was to get home.

"You know?" Draven's voice was uncomfortably close again. "I don't think it would be wise for me to be seen with both of you. Not right now. Ashyr's probably supremely mad at me. I mean the exchange I gave him—that *had* to have messed with his head! Not that he didn't deserve it. He shared some messed-up stuff himself. But...for right now... I think...I need to gamble a bit. Let his anger die down, stay low for a while, until you take care of things. But I still want to see you, and stuff. Like even…if not EnRapture…just I don't know…talk. Like, this isn't goodbye, it's just I need some time to figure out how to stay safe, while Ashyr cools down."

Yam's palm could push no harder against his forehead. *Please, Leilani*, his mind muttered a ridiculous prayer. *Please have some common sense here.*

"Draven." Her words came out slow and pained, like they weren't even from her. "I just want some time alone with my dad."

"Oh, good." A huge sigh followed. "Then I won't head right back into the city with you guys. I'll sneak in on my own. You got it from here." And then, he touched Yam's shoulder. "Right, mate?"

From the no-touch rule to a touching monster. Yam felt his shoulder tense and he drew away from the touch. He started to say, "See ya," but even that didn't hold. The last thing Yam ever wanted to do was see this phony again. So all he could do was nod his head, keep his feet walking, and stay focused on the city ahead.

"All right," Draven spoke to Leilani. "So glad you're back, and I'll find you at some point again, okay?"

"Whatever." Leilani's voice sounded distant, as if she wasn't present anymore.

Yam just sped up. His thighs burned against his pace, while he heard Leilani's footsteps close behind his.

FORTY-FIVE

FOSTER

The silence in his private drone must have eased Ashyr. Back to his old ways, he filled the void with his words while Foster looked helplessly over Los Angeles.

"You will be remembered." His tone was that of a funeral eulogy. "Your children, your grandchildren will all trace themselves, their blood, their upbringing, their lives somehow back through you. I had that, Foster. I had it too. Purpose. Right here." His hand knocked on the window, then pressed against it as if displaying emotion to the lives below. "I had such meaning. Never would I utterly be forgotten. My existence would carry on forevermore. I had found my relief. My voice. I was heard. And now, that all will be gone."

Foster held no energy to challenge Ashyr, but he couldn't stomach another word. He closed his eyes and tried to tune Ashyr out.

"I have two hundred children right now on the pathway to death. And one of my favorite youths, one who held great promise, turned against me. He turned against you too."

Foster nodded heavily, still trying not to listen while rolling Draven's name slowly around his mouth.

"I had a clear solution," Ashyr continued. "A plan of rescue, only for her to leave me. I hold Draven responsible for this. But Yam…" He paused until Foster lifted his eyes to meet his. "He's a loyal one. Loyal to his contracts with me, you, Brody. He's a pain. But a good kid, who wants to help others. I wish she had, too."

"Ashyr." Foster warned him with a look.

"I just want you to know I have it bad too. Royal hell is about to break out through my tribe. My children are dying. Draven…and others…I can't trust them. I no longer have a plan. Things are very messed up at the moment."

Foster looked to the gray nothingness below. "You messed up."

"Your daughter did too."

Foster met Ashyr's eyes. Fury rose near the surface again.

Quickly, Ashyr followed up with, "She used EnRapture. You get that, right?"

Foster turned again to the grayness below. "You will fix this." With no energy to deal with Ashyr, to threaten, to chastise, to point out the catastrophes he left behind, Foster kept his focus clear. "This isn't over, Ashyr," he said quietly. "We find her, and you redeem this for her, for me, for all of us."

"I am practically dead," Ashyr whispered. "I no longer will be able to help my people."

A beep sounded. Foster looked down at the device borrowed from Brody.

Yam found her.

He looked to the sky and exhaled a huge sigh of gratitude. He threw himself against the back of his chair and closed his eyes. His heart rate pulsed with relief.

Coordinates followed. With sudden purpose, Foster took over, shouting commands at Ashyr, including Ashyr's role to drop Foster off and then leave. He would reunite with his daughter alone, protecting her now from whatever harm he could.

* * *

Off in the distance, he saw her, walking behind Yam. And then he ran. She ran too.

He ran as fast as he could, nearly tripping on the cracks and divots of the broken road. He jumped over some debris, ran around a pile of junk in his path, and then he was there, wrapping his arms around her. Her head pressed against his chest. Moisture soaked his shirt. His own tears spilled down. The rise of his chest, the breath of Leilani, alive, back in his arms.

Her clothes were dirty, her hair matted, her face filthy. She spoke into his shirt. "I'm sorry, Dad." Her voice was muffled, between tears and breathlessness. "I'm...so...so...sorry."

His hand stroked her tangled hair. He squeezed their hug a notch tighter. "You're safe," he said. "That's all that matters. You're safe."

Off in the distance, Foster caught sight of a young man, moving alone, inward toward the city. He then turned to Yam, standing a slight distance away from them.

"Draven?" he mouthed to Yam.

Yam nodded and mouthed, "Coward."

Foster closed his eyes, offered a prayer to the skies above. She was found. He extended his arm and motioned Yam toward them. "Thank you." Emotion caught in his throat. "Thank you," he said again and wrapped his arm around the boy. "Thank you," he said, looking into the heavens. "Thank you," he said to the earth he stood on. "Thank you," he whispered to everything within his reach while keeping both arms around the two.

Finally, it was Leilani who stirred, breaking the embrace. Yam quickly stepped away. He gave her a short glance then shoved his hands into his jacket pockets. His Adam's apple trembled slightly, and he stepped farther away from Foster and Leilani. He nodded toward Foster, not quite meeting his eyes. "Glad she's found."

Foster met his face with a smile. "Thank you," he said again.

FORTY-SIX

FOSTER

Once back in the city, in the quarters Ashyr had arranged for them, after she had showered and cleaned up, Leilani asked Foster to stay with her. They sat on the bed and clasped hands. She didn't say much, offered nothing of her experiences, but leaned her head on his shoulder.

When she said she was tired, Foster shifted to go, only for her to add, "But don't leave me."

On the trek back into the city, she appeared exhausted. Her smile was there but her eyes appeared distant and haunted. And now, as her head nodded against his shoulder, he held to so many reasons he couldn't leave her side.

Ashyr had been too busy to face Foster again, but he had set them up nicely in a quiet place away from the noise of the city, a little apartment with three bedrooms, on the ground floor, decorated in neutral white tones.

Gift baskets of food covered the kitchen counters. Leilani ate everything Foster offered her. Crackers. Cheese. Dried fruit. Cookies. Nuts. Cereal.

"I want real food," she said between bites. "Not their shakes or their vita-meals they swallow around here. Or that little compact sandwich bread."

"Got to leave time for EnRapture," Yam mumbled into a bowl of oatmeal.

After the food was eaten, Yam excused himself to his room.

Now, as Leilani slept against his shoulder, Foster replayed what little he could piece together from their walk back through the city.

At times, she would pause, only to hug him again. Sometimes they would walk in a half-hug where she would clutch him as if she would never let go. Memories swirled around him like sleep dust. Her as a young girl, him taking her out into the water, farther than they had ever gone before. Waves crashed in around them. Her arms tightened. In his ear, she whispered, "Don't let go, Daddy. Don't let go."

And now, as he looked at his nearly grown daughter, asleep with purple discoloring around her eye and a cut over her lip, he choked out a whisper, "I won't let you go."

But eventually, he had to. As if she were a young child, he scooted himself out from under her. He left, hoping she wouldn't wake, as other words tugged at his heart. Her request to go home. Her request to see her mother. Her request to go back as things once were.

Once, right after she had nodded off, she had called for Mariana as if Leilani were in pain. "You're okay," Foster had reassured her. "I'm here."

"I want Mom. I want to go home, and I want Mom."

Earlier she had said those same words, but calmer. Yam had been with them, and he also had said, "I want to go home too."

Mixed in all his emotions, Foster had said, "Let's make that happen." Now he headed to Yam's room. They had a one-passenger drone and a lot of unknowns. They needed a plan.

When Yam answered, he looked ghastly, as if fighting his own demons. "How is she?" he asked.

"Asleep. How are you?"

"Just heard the status…" he swallowed, as if unable to complete his words. "This is tough…" He shook his head like he was about to break.

Lying there on the table, Foster saw the same communication device he'd used earlier in the day. It vibrated as if still alive. "You and your dad have been talking?"

"Yeah." Yam motioned Foster into the room then retrieved the device. "He asked me to share this message with you." He glanced down and shook his head. His hair, unrestrained by his typical bun, flopped against his chin. "Baba and I…" the swallow of emotion was audible. "We've been having a lot of thoughts… lots to discuss, to work through." Foster wanted to touch him, play surrogate father, and place a hand on his shoulder. Yet he refrained, afraid himself over what Brody shared. "He wanted me to share this with you…" Yam kept hold of the device. "Tomorrow… when I come home…I'll have a choice to make."

Foster nodded, knowing whatever Brody wanted to say had just been shared. The island was no longer a part of those choices.

Yam handed over the device. He took it to read: *Tell Foster Bingo! The underground gave the reveal.* But one look at Yam and Foster knew the rest. Still, he scrolled to the next statement.

Tell Foster—not fixable. Not now.

Microorganism apparently likes metal.

A lot.

Foster rolled his shoulders back, drew in a breath, and continued.

If the island was a heart, one valve is still functioning, but it's not going to last. We are too late to stop it. We're coming up on the end.

Foster met Yam's eyes. All he could do was nod. "Mind if I take this now?"

Yam waved a hand at the device. "Go ahead." He retreated onto the bed, while Foster slipped into a seat and composed his message.

Foster here. Hoping to bring Leilani back to my island. Mariana too. Is that feasible?

As he waited for a reply, he added, *Can you send a message to Mariana for me too?*

Foster looked across the room at Yam. His head was pressed against the headboard, his eyes closed. Heaviness covered his face. His chest moved up and down in a strong rhythm.

The device vibrated in Foster's hand.

Sure. Send what you want. The PIGS will deal with sending it out.

Then another vibration followed. *Let's connect again tomorrow. I'll have a reading on how much time we have left.*

Thanks, Brody! Foster replied, then he stared at the device and tried to formulate his message for Mariana.

Glad you found her, Brody shared.

Again, Foster glanced at Yam. The face still appeared tense while the boy processed the news. Foster typed *Thanks to your son* right as another message appeared. *Brody out.*

An automated response followed. *Message to be sent to Mariana. What is the message?*

Now it was just Foster and the PIGS. He closed his own eyes and pictured Mariana. He missed her, today more than ever.

Leilani safe. He typed.

He hit send, then processed the next words.

Come to the island.

He watched Yam shift. The boy's eyes opened only to stare down into his lap.

Suddenly, Foster's fingers took a life of their own and fired off the plan.

The order of events:

First, send drone to us.

Yam use single to go home.

Then his comes for you.

Brody would say stop. He had shared enough. There already would be significant delays between each message. But Foster couldn't stop.

Family there to act for you.

LIES A PLACE

Need you with us, please.
Come home.
Leilani safe.
We need you.

FORTY-SEVEN

YAM

At the sound of the chair moving closer, Yam opened his eyes. "What a day," Foster said, sitting near him. "Things aren't ideal. No perfect world to pretend we're in, but we all...we'll be okay."

Yam looked back at his hands and nodded.

"We just focus on today," Foster continued. "An increment at a time, and it's going work out. I don't know how, but everything eventually will be okay."

Yam's grin back was weak. The high of finding Leilani was over. Now, what Yam wanted was just to be back with Baba. With Mum.

"I promise to get you home. First thing tomorrow, okay?" Foster said.

Home. Yam ran his hands through his hair. Baba had said the choice was his. Whatever that meant—joining Baba, joining Mum—either way, Yam's L.A. days were done.

But before he could go, there was one last thing to address. He tried to look at Foster but struggled with eye contact and finding the right words. "I need...before I...there is still something...I need from Ashyr."

"What?" Foster leaned forward. "Ashyr owes all of us. You tell me and I'll make certain you get what you want."

If Yam had the courage, he would have gone straight to Baba with this request. Instead, with eyes that burned, he looked at Foster and hoped for understanding. "The youth are still dying. The children are still going to go through a lot of pain. Everything we did has no meaning."

Foster lowered his head and slowly nodded.

"But Ashyr has a proposed solution." Yam forced the words out. "And he's right."

"There are no other eggs." Foster spoke to his hands.

"Not with her." Yam couldn't say her name. "Does she know?"

"I don't think so." His voice was nearly a whisper. "We will tell her. Her mom and I. We'll discuss when it's right. For now, she's dealing with enough."

"If it had been the training stuff…"

Foster gave the slightest of a shrug. "Yeah." Then he let out a loud exhale. "Ever wonder why he never sought help from those in Australia?"

"Nope. They all hate him there."

Foster made a noise like a pained chuckle.

"I don't want to talk about it," Yam said. None of it. Not even his donation left for Ashyr, the emptiness Yam felt, the regrets he held. Still, he had to finish what he started. "But…Ashyr is asking for our help."

Foster sat upright in his chair. "I'm not surprised. But we have bigger issues right now—thanks to him."

"So was it his airship that destroyed our atmosphere?"

"Timing sure suggests it was. Too odd to be a coincidence."

Yam nodded, while still feeling the unrest of what he needed to say. "I haven't told Baba yet," he paused, digging deep for the courage needed. "But... Ashyr wants access to Baba's AI, his information bank with the hope the system can identify a solution for his people. He thinks it could find another way to cure his youth."

Foster grimaced at Yam's words, just as Yam feared Baba would. A long inhale, then on the exhale Yam closed his eyes. Although it was an extremely difficult request, it needed to be asked.

When he opened his eyes, he met Baba's resistance in Foster's face. "Enough is going on right now. Your father is dealing with time-sensitive, critical things. Did you know he's working on a spaceship?"

Yam couldn't answer the question. Baba had unlimited projects going on; it was why he was who he was. The islands were a spaceship in their own way. *This project*, what he was asking of Baba, was important like his other projects too. He pressed his head firmly against the headboard. Then he ventured forward again, "There is a girl, Aria. You wouldn't be here if it wasn't for her. The message from the airship, it was her idea—she risked everything for us so…Lei…could be found…so you could be here. It's thanks to Aria."

"So we thank her," Foster said, then shifted in his chair like he was ready to move on. "Thanks for telling me. I want to thank her. That's important. Tomorrow, while we wait for our ride, Leilani and I will thank her."

"No. It's more than that."

"What else?"

"If Ashyr punishes her for breaking his rules…if he hasn't already…he plans to send her to Australia."

"Then we tell him not to. He'll listen. He owes me, you, all of us."

Yam stared forward. He couldn't look at Foster. Slowly, he shook his head. "No. It's still more than that. She doesn't want to live here anymore. She helped because I made a deal that she could come be with us."

"Oh. Well, that's a problem."

Yam glanced over to meet Foster's wide, concerned eyes. "I was hoping Baba would…"

"So our homes, our families, everyone is relocating to Australia. We work with Ashyr to have her join us."

Yam drew in a weighty inhale; the sigh that followed was even heavier. "It's even more than that."

A small look of frustration covered Foster's face.

"She leaves here, and she will die," Yam said. "We don't help Ashyr, and she dies. All the youth will die. And they shouldn't. It's not right."

Foster scratched at his neck. "You want to make Ashyr's society continue to work as he wants it to?"

"No. I don't agree with so much here. I want out as soon as I can leave. But I can't let her get shipped out to die. And I can't not help her, or any others that we might be able to help live. I believe that's why Baba invents what he does. Why you invent what you do. To help others. And these people need our help...so we help them." He exhaled and leaned his head against the headboard.

When Foster didn't say anything, Yam glanced at him from the corner of his eye. Foster's hands were clutched together, and he was looking down at them.

"So...she needs to stay here," Foster offered.

"Yes. At least until there is a cure...then...I don't know what happens then."

"None of us can think that far ahead right now."

"But Baba needs to be persuaded to help."

"And Ashyr..." Foster released a long sigh. "What do you need from Ashyr?"

"Let Aria stay here, unharmed, until there's a cure. That's what is right. What is best for her, and all the others. And we need to do what's right."

Foster sat taller and nodded. "I agree."

"Thank you."

"You're a good person, Yam."

"I'm just trying to do what seems right."

"I wish we all were."

"Me too."

FORTY-EIGHT

LEILANI

I slept in late. When I awoke, Yam had already flown out. A goodbye would have been nice, not that I deserved one.

Meanwhile, Dad kept talking to me about a plan. I couldn't follow the details. It didn't help that Dad said the plans kept changing, hourly. The one detail I partially gathered was that Dad and Ashyr had been in negotiations all morning. Something was taking shape, something about Dad and me flying home in the airship.

"This allows for the quickest evacuation," Dad said, his voice sounding as dead as I felt. "With the use of Ashyr's airship..." My body tensed each time Dad said that name. I didn't want to see Ashyr; I barely heard the rest of Dad's words about transporting the family.

I just wanted home. I wanted Mom and how things were before, but each time I met Dad's eyes, they held such concern, like he could see all the brokenness I felt inside. And when he spoke of the island, I heard it, a shattering inside him too.

His words became too hard to listen to. So as soon as it was time, I walked right onto the airship, right into Ashyr.

I only had empty words. He turned from me, making it clear he didn't want to hear anything I could offer. That was fine with me. There was nothing he could say to me either. Fortunately, Dad balanced things out. While I moved to a chair far from them, I listened even though part of me wanted to shut out their words.

"So I will speak with Brody," Dad said.

"Foster, remember. I keep my word." Ashyr turned in my direction. Quickly, I looked away. "Aria has been issued a warning. She is back with her group. You have 72 hours with my airship." His throat cleared, only for him to add, "I keep my word."

"Enough!" Dad said. "The last message from Brody is, 'Let's put a stop to the world is ending crap. It's getting old.'"

"Yes." Ashyr turned too quick this time; our eyes met. I closed my eyes. My heart raced. "I'm happy to be done with your family."

"Let's get through this." Dad sounded tense.

"Let's just see what we can solve…and hope it's not too late."

I stood. I was tired of listening. Tired of him, and tired of hearing the brokenness in Dad that mirrored my own. I walked away.

After Ashyr left, Dad joined me. Soon the airship took flight and we watched as it lifted over the city.

Dad placed his arm around me. With our departure, a lightness emerged. I leaned into Dad's hug. I never wanted to come back.

"I won't ask you anything," he said. "But I'm here when you're ready to talk."

For a long time, we just stood there, watching the city disappear, seeing the great Earth grow. I didn't want to talk, wasn't sure what words to share. But finally, when I knew I was far enough away from them, I quietly said, "Strange creatures."

His arm tightened around me. "You were never supposed to be hurt by all this."

His words just hung there, with my response lodged painfully in my throat. Best not to think.

To stop the confusion and chaos inside, I pressed my head against his chest and closed my eyes. Right then, I was wrapped in Dad's arms, that was all I needed.

"Leilani. Your mom and I…we are here for you. Whatever you need…we are here for you."

Tears came. Choking ones. The kind that made me feel like a little girl again. Dad did nothing other than hold me and let me cry. It was what I needed. And even though I didn't want to speak, in a small whisper, I did, "Dad, they weren't human."

* * *

I was different. Home was different.

All I had wanted was to get back here, only to finally see what Dad had been trying to tell me. I couldn't go back home. I was lost. And home was gone.

But still, I tried. Even though it was nearing the end of the day, I slipped into the familiarity of my morning routine. I looked to the waves and reflected on the reunion with family. A quick whisk of hugs, tears, me exiting the airship, them entering it. From there I felt tired, and Dad encouraged me to take a nap, in my bed. I pretended to sleep like if I could, I would wake up and find all to be well.

But I couldn't sleep due to the recurring terrors that would come, so in time, I got up and went down to the beach to track the swells. Each wave stirred new awe, the physics and mechanisms that went into each generated wave.

I needed something stable. I missed Huck. But he was now gone. I missed all my family too. Their absence left a lifeless silence over the island.

Footsteps approached me in the sand. Dad cleared his throat so as not to startle me. "Hey, sweetheart."

Such a paradox inside. Feeling so lost yet hearing his voice and feeling so found. I faced him to see dread, fear, concern, worry all creased into his face. Together we sat in the sand.

"How are you holding up?" He put an arm around me.

The word I told my brain to say was *fine*. That had been the command. But what came out was nothing like the command. Instead, other words broke out. Talons. Snake tongues. Squirrel person. The capture. The witch woman. The cell. EnRapture. The awful. The good. Confusion. Moments that weren't real but seemed to be. Details spilled out. Ridiculous ones. Fairytale horrors. One crazy giant fairytale, except the story was mine.

"I don't know what's real," I said and ran a wrist over my wet cheek. It felt real. I had experienced it. I struggled to breathe. My chest shook. Dad's big strong arms tightened around me.

"It's okay," he said. "You're here now. I love you. And you're safe."

I gasped for air. The depleting oxygen around us suddenly felt so real. And with my gasps, I was robbing us of what was left. But I couldn't stop as I held to his words that he still loved me; I just teared up more.

He ran his hand over my head. "It's okay, Leilani."

"Don't say…" I could barely speak. I needed air, and strength to say… 'Don't tell Mom.'… 'Please don't tell Yam or his dad'… 'Don't let others know I went crazy'… 'That I still feel crazy.' Instead, I whispered, through struggling breaths, "Do you believe me?"

The sun shone on his face. His eyebrows scrunched together with a look that made me not want him to answer. His response matched what kept running through my head. "Do you?"

Do I? Do I believe me?

Lies—wasn't that what EnRapture was all about? So…truth—did I even know what truth was? What remained for me to believe?

The generated waves in front of us served as a reminder that I couldn't trust Dad…not regarding this island. But from what I just shared…could he believe me? Could I even believe myself?

Dad started talking about detoxing. That my brain was working to reprogram itself against the errors I'd fed it. Neurons had fired inside my head, sending strange, odd messages. Messages I had believed in.

So…what was truth? Did I know? Doubts pinged through me, leaving me with questions and uncertainty over what I had experienced.

Real or not…I was left with horrible, horrific terrors. Every night they disturbed my sleep. In the day, they loomed near, ready to ascend again on my mind. I wanted to ask Dad if this was part of the detox. If in time, I would be okay again. Instead, I just let him keep talking about misfired neurons until he said, "Does that make sense?"

I made a weak attempt to nod while my mind answered Dad silently, *I don't know what's real… what's true anymore…I wish I did.*

FORTY-NINE

MARIANA

She didn't want to go here, not to the large three-story white colonial-style building, not through the French-style doors, down a hall where smells turned her stomach. An odor was there, one Mariana felt she should be able to place, but she couldn't. Sweet, like hyacinths, overly fragrant, too sugary, like something was trying too hard. Too potent to be real.

Her escort led her past closed doors to a new smell of a musky, spicy scent that caused Mariana's lungs to burn.

Bile rose in her throat over the smell, over Misty's words, once accusing Mariana that she only saw what she wanted to see.

"What is this place?" Mariana asked her escort ahead.

The guard turned back and with his yellowed teeth gave her a grin. "Everything."

Her knees weakened but she kept following, immediately regretting she had asked, while he kept talking. "Everything we want out. Everything we want in. It's our *everything* castle. So make your time good here. Tarthur doesn't let just anyone into this place."

Up the stairs, and the sounds came stronger now. Laughter. Screams. Crying. Fighting. Noise sandwiched between rooms above, below, on both sides. None overbearing to drive the others out, just an awkward orchestra of noise. As the notes came, the house held them all as if they all belonged here.

As long as she didn't have to see faces, no eyes, no mouths that formed those sounds, no hands that reminded her of the abuse that was here, what never should have become of Em-Path. No faces to reveal the victims and victimizers. These were just rooms.

And then she was led into one. A small, safe room with a table to make Tarthur an offer and be on her way. It was all Mariana could hope for...a negotiation and a way out.

*   *   *

Tarthur didn't like change—and the plan had changed. Again, she sat at the directed three o'clock. He sat at the twelve. She missed Sunny's support, but she understood the deal. She stayed focused as a guard roamed around her.

"The arrangement was two at a time." His gorilla-like forehead leaned toward her. "They, your people, have already started coming according to our arrangement. But now you're asking to change it?"

"We've moved into a state of emergency." Her voice remained firm and in control.

"And…" His fingernail flicked at the metal cap of a heavy stainless-steel canteen. He flicked it again. "How do I know you're telling the truth?"

Internally, Mariana recited the mantra that sustained her: *War.* But when she spoke, her words stayed balanced and focused on the current facts. "The hope was our home was repairable. Instead, when Brody finally found the microorganism, it was too late. It survived by eating undetectable holes through our equipment."

"Brody found it, huh?" Tarthur shifted in his seat. He reached for the canteen.

"He did."

His eyes appeared intrigued, watching her as he uncapped the lid and took a drink. "Well…" he finished, setting the canteen back on the table. "Can I help Brody?"

"You?"

His forehead lifted. A large grin exposed his teeth. "Yes. Me. Can I help your island? Repair your equipment?"

War. The watchword continued to hold Mariana. "If there was any way to help Brody, he would have asked."

Tarthur's grin widened. "Nice to know he would have asked *me*." He slid farther into his chair. "So your people, all of them, will come at once. How?"

"Through an airship of Ashyr's."

The smile flashed into a glare. "So Brody works with Ashyr?"

She couldn't retract the sarcastic smile. "Hardly."

"But Ashyr's helping you?"

"He is."

Tarthur snapped a finger at the guard and pointed at Mariana. His thumb and forefinger mirrored the gun that the guard now held next to Mariana's head. "Why?"

Her shoulders tightened. She fumbled with a breath, trying to deflect her situation. She refocused on Tarthur's eyes that peered at her and kept her tone even. "I don't know the exact details. I suppose Brody or my husband, Foster, asked for his help."

"Hmm." He leaned back. His hand motioned a downward release to the guard, who stepped back. "So you will need buses. Probably two. Maybe three to help your people relocate."

"No," she said firmly. The guard shifted, sounding closer, as if the gun were still raised at the back of her head. But she kept her focus on Tarthur. "The airship will land right in our town."

His chest drew up. A long second passed. He watched her as if waiting for her face to break. "What if I want to see this airship?"

"It's not mine." She kept her tone firm. "You'll have to take that request up with Ashyr."

He cleared his throat. His face did not appear pleased, but he again raised his hand, waving the guard to step back. Mariana listened to the swoosh of the sports coat; the gun being put away. "What else do you need?"

The worst was almost over. Mariana took the moment to regain her breath. When her granddaughter Olivia arrived, both she and Kate were overjoyed that Olivia's acute respiratory problems had diminished once she left the island. Zane also reported a positive shift in energy after arriving in Australia. Next to come were Clark's boys, who also had been struggling with the island's unbalanced air.

"As soon as the drone arrives," she regrouped again, making certain her voice stayed firm, "I need to use it to return to our island."

His eyebrows raised. He growled, then said, "No. That was not our arrangement."

"I need to leave. And then I'll come back, like Sunny does."

"That's Sunny's and my arrangement." He leaned forward. "She always brings back gifts from Brody."

"I can too, not from Brody, but from Foster."

"Like what?"

She did a quick inventory. Nothing that would harm another. But something of value. "Grady Juice."

He scowled. "What's that?"

"It's wine, more or less. It's good, very good. You will like it. It takes some skill for even one bottle, but it's like a grand cru—"

He raised his head. "Three bottles."

She gave him a light smile back. "Four."

He raised his eyebrows high. "Five."

She lowered her smile. "Four."

"Four. With an order for more if we like." He snapped his finger. "Then you return." He gave a confirming nod. "And you do not continue to go back and forth. You are not Sunny."

"I can only give you four. And when I return, I will stay here—to help my family get settled."

"Deal."

"Deal," she said.

*   *   *

After all Mariana had been through, nothing felt as sluggish as sitting in the two-passenger drone flying back to the island. Like a sloth crossing the street, the movement was a meandering stroll across the sky.

Her heart felt split, even more so after hugging her grandsons, only to see them join a bus of miners to head toward their new village.

But she needed to return, to wrap her arms around Leilani, look her in the face, and know she was okay. And she needed to be with Foster.

Kate first vocalized the concern. She had said, "Will Dad actually be able to leave?" Then she added, "He and the island evolved together. They are one and the same. Clearly, the island will die without him, but will he be able to survive without it?"

Zane had echoed Kate's words, sharing how obsessed Foster had been to save it, not sleeping, barely eating, hardly changing his clothes. Zane speculated that if the island could not be saved, Foster planned to die with it.

And Liam shared the emotional pain of watching his father hurt like his body was physically aching while the island struggled chronically to repair itself.

Such concern made it clear. Yet Mariana still felt torn. How could she be gone as the rest of the family arrived?

Although Zane, Liam, Sunny, and Leif assured her that while she was gone all would be well, it was Kate who finally convinced her. She pointed out the resourcefulness of their people. They had lived off the island for a long time, respecting their place, reusing, recycling, rewarding the land. Even if the terrain was completely different, they would master it. Their skills and resources would be valued by Tarthur and others, which would help them in the days ahead.

"The family is strong enough," Kate assured her. "We are a society of skilled, talented, productive individuals who have lived in harmony for years. We aren't losing that. Our rhythm, our community synergism remains with us."

What Kate shared was true. Their family was strong. And now, as the navigation panel showed the island dot approaching, Mariana's heartstrings pulled her forward. She was nearly home!

*   *   *

The entry into the belly of the island was auto-programmed, leaving no one to greet her as the drone moved through the safety protocol. Then, as soon as the 'all clear' sounded, Mariana unbuckled and leapt from the craft.

The underground held an eerie sound. No voices, no footsteps, just a continual churning of compression and decompression noises from the pipes above. The systematic gaps and flows made Mariana feel like the island was on a ventilator, working to stay alive, but knowing it was no longer going to live.

Briefly, she paused, giving the island its moment, as if she were holding its hand and sharing that *all would be okay*. It had done well. The people were almost safe, and they would live on, even after the island's last breath.

"Mariana!" Foster's voice came from the overhead speaker. Urgency and joy were there.

"I'm here!" she yelled, practically singing her words. "Where are you?"

"Up on the beach."

"I'm running to meet you there!"

And run she did. As fast as she could, through the metal hallways. Snatches of memories tried to catch her, the beginning—building the island, the middle—the peace and happiness shared, and now the end. But Mariana moved fast, to the ladder, up the stairs, through the door, out the tree, and there, there on the beach, the humid air meeting her. Immediately she caught the tightness in her chest. After all the running, she felt the lightheadedness, the dizziness, the rush to sit down. Yet it was so difficult to stop.

In the distance, she saw Foster and Leilani.

Leilani!

But even they moved slowly. Like the sloth drone. Like the air coming, so slowly, into Mariana's lungs.

She felt more dizziness, her body slipping back; she was fainting.

Instinctively, she tucked her body into a roll as she fell toward the sand, automatically using her elbows rather than a wrist to stop her tumble. A broken wrist would be very bad, she thought, just as she lost consciousness.

When she awoke, Leilani stood above her. Such beauty, her smile there mixed with a distant look of concern.

"I'm all right." Mariana wanted to ease the worry from Leilani's face. "I'm all right." She tried to sit up, but again too fast. Her head whirled a bit.

And then Foster was there. His warm hands, his body, all of him, slipping down onto the sand, him cuddling around her as if he were too tired too. She could hear his laborious breath. Propped against the sand, they leaned into each other. A sitting hug—Leilani joined them, a ridiculous dog-pile of husband, wife, mother, daughter, father, family, all together again.

Laughter, short bursts of laughter.

Tears. Hugs. Smiles.

With no words tumbling out, Mariana brushed the hair away from Leilani's face, wiping her daughter's tears. Foster's arms tightened around her. Mariana squeezed his hand.

Leilani was in the crux of their hug, like a little girl again. Like when she would climb into their bed to sleep with them. That same love that welcomed her, perhaps seen as a weakness then, now encircled around her.

Among short laborious breaths, there were smiles, so many smiles. Yet Mariana caught a blankness in Leilani's eyes. An entire story seemed trapped within them.

In the days ahead, Mariana would seek to understand; she would listen to hear what had transpired. But for now, at this moment, what mattered was they were there.

The present moment, this was what mattered! Right there, her family together, wrapped in abundant love. At last.

FIFTY

FOSTER

The reunion with Mariana had left all of them more breathless, more oxygen-deprived than Foster would have suspected. Such overpowering emotions appeared to have caused them to not ration their intakes.

Moderation. It required moderation.

If they were smart, stayed calm, and kept their heart rates at a resting stage, using slow, controlled breaths, they would manage better.

"I wish we had more time," he said. The waves shared such a different hypnotic tale. Day after day, every morning and every night they would be there, tumbling along as they had been for the past several years. If there was one more day, one more ridiculously ordinary day, Foster would surf with Leilani, he and Mariana would enjoy another quiet evening at the house, he would take another private hike up to his highest cliff. "But..." he kept his focus, "we are limited and we need to discuss what happens next."

"Yes." Mariana moved her nose around like a dog trying to assess a smell. "Where is the air best?" Her breathing sounded raspy.

"Well..." He tossed his head toward the waves. "It's not as nice a view, but downstairs, near the tanks."

"Here we are." Mariana gave him a sad smile. "Our final day, tapping into...the emergency supply."

"What's left," Foster said.

With arms still wrapped around Leilani, she shifted to rise. "Might as well finish it off, right?"

"Well..." His body kept adapting, and Leilani was young, but Mariana's breathing made it clear. "We'll pass around a mask, get a refill of oxygen for some clarity of mind. It'll be good for all of us."

She leaned on Leilani, who appeared to have no intention of letting go either. "The end," she said softly.

Amid the sad looks of the mother-daughter duo, an inner smile tugged at Foster's heart. No longer enemies, these two were cohorts in a broken happiness brought on by their reunion.

It was like watching the others. Special bonds surfacing among the entire group, happening all around, a mighty evolution, a shift within the family. Like a living organism fighting to survive, each member had joined their united mission. Support, service, combined preparedness—the connection between all their unit ran deeper than before.

Survival meant adapting, transforming, together as a stronger whole, leaving Foster with a strange peace, a clear momentary hope for their future.

Once they reached the tank, Foster unhooked the mask. Each took turns pulling in rich oxygen. As his breathing softened and his mind opened, Foster utilized the renewal to move their actions forward. "So how are things?" He looked to Mariana.

She chuckled as if he had shared a joke with her.

"Yes, Mom..." Leilani sounded like a young child. "What's it like in Australia?"

Mariana's eyes didn't retreat from Foster's "How much do you know?"

He responded with his eyes. "It's the best bad solution."

She confirmed the rest with a nod and Foster felt his heart ache. "I don't know details," he added. Mariana's eyes told him she wanted him to elaborate on this, so he did. "Unless Brody's full focus is there, his words are pretty brief. I know there's a coup...that's made things very difficult...but within boundaries, conditions are currently livable."

Mariana squeezed Leilani. "That's a fair summary. Yes, it's not like here."

"I didn't think so." Leilani still sounded so young. She kept looking at both parents. "What's your favorite part?" she asked as if trying to sound brave. He'd heard that same effort demonstrated by the other children.

Mariana reached for the open oxygen mask. She drew a round of large breaths. When she lowered the mask, she kept her eyes on it. "That's a good question. A difficult one too. I think my favorite part will be when we're all there. Right now, it's a lot of labor, but thanks to Sunny, and our incredible family, we're making it work. And so will both of you." When her eyes lifted, Mariana looked to Foster, not

Leilani. With her exhale, her shoulders dropped. A message for him was in those eyes: she had so much more to share if their daughter wasn't there.

"It's not permanent, right?" Leilani asked.

"Definitely not."

"Absolutely not."

Hastily, both parents spoke on top of each other.

"Just until—"

"We find what's next," Foster raced to the end.

But Mariana took it even further. "Basically, let me explain it this way…to my two scientists." She winked at him. "We only all reside on the southeast side because at this time the rest is not accessible. But imagine it like this: Our people, the people we want to associate with—we are like the nucleus. And then, there are outer rings, and out there is where we don't want to be. The electrons, the mafia, or the *drangs*, they want to run everything. They think they rule over the entire nucleus. And if we let them, their influence will take over us. We, our community, along with the others before we came, we are the protons. We are positively keeping the continent running with the work and labor we do. We try to stay close, support each other, keep things going smoothly. We work to make up the difference in how the electrons want to change everything. So as long as we keep an equilibrium, we are okay. We'll be okay, until—" her voice heightened with intensity, "until we find the next solution."

"Which is in the works." Foster wrapped an arm around her. She leaned into his hug.

"What's in the works?" she asked soberly.

"Well…it's a bit of a far-fetched plan."

"But it's another option?" she asked cautiously.

He released the hug, replacing it with a calming smile. "According to Brody, it's an option. I'm not completely sure how viable this option is…but we should first talk about it."

"It's an option." She gave him a meek smile. "From Brody, so we go for it."

A broken laugh followed. Foster hugged her again while turning to Leilani. "Would you like to hear about it?"

While Leilani nodded, Mariana's tone shifted into a flirty voice. "It doesn't matter. We go for it."

He pressed his lips together, finding amusement in the strange moment.

"Even if it's to shoot a rocket to the moon," she said playfully, "we go for it, okay?"

Foster gave another laugh, this one tired and more of a surrender. "So Sunny must have told you."

Her eyes were cautious. "Told me what?"

"What is it?" Leilani asked.

"The rocket." He shrugged. "It's that. Sort of. A crazy launch into space."

Mariana's eyes grew huge. "Really?"

He reached for the oxygen mask and breathed. Mariana's face suggested a concerned shock. As soon as he was ready, he ventured the rest of the way. "He wants to head to the abandoned Space Station. After two decades, Brody thinks it's still in orbit and he has this belief that if we can just connect his technology to what is there...I'm cautious about it...but he thinks we may be able to contact other intelligences...and seek refuge away from Earth."

Mariana's mouth dropped.

"I know," Foster said.

"Sounds fun." Leilani's smile almost met her eyes.

"So..." Foster looked to Mariana.

"Are we all going?" Leilani asked.

"No." Mariana shot the word out while Foster shook his head.

"There are four seats in the rocket. Brody says one seat is mine, if that makes sense for...and then the other..." He used his eyes to communicate with Mariana, asking for her permission regarding his seat, asking who else they should send, asking so many other questions in between this next decision.

"You really think this will work?" Mariana asked.

"If we move forward with this, then we move necessary resources over to Brody's island, where he buys us a little more time. His little island has enough to..."

"Foster?" Her voice was stern. She expected an answer.

To hide his doubts, he reached for the oxygen mask and took an inhale. As her eyes waited, his exhale became a long sigh. "Brody does."

"Okay then." She gave a firm nod. "We go forward with this."

"He's been collecting a lot of junk from the 2020s private space era...and a few other things from the skies. I haven't seen it yet, but he's got something in the works. He basically has given up on Earth, on any real solutions. He is adamant there are other life forms out there...with more advanced technology than us. And that reaching out to them is our best hope."

He gave Leilani a quick look, regretting how much doom he had just shared with her. Such words reminded him of his grandfather predicting the world would end in Foster's lifetime...which perhaps was correct. But it was Brody who believed that Earth was done. Foster wasn't quite sure what he believed.

Leilani looked back and forth between him and Mariana. "Can I go?"

Foster jumped to the answer before Mariana. "I think you need your mom right now."

"Dear." Mariana slipped from Foster to pull Leilani into a hug. "I think..." Her voice cracked. "You need a lot of things. So let's give you what we can."

Leilani stepped back, fracturing their little circle huddling around the tank. She searched Foster's face. "You told her?"

He gave a slight headshake. "Sweetheart, no. Since your mom arrived, we've all been together."

"You know?" She looked to her mom.

"I don't know anything." Hurt crossed Mariana's face, their relationship hitting a fractured moment again. "But...I'm here to listen," she said weakly.

"Mom." Leilani's eyes danced wildly. "It was crazy. Awful. Horrible."

Mariana opened her arms, inviting her daughter into a hug. "Oh, Leilani."

Other than the island's systems working laboriously around them, silence held as fear clung to Leilani's face.

"I don't know what happened," Mariana said, "but you're with us now."

"You're safe," Foster added.

"And…" Mariana's arms still waited. "I'm here for you."

Leilani fell into the outstretched arms. Soon her body shook through the sobs. "I messed up, Mom. I messed up really bad."

As their daughter's face pressed into her neck, Mariana looked to Foster, confused and worried. Then slowly, her eyes revealed she understood. "EnRapture?"

Leilani's whole body shook furiously, up and down, in her mother's arms.

Mariana's face shifted from sorrow to terror. "No," she suddenly said. At first, she looked as if she would release the hug, only to tighten her arms around Leilani. "You will not come back with me." She looked to Foster. Panic filled her face. "She won't come. She's not welcome in Australia. Not if she's used EnRapture."

FIFTY-ONE

MARIANA

Mariana's unpainted toenails slipped down into the sand. If she stepped farther out, the waves would wash over her feet. The waves still churned a rhythm that seemed to soothe, a promise that life continued, upward and onward.

This wasn't the end.

It just felt like it.

Back at the tanks, Mariana had tried to quickly recover for Leilani, to compose herself and not add more blame to Leilani's distress. But with a few firm remarks, Mariana designated the next steps. Foster and Leilani would follow Brody's plan while she returned to Australia.

After they acquired the box of Grady Juice, Leilani requested to make a final stop on the beach for their individual goodbyes. Now in a state of reverence, daughter, father, and mother stood a few yards apart, looking out into their ocean.

Each deep breath reminded Mariana of her lightheadedness, the tightness in her lungs, the shortness of each exhale, as if she had just run some rapid race. The vibrant headache, the lethargic movements, and yet Mariana would fight to see this goodbye through, to not rush it.

But how did one properly say goodbye to a home that had served them as the island had?

Had she the energy and time, Mariana wished to walk the entire circumference of the island, weaving in and out, visiting homes, doing a final look through each place to validate it was ready to be closed up for good.

What would be left behind now?

Foster's Grady Grape press. His books. His research.

Leilani had already packed her things. When she told Mariana this, such emptiness was in her eyes, as if nothing she possessed could fix what was gone. To visit Leilani's room would break Mariana, tipping her into unconquerable sorrow. In so many ways, leaving the island also simultaneously felt like leaving behind the strong-willed girl that Mariana had butted heads with so many times. How she missed that girl.

While Leilani and Foster continued their quiet goodbyes to the island, Mariana fought against herself, this desire to mentally go through her home.

She didn't need to see her office or the family photos which lined the walls. It was over sixteen years of togetherness, a visual gallery that displayed the growth of her and Foster's offspring. Leave the photos, get back to the rest of the family, see them for real, and work toward their future.

Her mind traveled toward Caroline's salon, then to Caroline's home on the island, the toys of her children, their beds, their bath toys, their colored plates and cups probably still drying on the dishrack. If Caroline had orchestrated the exodus then it was likely Caroline never had time to pack herself.

Or what of Zane Jr, his family, those precious twins, their board games, the dog bowl?

As the waves rolled now over her feet, sinking her into the sand, her thoughts carried on, through Clark's home, through Rex's, Kate's, Liam's—only for a hand to touch her shoulder.

She couldn't meet his eyes or face the sorrow, the weight, the heartbreak in them.

Instead, she kept her face planted ahead, letting the waves mesmerize her, letting water lull her, as it always did, into a sense that all would be well. They would all be okay.

"You ready?" he asked. Still avoiding his eyes, she appreciated his touch.

"I'll never be ready to leave. But that doesn't change anything, does it?" She turned to meet him. The lack of solid oxygen made her feel weak. "It's time, Foster."

He nodded, appearing more prepared than she suddenly felt. His hand slid around her waist, and she leaned into the hug.

Leilani's hands pressed against her cheeks as she watched the waves. With a bit of resistance, Mariana lifted a buried foot from the sand to approach her. "We need to go," she whispered.

"No!"

Even though the defiance in her daughter was back, Mariana braved forward, touching her daughter's shoulder from behind. "I'm sorry," Mariana said quietly.

Then, like so many times before, Leilani mumbled out her words, making them indecipherable. But Foster, who now joined them, must have heard because his body stiffened.

"What did you say?" Mariana asked.

Leilani turned to face her directly. "Why did you lie to me?" The words were clear and strong. "About this—about where I live, about our home?"

A rueful quiet followed until Foster said, "Ironic, isn't it? We did it to protect you."

"We didn't lie to you," Mariana jumped in. "The world we knew, how life was before you were born—that was all gone. What Ashyr created wasn't our world."

But Leilani just shook her head. She turned back to the water's rise and fall. When more of her daughter's word came, Mariana had to lean in to catch them. "I don't get why you didn't tell me the truth."

"It was a mistake," Foster said. "One we deeply regret."

"I don't understand why you didn't just tell me," she said.

Mariana cleared her throat, pushing past the throbbing headache from the island's lack of air. "We thought if you didn't know about Ashyr's society, you also would never know of its wrongs either."

"Instead," Foster added, "I now wonder if we were more keeping our wrongs from you. And keeping the truth from you led you straight into what you weren't prepared for."

"You couldn't have prepared me for what I found."

"We could have warned you," Mariana said.

Leilani faced them again. "I would have liked to have known before, like Clark, and Rex, and Kate, and Zane, and Liam and Caroline. Why did you treat me so differently than them?"

Mariana nodded with the explanation straight on her lips. "We kept it from all of you, those your age and younger." But now the clear explanation sounded flat and wrong.

"We regret it," Foster repeated.

"We do," Mariana added.

"Were you ever going to tell me?"

"Of course," Mariana said.

"When?"

Thankfully, Foster took this one. "We had planned to, soon. We hadn't decided for sure when, but it was going to be soon. And in a much better way than Ashyr did."

"So you built it, huh? Not EnRapture, but the first one." Leilani looked to Foster. Mariana did too.

"Em-Path. And yes..." He wrapped his arm around Mariana. "We did. And yes, Leilani...we were going to tell you about all of it. About the island, and what led us here, how it was going to be yours...how I hoped you would be its caretaker, like I had been."

Leilani didn't say anything.

"So...with Em-Path..." Mariana tried to clarify the details. "When we would have explained it... well...we wanted you to understand the good. We—your father—his purpose for it was good. It was a goal for more empathy. That was what we were trying to do. Never was it intended to be like it is now."

Leilani looked to the sand. Again, Mariana could barely make out her words. It sounded as if she said, "It creates a lot of confusion."

Foster followed up with, "EnRapture feeds off a lot of lies."

"That's how Ashyr's world lives." Mariana spoke slow and clear. "It exists on lies."

"It's the only way to survive there," Foster said.

"Sweetheart," Mariana stepped closer, putting her arm around Leilani. All three now stood in a line, with Foster's arm wrapped around Mariana's waist and Mariana's arm draped over her daughter's shoulder. "We didn't tell you about Ashyr, about Em-Path, about the past, because we wanted... we thought we were protecting you. We wanted to keep you from some of the evils of humanity, but our island...in truth, it was a grand scientific experiment. If it didn't work, if it were to fail, we didn't want to return to a place that we had taught you to be alarmed over. I want you to know our actions were done with a lot of thought, what we did was with love and with an effort to not build your childhood in fear."

"But," Foster spoke strongly, "sometimes we get lost in fear... Fear against the truth. And...in this case...we made a mistake."

"So did I." Leilani spoke clearly, without any mumbles. "And I don't think I'll ever stop hurting from those mistakes."

"You will," Mariana said weakly.

Leilani shook her head. "All I've learned about myself is I'm selfish. I'm not trustworthy. I'm unreliable. I'm stubborn and I'm proud. I don't want to be this person. I hate this Leilani—I don't trust her."

Foster's arm tightened around Mariana. Neither spoke. Then Foster stepped out, breaking their line, placing himself directly in front of Leilani. He gave his wife a quick, cautionary look, then pulled Leilani out of Mariana's embrace.

"Hey." His hands clutched Leilani's. "Look at me." She did. "I need you to listen to me. Truth—that is what will heal you. Even if it hurts at first...right now, everything may feel broken and confusing, but it's okay. Keep looking for what is true. If you do, you'll be on a journey...and on that journey, you'll find what you *truly* need. Do you understand?"

She shook her head.

He shot a look of helplessness at Mariana. Mariana felt it too. Helpless and confused.

He tried again. "I know that sometimes the truth hurts. It's painful, it's scary, and it brings with it a lot of unknowns. We were scared to give you the truth. But the truth is better than lies."

From behind them, Mariana added, "Your father is right."

"Here's the thing…" Foster let out a huge sigh, then clutched at his head as if feeling the unbalanced air's impact. "When I built Em-Path…the neurons were never meant to send out lies. In fact, neurons lead a very sheltered existence. Here…for just a moment, let's sit." He looked aged and exhausted as he sank onto the sand. "I want to explain this to you." Leilani followed. Mariana too. In a little circle, they sat while Foster paused as if to rebalance his breathing. "Neurons…are buffered, both physically and chemically…from the rest of the body. Through glial cells, which are the nerve glue of the central nervous systems, they do this. These glial cells… they surround the neurons, and hold them in place, and control their supply of nutrients, and some of the chemicals needed to exchange messages with other neurons. They also insulate neurons from one another so that neural messages don't get scrambled. It's incredible…and it's how our brains protect us. But what I did was create a temporary way to weaken the glial cells while strengthening others, and I removed the insulation, the protection.

"But Sweetheart…" his voice was tense. "As soon as I saw the risk of what could happen to people's neurons, that without this protection, lies could be transferred instead, I tried to stop Em-Path from being shared. It was dangerous now. People's lives could get scrambled in bad ways. I tried to stop it. And when I couldn't…and our world was changing all around us…I removed you from all of it. Fate let me protect you from my mistakes."

Mariana placed her hand into Foster's. She looked directly into her daughter's eyes. "You now are like the rest of us adults. We have regrets. We have made mistakes that hurt. And all of us are trying to heal."

"It's a long road ahead," Foster said. "But you are going to get through this. And the way to heal is to now give your neurons accurate messages."

"I want to heal," Leilani said.

"That's just it. Lies change you." Suddenly, Foster spoke animatedly. "But the truth does too." He nodded at both of them as if understanding something for the first time himself. "When you let truth be your message, it gives you the ability to see life accurately. So use that, Leilani. See the truth!"

Mariana wasn't completely following, but Foster's enthusiasm was contagious and problematic. "We were wrong," she said, placing an arm on Foster to calm his oxygen-depleting energy. "We never should have kept the truth from you…but we did. We made a mistake. And we are sorry."

Even while his breathing turned raspier, Foster remained animated. "But now you have the chance to rebuild the messages happening in your brain. So let truth free you—it wants to heal you. That's how you are going to get through the pain. Because at the end of the pain is truth… it's real…and it's better than lies."

"We need to go." Mariana became the voice of reason.

"I know." Foster stood. He motioned for them to do the same. Then he pulled them into a group hug. "We are committed to you. Together…we will find the truth…and we will heal."

* * *

As the drone carried Mariana away, Foster gave her a gift. Through his programming, the craft flew upward first, so she could have a final flight over the island before heading back to Earth.

In the evening haze, sunbeams danced along the water. So stunning. So misleading, as if the island suggested their worries were in vain. But if there was another way, it would have been found.

She trusted Foster. Trusted Brody. Without them, there never would have been this paradise.

With a thankful heart, Mariana gave the island her last goodbye. As tears fell as the drone descended away, she reached into her pack and pulled out the small pyramid. Her fingers ran over its beveled edges while she contemplated a thought Sunny had stirred, a question that Mariana had no answer to. *Why did they, Foster and Mariana and their family, get to experience all these years safe and protected, with so much incredible happiness, while others did not?*

They had been spared, while the rest of the world suffered.

At the time, it had been a difficult choice to leave the world behind. And now it was a difficult journey to return. But they were different people from before.

Somehow, their changes during this time, their evolution into something new, had to be enough. Perhaps through this change, Mariana really could see what she needed to see. Like Misty had said, maybe it was time to see. And maybe with Sunny, Mariana could help where she needed to help. Maybe her family was strong enough to make it through this new chapter of change.

With a reverence, she closed her eyes, separating herself from the outside sea of darkening blue. With a grounding mindfulness, Mariana placed the pyramid back into her pack. Then she tried to pray like Sunny did: a prayer of gratitude for the past; a mindset of peace for the present—that it was what it was; and an expression of hope for the future, of all that was outside of Mariana's control. Ultimately, she needed to put her trust in Mother Goddess, that she would protect their family, like they had been protected before.

When she looked again into the expansive sky, stars began to appear. In time, Foster and Leilani would be even more a part of this vast wilderness above, looking down on her and the rest of the family.

They would look down and she would look up, and their love would connect them somewhere in the middle. Love that was big enough to keep each fighting, working toward another reunion again.

Soon, like an explosion, numerous stars appeared. With the abundance of speckled lights, she couldn't make out any constellations. Instead, the galaxy clusters made her feel small, yet not alone. The view was like a great army. An army that cared about her—who she was and what she was doing right now.

With closed eyes, she felt a blanket of care wrap around her while the drone carried her through the sky back to Australia.

As she slipped into a state of extreme reverent sleep, she dreamed of an image projected against the night's landscape. A large, beautiful face took over the celestial sky. Brilliant long flowing blue hair entangled itself among the stars. When the face spoke, the sound was soothing, another blanket of securing comfort.

Then the woman even said her name. "Mariana." The voice was clear and confident, with the utmost compassion. "Dear child, we will help you."

Without speaking, Mariana communicated from her heart. *Who are you?*

The woman's mouth remained still, but the answer still came, a clear communication back. *The message, sent with love, from Mother Goddess. We are coming.*

FIFTY-TWO

YAM

He knew what this was. It was a "keep the boy busy" activity, like his parents used to do when he was young. "Keep watch for the drone," as in, "Here is a chore to keep your mind and energy attended to."

Not that Yam really needed to be doing this, looking to the recent dark sky to send a command to the PIGS when it was time to open the knob. From the drone, Foster could send a communication message directly to Baba. But Yam knew what was happening. His nervous energy was impacting Baba, making it so Baba couldn't focus.

So just like the first time Yam had met her, Leilani would enter again through the upper knob of the island's dome.

Baba said this entrance plan would diminish the impact on the air equalizer contraption at work within the belly of the island. So Yam sat on the dock, letting his legs dangle above the water, watching the moonlight ripple below, accepting he was here to help Baba focus. There was some truth to Yam's purpose, waiting there. Even an incoming message from Foster could throw off Baba's concentration. And all their lives depended on Baba right now.

Still! Yam just learned who would be taking the last seat on the spaceship. Knowing *she* was coming was enough to send Yam's hyperventilation into overdrive.

This *mission of hope* would be ruined by how Yam felt toward her—the anger, the hurt, the confusing despair. How could Baba do this? Even with his extreme mental focus, how could he miss this? Did Yam have to spell it out? He could *not* go on this mission if Leilani would be there!

But the other option was for Yam to join Mum and his sister in Australia—and he didn't want that either.

Yam closed his eyes and worked on his breathing. When he first returned home, Baba threw his arms around Yam and kept repeating, "You did good, son. You did good."

From there, from all the explanation Baba shared, Yam felt excited, eager for this mission into space.

Until this.

His mind kept harping on this question: How could he be in such tight quarters with her? As if being in Ashyr's apartments wasn't bad enough. They had gotten on each other's nerves there, so much that she had run away. This would be even worse!

Every single day, he would see her face. Again, and again.

He might as well go mad.

From the FID, Yam received the PIGS notification. He looked up to see the speck of drone light. Right on time.

He drew in a long meditative breath before sending the command for the knob to open.

It came down to two choices. Leave Baba. Miss out on this incredible adventure. Or deal with Leilani.

To find meditation in his breath was pointless; all he felt was lightheaded, headachy, and confused.

High above, the drone's light settled into place. He sent the command to close the top knob. Once complete, he sent the next for the overhead entrance to open. She was coming. How he disliked the emotion of hate. He felt it as the drone lowered down. Such exhaustion. Such detriment to the body.

It just wasn't worth it, holding onto such a feeling.

Still, what other options did he have?

He struggled to find any calmness in his breath. Nothing good would come of this. He needed to stop hating, but he wasn't ready to forgive. He couldn't be her friend again. He could never trust her. Yet she and he, in a small spaceship, flying to the space station, staying for as long as Baba said they needed to—he had to find a way to make this work!

A sister.

He had three already. He loved—and hated—them all the time. That's how he had to view this: She was like a sister.

Maybe in time, when the anger dissipated, he could tease her like he did Aya, or laugh with her like he did with Ivy-Mai, or just put up with her like Rani.

No matter the good or bad, his sisters were family, and he would do anything for them.

And he would for her too.

It would have to work—she was his sibling. Nothing else.

Sibling spats. Torments. Teasing. Care. Concern for her. He could do this.

Just as the landed drone's door opened, Yam pulled himself up and walked off the dock.

Her thin body slipped out. She pulled off her helmet. Her long hair fell past her shoulders. "Hey Yam," she said, soft, guarded, and sad.

And then he made his mistake. He looked straight into her soft gray eyes. This was going to be tough! Very tough indeed.

FIFTY-THREE

LEILANI

We sat around a table, Dad, Yam, Brody, and me. Brody had a diagram, a map, and a miniature rocket modeling the plans. Animated robots churned at his words. The smallest, mismatched one, WatSiri, kept making a *chunk* noise that pierced my mind.

The old me would have watched intently, wanting to be a part of all this. With eagerness, I would have listened while the questions filled my brain. But for the new me the noises, the details, Brody's words stirred triggers of sharp pain in my skull. I couldn't place myself within these plans.

I watched Dad; he was so focused, keenly interested in all that was being shared. He had lost weight, his beard was thicker, his hair had lost more color. He hunched now, and looked older, drained.

I watched Yam. But I couldn't for long. Every time I did, I saw his eyes working extra hard not to look at me.

I just wanted him to know how sorry I was. I messed up. And although I understood things differently now, I didn't deserve his forgiveness.

I tried to watch Brody, but I just didn't want to listen to him. Something was wrong.

I wanted to be with Dad, but not on this quest. It just didn't feel right.

With each word Brody shared, I just felt more dead inside. I didn't belong with them.

I couldn't go back to the island.

And Mom was adamant I didn't belong in Australia either.

So where did I belong?

I looked down at my hands. There were still scars across my knuckles and along my arm. I still had bruises. But my heart and mind felt the most scraped from all this.

I closed my eyes, losing focus on Dad's questions, on Brody's answers, about when we were leaving, how we needed to prepare, on what these plans meant.

I should care.

I just didn't.

An image began to take shape in my mind. I tensed, fearing my brain was taking me toward an EnRapture memory. I felt the fight happening. How much I didn't want to go there! How bad would the memory be? How disturbing? I couldn't make a scene. Not right there. I had to stop it.

I didn't want anyone to know what I was fighting against, how much EnRapture still haunted me. I tried to calm down, to let my breath take me to a safe place, like the beach, where I had returned to so many times, especially when I was scared. But the beach held memories I didn't want to see. Not at this crossroads. A beach memory would only trigger more uncertainty, not safety.

I just kept closing my eyes, trying to go someplace other than where my brain wanted to go... and then I saw him, the red-headed monkey-like boy from the care center. He was touching his nose and he was laughing. He waved. I waved back.

And then he kept waving.

He saw me.

He saw me and he needed me.

And I left. I was there...to save him.

But I left.

My eyes shot open. "I need to go back!"

Brody stopped talking. All three faces stared.

"Where?" Dad spoke with so much concern.

I turned to Yam. "You were right." My words wouldn't stop. "I left the island for this." Nothing, not my fears or anything else, would hold me back. "I have to go L.A."

"It's too late for that," Yam said.

Dad's face told me he wouldn't listen to what I said next.

"You can't help them," Yam said.

I looked back and forth between Yam and Dad.

"It's too late, dear." A sadness filled Dad's eyes. "Going back won't help you."

"It's not about helping me. It's about helping them. I need to do this." I closed my eyes to shut out the noise and focus on what I knew. "I need to return for them."

The rest of the story continues in
the final book, FOR THE ETERNAL,
Book 3 of The Existence Series.

Thank you for reading LIES A PLACE.
Please consider leaving an honest review
on Amazon.com, Goodreads, your blog, or
another form of social media. Reviews can
dramatically boost visibility for a published book,
effectively increase sales and allow an author
to continue their craft—and you
to continue reading!

ABOUT THE AUTHOR

TARA C. ALLRED is an award-winning author, instructional designer, and educator. She has been recognized as a California Scholar of the Arts for Creative Writing and is a recipient of the Howey Awards for Best Adult Book and Best Adult Author. She lives in Utah with her husband.

In addition to the Existence Series, her other published works include the *John Sanders* series, *Helping Helper*, and *The Other Side of Quiet*, a 2015 Kindle Book Award Finalist and Whitney Award Winner.

For more info, visit www.taracallred.net.